It was darker in the hotel foyer than any place I'd ever been.

There was a stiff draft coming from somewhere, a ragged stream of cold that made its way up my legs until the muscles in my thighs and calves felt frozen solid. I forced myself to walk forward. A draft meant, I thought, a window. A window might mean light.

Shakily, I reached out and touched cloth: curtains. I took a deep breath and went at them.

There was something—a bench? a sewing box?—lying on the floor at my feet. I pitched forward, stumbling uncontrollably. The palms of my hands hit the cloth of the curtains and then a flat surface that felt thin and fragile and had to be glass. The flat surface gave way.

I was already out in the rain and cold before I realized what had happened. It hadn't been a window—it had been a set of French doors, insecurely latched. They'd popped open and dumped me in the back garden.

Abruptly, someone turned the garden lights on. I blinked hard, trying to focus—and then wished I hadn't.

I was standing in a garden, all right, a rose garden. I was surrounded by hundreds and hundreds of white roses. . . .

WATCHER IN THE GARDEN

WATCHER
IN THE
GARDEN

ANGELICA PAAR

POCKET BOOKS

New York   London   Toronto   Sydney   Tokyo

This book is a work of fiction. Names, characters, places and incidents are either the product of the author's imagination or are used fictitiously. Any resemblance to actual events or locales or persons, living or dead, is entirely coincidental.

An *Original* Publication of POCKET BOOKS

POCKET BOOKS, a division of Simon & Schuster Inc.
1230 Avenue of the Americas, New York, NY 10020

This book is for Marian Babson.

From the *Boston Globe*, February 25, 1988:

ORLEANS—The mutilated body of a young woman was found here yesterday near the Cape Cod waterline, partially concealed in a pile of driftwood collected by local sculptors and left on the shore for weathering. According to police, the body, its facial features badly obscured by several days' exposure to the elements, was found at 6:05 A.M. by a member of the Orleans Community Artist League who had gone to the driftwood pile to acquire several pieces for herself and other members of the League.

Police estimate the young woman's age at approximately twenty and are proceeding on the assumption that she was a student at one of the colleges in the Boston-Wellesley-Northampton area . . .

PART ONE

PRELUDE

—— ONE ——

There are people who will tell you that England is a more civilized country than the United States. In some ways, they will be right. English shopkeepers say "hello" when you walk through their doors and "thank you" when you pay your bill. English cabbies never tell you war stories about muggings and never try to make you hurry up. English policemen not only don't carry guns, they also don't carry that he-man machismo chip on their shoulders as so many American cops do. English policemen are not only polite and well-spoken and helpful, but they're often friendly as well. Unfortunately, most of the people who tell you England is a more civilized country than the United States don't live in England. They live in the United States. When they come across for their yearly visits they put up at outrageously priced bed-and-breakfasts in South Kensington and miss the one thing that might let them know they could be wrong. I've always had a very hard time understanding *how* they miss it. God only knows, it must be staring them in the face every morning they spend in London. These are not unobservant people. They can spot a copy of *Playboy* half buried under a pile of *Ladies' Home Journal*s at two hundred yards and read you chapter and verse on why that sort of thing causes rape or saps the strength and virtue of the children of America. They stand in supermarket check-out lines in Topeka and cluck over copies of *The Star* and *The National Enquirer,* convinced that the popularity of papers like these proves the superficiality and will-to-violence of their own countrymen. Then they come to London, and every day they walk past the arched arcade that leads to the South Kensington tube stop, missing the most obvious thing of all: the newspapers. They not only miss them, but they'll lecture you for two hours on how wonderful London is for being able to support eight daily papers, while a city like New York can only support three. They will tell you that, of the three daily papers in New York, only two count. They consider the *Post* tantamount to the *Enquirer.*

I do not live in the United States. I used to—I was born in California—but I moved to London five years ago, and I have been living ever since in a tiny section called Putney. Maybe because I'd had such a spotty education, or maybe because I'd never had any pretentions to being an intellectual, I noticed the newspapers right away. Yes, London manages to support eight daily newspapers. Unfortunately for the American Anglophile, only one of them is the London *Times.* The rest of them are—well, good Lord. Look at it this way: In America, if you print something about somebody that is not true, and they can prove it is not true, you might go to jail. In England, you might go to jail for printing something that *is* true and that may be considered damaging to your victim's reputation. If all you did was lie—called the man a homosexual when he wasn't one, declared that the head of the Bank of England had a drug habit, whatever—what you have done is not considered libel, and as long as you don't bother Maggie Thatcher or the Queen, you cannot be prosecuted for it. This has had a very curious effect on English newspapers. With the exception of the *Times,* the London dailies are full of violence, scandal, sex, hyperbole, and bad grammar. A number of them also feature what are known as Page Three girls—half-page spreads of pretty little eighteen-year-olds who are stark naked from the waist up. Some newspapers are politically affiliated, and haven't given a flying damn for accuracy or sense for years. (One of the conservative papers reported on the nomination of Geraldine Ferraro by saying that she brought Walter Mondale "the combined support of the traditional Italian community of Queens and the women's liberation movement of California.") Some newspapers are

12

so wild, you begin to think everyone who writes for them must be on hallucinogens. Rupert Murdoch doesn't dare pull this stuff in America. He'd be laughed off the newsstands. Either that or he'd be banned by act of Congress.

Whatever. I am not, God help me, a snob. I started reading the London tabloids as soon as I moved to Putney, and I've been reading them ever since. I read them the way everybody else does—on the underground on my way to work—and I find them very enlightening. If I ever want to give up what I'm doing and become a sex-and-sin bestselling novelist, I'll have my research all done. Before that late-September day when I met the godmothers, though, I'd never taken the newspapers seriously. Dear sweet Jesus, how could I? These are the kind of publications that tell you with all due solemnity that a psychic in Brighton has just determined (by telepathy, of course) that the Archbishop of Canterbury has a tail. The power of the British press lies in the fact that nonsense like this would almost inevitably force the Archbishop into holding a press conference to deny the rumor, and hardly a single soul in the United Kingdom would find anything strange about *that*.

Putney is on the "wrong" (meaning South) side of the Thames, but it has its own charm. It is very pretty. Its high street is laid out on a hill and lined with small stores and solid pubs. There is no urban decay. The Oxford–Cambridge boat race starts right under Putney Bridge, and about a dozen other schools use that part of the river for rowing practice. If you go down to the little park in the late afternoons, you can see them, girls and boys in different shells, pumping away across the choppy water. Putney also has this to recommend it: Although there are moneyed sections—the hills above the high street are the haven of choice for British television stars—most of Putney is dirt cheap.

I have a small flat in a two-block-long street called the Roskell Road, a "garden flat" with a square of flagstone surrounded by rose bushes in the back. That morning I woke up and made the dreadful discovery that the heat had gone out sometime during the night. My heat had gone out for the same reason it always did: because the system had been put in at about the time of the Roman invasion. I lay in bed under two comforters, four blankets, and a set of Irish linen sheets, wondering what I was going to do about it. Then I reached for the night table to turn on the lamp. I also dislodged the tower of papers and cards I'd left on the night table and sent them skittering through the bedroom door and into the hall. The papers landed wrong-side up. The cards, worse luck, did not. They were small, square, shiny-new thermoplates and they said: *Avra Mahon, Country Tours.*

Avra Mahon, Country Tours: me.

I sat up in the surrounding coldness, glad I'd worn both my flannel nightgowns to bed the night before, and reached for my cigarettes. Cigarettes are my only real vice. Given the way I grew up, an addiction to them was almost inevitable —but then, given the way I grew up, addictions to a lot of things were almost inevitable. I have managed to escape the really awful ones: drink, dope, prostitution. I try not to think about my childhood, but maybe childhood is something that none of us can ever be free of. Once or twice a month, I find myself at that immense international newsstand across the street from Harrod's, and what I always do there is buy the papers from Santa Clara and the surrounding towns. Then I take the papers to Green Park and read the back pages, looking for names I recognize. You'd be surprised how often those names appear—Shirley Monahan, Lisa Mark, Anita DePezo: the third tier of the west wing of the Santa Clara Facility for Girls, orphans, bastards, foster children. During one three-month period of my second year in London, I bought those papers every day, because a name in them was the Ultimate Name, one of the two which never failed to blow my cork from here to Istanbul. That was Mrs. Catherine Hobart, my sixth and last foster mother, the one I ran away from, finally and for good. At the time, she was being tried for gross neglect, gross abuse, and fraud. The people of Santa Clara were shocked. I wasn't surprised at all.

That morning, I was thinking of another Ultimate Name, Miss Anne Durbin. Miss Durbin was my social worker. I am sure there are many wonderful social workers out there, dedicated and kind, but I never met any of them. Miss Anne Durbin certainly did not qualify. She was a petty tyrant and

14

a closet megalomaniac, and to this day she's what comes to mind when anyone uses the word *evil*. You could see it in her face: the malice and the hate and the need to destroy; the will to grind everyone around her into the dust she was afraid of being ground into herself. She liked helplessness, Miss Anne Durbin did. She liked the helplessness of children most of all. She could do whatever she wanted to children and they could not do anything back.

What Miss Anne Durbin had said to me, in the last of our sessions before I ran away and got away, was, "I don't understand why you don't just buy a pair of heels and hit the streets right now. You're only postponing the inevitable."

On the day she said that, I was still a virgin and such a devout Catholic that the mere mention of sex sent me scurrying to confession. I was also fifteen years old.

Ten years ago.

I got out of bed and headed for the kitchen to light the heater. I kept a box of wooden matches on the counter next to the heater for just these emergencies. Then I thought about my shower—which wasn't a real shower but one of those nozzle gadgets you have to hold in your hand up over your head—and about the fact that I had about one pound forty in my wallet, and about the fact that I didn't have a single client on my schedule. After that, I thought about my winter coat, which was beginning to look like a rag. Gloom, gloom, gloom. If you were going to be depressed, I decided, you might as well be *thoroughly* depressed. If I worked at it, I could probably keep up this litany of misfortune right on through my shower and dressing and the walk to the Putney tube station.

On the other hand, I could never really depress myself on any day I'd thought of Mrs. Catherine Hobart and Miss Anne Durbin. Let me tell you something: Anything, not only relative poverty, job problems, and the lack of someone to love in your life, but even the drink and dope and prostitution and petty crime so many of the girls I knew had finally succumbed to, are better than Mrs. Catherine Hobart and Miss Anne Durbin. There are people who moan and groan about girls like Shirley and Anita, who say they weren't *thinking,* who picture them as wayward and without direction. It's not true. Those girls were the most stubbornly self-directed people I have ever known. Their direction was clear-cut and without qualification: *out*. If you have not been through it yourself, you cannot imagine what it means, that need to be *out*. The juvenile system is like a spiderweb made of catgut. It is sticky and eternal. If you don't find a way to escape, the system will beat you into a screaming, bloody pulp whose only emotions are terror, hopelessness, and self-hatred. Suicide is better than that, and suicide is what these kind of girls choose.

I headed for the shower, humming a little because I'd thought of what I always ended up thinking of when I got started on the subject of Mrs. Catherine Hobart and Miss Anne Durbin: Sister Thomasina Marie, C.S.J. She's dead now—she was past sixty when I first met her—but I am determined to believe the Catholic Church is right and there is a heaven somewhere, where Sister Tom is sitting on a cloud playing Bach concertos on a harpsichord, resting at last from the parade of foster children who filled her life and often made her crazy. In the years since I went out on my own, I have heard a lot of bad things about the Catholic Church, most of them probably true. I don't really care. The Church may harbor malicious priests and insensitive cardinals and the kind of self-righteous lay people who think they have a right to legislate their prejudices for the rest of the world, but it also harbored Sister Tom, and without Sister Tom I'd have been dead of heroin abuse and venereal disease before I was twenty-one. Because of her, I never got started in that direction at all. What Shirley, Lisa, Anita, and I lived through was not a game, or the background for one of those heartwarming made-for-cable movies that show up on television every Christmas. It was a war in which the other side had all the weapons and all the experience. Sister Tom was on my side in that war, and when the crisis came she didn't stick to regulations. When she knew I had to get out, she opened the St. Rose of Lima poor box and counted out five hundred dollars. Then she gave me the address of a convent in Albany where I might be able to get a job. I made her a promise then that I have always kept and always will. I go to confession every Saturday and to Mass every Sunday, even if I have to drag myself out of bed while suffering from pneumonia. Whether or not I believe in God has nothing to do with it. Whether or not I believe in the Church has nothing to do with it, either. I made her a *promise*.

I turned on the little nozzle gadget without looking at it. It went off in my face, drenching my hair and my shoulders and all that thick-pile flannel until I felt as if I'd been dumped into a swimming pool. I dropped the idiotic thing and went for the faucets. When I finally got the flow turned off, I looked down to see my bathroom floor flooded, an inch of liquid lapping around my toes and heading inexorably for the hall carpet. I reached for a towel and sighed. Gloom, gloom, gloom. Then I couldn't help it. I burst out laughing.

The truth of it was this: I had a small business with offices off Linden Grove that was not doing very well; was going broke; I was lonely; I had no idea how I was going to survive through the winter. The truth of it was also this: It was all wonderful. Shirley and Anita were dead, Lisa had AIDS, Mrs. Catherine Hobart was in jail, and if there was any justice in the world, Miss Anne Durbin had had something terrible happen to her, too. (Although just being Miss Anne Durbin might be terrible enough.) I, on the other hand, was living in London. I had a nice flat, even if it was small. I looked like one of those English girls in a Miss Marple movie. I had tea every afternoon at a little hole-in-the-wall place called The Gaslight House where the walls were made of brick, the lamps were made of brass, and the whole scene could have been part of a Sherlock Holmes story. My childhood might have taken place on another planet; life as it was lived there never touched me at all.

I got the nozzle straightened out and turned on the water again. I didn't have any clients, but that didn't mean I wouldn't *get* some. Going into the office was definitely a good idea.

I stepped into the bathtub, sat down, and held the spurting nozzle over my hair. The water was cold enough to freeze meat. It woke me up.

Welcome to English plumbing.

Half an hour later, I was at the Putney tube stop, running a little because I was late. I bought the *Sun* at the kiosk and a yellow ticket at the counter and then went barreling up the stairs to the London-bound train platform. My heels sounded like gunshots against the concrete, and my hair kept getting in my face. A few people smiled and waved. I was a familiar figure in the Putney tube stop. Anyone with hair as red as mine becomes familiar very quickly. I smiled and waved back, my way of letting them know I was not an Irish terrorist.

When I got to the platform, the train was just pulling in. I went through the first open doors I came to. In the old days there used to be smoking cars on the London trains, but that has been done away with. Now I rode cigaretteless through Knightsbridge and South Kensington.

I took a seat next to the window, stretched my legs, and reached for my paper. I was just about to unfold it when I heard one of the men in the seat in front of me say, "You just watch, mate. It's going to be one of those mass-murderer things."

"Don't be wet," the other one said.

"I'm not being wet," the first one said. "You just look at what it says here. Mutilated. *Cut up* is what they mean. Parts of the body missing, it'll turn out. You just watch."

"Rot."

"No rot. Killed her in the Kensington Gardens, he did. Ordinary murderers don't kill girls in the Kensington Gardens."

I looked down at the paper in my lap. The *Sun* is the worst of them, which is why I bought it, but suddenly I wished I'd gotten something a little less colorful. The *Sun* can make a bloodbath out of a simple robbery. If there really had been a nasty murder in the Kensington Gardens, it would read like *Dawn of the Dead.* I unfolded the paper to the front page and there it was, in sixty-four-point type, complete with a mercifully muddy picture that took up most of the bottom half of the page: RIPPER STALKS LONDON.

Welcome to the *Sun.*

The story was on page eight, and I turned to it, reminding myself all the while that I was going to have to be careful to distinguish fact from fiction. It turned out not to be possible. I stared at all those columns printed in cheap ink and realized there was going to be no way of knowing what was true and what wasn't. The whole thing was just so outrageous. The only part of it that made any sense was the picture they had of her from before the murder, one of those little square snapshots you get from photo booths in the Camden Town arcades. She looked like a perfectly ordinary girl, not particularly plain and not particularly pretty, maybe a little shy. She could have been anyone.

What had happened to her, at least according to the *Sun,* would have been a bit much, even for George Romero. The London papers never print hard details of mutilation crimes for fear they'll encourage copycat killings, but the *Sun* walked a very thin line. The *Sun* printed hints, and the hints were so broad it was impossible to mistake what they were getting at. It had been worse than a nasty murder. It had been carnage: Her face had been slashed to pieces, and not one but four knives had been left sticking into her chest. She had not died from either of these things; she had died from a severed carotid artery. She had bled to death.

I looked at the name under her picture—Sheila Ann Holme—and then at the little paragraph under it that explained her life. She hadn't had much of a life to explain. She had had no family, few friends, no job, no visible means of support beyond the dole. She had had only one thing to distinguish her, and when I got to that line in the paragraph my mind went over it and over it in growing shock. Sheila Ann Holme had had very long, very red hair.

It was silly, of course. There are a lot of young women in the world with very long, very red hair, and a number of them must be, as I was and as Sheila Ann Holme had been, without family or any other close connections. Of that number, some of them must have—as I had, as Sheila Ann Holme had—moved to London from someplace else. England is a very small country, and London is a very large city.

The *Sun*'s writer was very good. Reading what he had written, I could almost feel the blood, sticky and slick against my fingers.

I closed the paper, folded it up again, and put it down on the seat beside me. I didn't want to look at it anymore. I especially didn't want to look at that small square picture. I suppose this is sillier than anything, but I thought I recognized it. Oh, I didn't know Sheila Ann Holme. I could have passed her on the street a hundred times without noticing her. I did, however, know The Look. I'd seen it in my own mirror countless times. The *Sun* hadn't gone into it, but it hadn't had to. I could have supplied anyone who wanted it with Sheila Ann Holme's biography, at least until she was eighteen: children's home, foster parents, wretchedness, loneliness, and despair. The Look.

The train pulled into my station and I got out of my seat, leaving the paper behind. Half a dozen people stared first at the paper and then at me, trying to shame me into picking up my litter. I paid no attention to them. I wouldn't have put my hands on that thing again on threat of summary execution.

I moved through the great maw of Marylebone Station, feeling raw. I passed the Bomb Alert sign—WHAT TO DO IF YOU FIND AN UNATTENDED PACKAGE ON THE UNDERGROUND—without even blinking. Usually it made me slightly sick. When I got to the kiosk, I bought a copy of the London *Times*. I trusted the *Times*. Maybe it would tell me all my conjectures were wrong. It didn't. I read it while I was walking to my office, nearly getting myself killed twice in the bustling London traffic. What I found out was that I had been damn near clairvoyant. Sheila Ann Holme had been orphaned at the age of two and then raised first in an orphanage called St. Anne's School in Chichester. Later, she had been placed in families once or twice, but never lasted long in them. I knew about that, too; that compulsion of orphaned and discarded children to fight the people who want to love them, that miasmic sentimentality of adopting parents who will have perfection or nothing. After the third try, Sheila had been returned to her school and kept there until she was sixteen. After that, she had disappeared into the roiling mass that was Camden Town and punk defiance, a style that had been developed by children whose hopes were dead and whose dreams had been shattered before they were born.

The *Times* had another detail. It seemed that—probably at the last minute, since the object was identifiable—the killer had taken a white rose bud and placed it in his victim's chest wound.

I don't know what shocked me more: the image itself or

the fact that it had appeared in the *Times*. It was just the kind of thing the police do everything possible to keep out of the papers, and England's idea of freedom of the press is somewhat more limited than ours.

I put the *Times* in the rubbish bin on the corner of my block and headed for my building, past the Sea Shell restaurant and a lot of little shops selling spices and antiques. The day was clear and cold enough for a heavy jacket. All I really wanted was a chance to regain the mood I'd been in when I had left my flat. I could not do anything about these children. I had had a hard enough time doing something about myself. As for the usual solutions, they were just not something I could commit myself to. I had seen government facilities in action. I wanted no part of them.

I let myself into my building and half ran up the stairs, sending up a little prayer to Sister Tom and her fellow saints that someone would walk in this morning and give me something to do.

As it turned out, I wasn't the only one who had been clairvoyant. The man on the train who had predicted that this was only the first murder had done a pretty good job himself.

Even more important was the fact that Sheila Ann Holme wouldn't be the last.

—— TWO ——

She was sitting on the floor in the hall when I came into the wing from the stairwell—a tall, impossibly skinny girl with spiked hair badly dyed all colors of the rainbow. At first, she almost didn't register in my mind. I was in a hurry *(God only knew what for)* and that get-up didn't mean what it probably would have in New York. There are dangerous punks on the streets of London, but their style runs more to heavy metal and ornamental weapons. The punks with rainbow hair are painfully polite. They even call you ma'am on the bus.

I was halfway into the wing before I realized she was sitting right in front of my door, and I was almost on top of her when the important thing registered: The Look. I blinked. It was a little like being caught in that old cliché about when once you learn a word, you start to hear it everywhere. I'd thought about all that for the first time in months this morning, and then there had been Sheila Ann Holme, and now there was this girl. She got to her feet, holding her hands behind her back, trying to look intense and respectful and cocky all at once. It wasn't working. She was intense enough, but she was not cocky. There was a vein in the middle of her forehead sticking out like a swelling river, and it pulsed. She was scared to death.

I started to get my keys out of my purse and she stepped back quickly, as if she were afraid I'd touch her.

"Miss?" she said. "Are you Miss Mahon?"

"I'm Miss Mahon," I said, and filed her accent away for

22

further consideration. She sounded cockney but not quite, as if cockney were something she'd learned later in life and not her natural way of speaking. I wondered why anyone would adopt a cockney accent. Accents are very important in England, much more important than they are in America. You can speak with a Texas accent so thick it would be nearly impenetrable to a person from Washington and still get into Harvard. You cannot get into Oxford if you sound like a cockney, and if by some strange chance you manage to, you cannot survive. In England, accent is class, caste, and destiny.

She took a deep breath and said, "I'm Ne—Eleanor Morgan."

I smiled. "Do they call you Nell? Was that what you started to say?"

She stiffened immediately. Behind her stiffness was an anger almost like violence. "I'm *Eleanor Morgan,*" she said again. "I've come about the job."

She took her hands out from behind her back, and I saw she had a paper in them, undoubtedly the *Telegraph* from three days ago. That was where my ad had run—I was looking for a receptionist. I didn't have any clients at the moment, but I did have inquiries, and with the inquiries came research. I needed someone to answer the phone while I went out looking at hotel accommodations and started fights with the railway people. I needed someone to help me answer the mail. Eventually it would be spring again. When spring came, I wanted to be still in business.

On the other hand, I had been reasonably careful with that ad. After a triple dose of Maggie Thatcher, London's unemployment rate was no longer fifteen percent, but it was still high. I didn't want a stream of hopeful young girls crowding my corridor. There was no address in that ad, and no phone number, just a post-office-box number where people were supposed to send their résumés.

Which left me with the question of just how Eleanor Morgan had known to come here.

I got my door open—it had a skeleton key instead of the modern kind, and it stuck—and gestured for her to come in. She hesitated and then rushed past me. I could smell the panic on her. Like most young girls with The Look, that panic had something feral in it. She was as ready to fight as to flee.

I walked in after her, then I shut the door behind us. I headed for the kettle and hot plate I kept on one of the bookshelves, thinking that if I could get some tea into her, I might be able to get some answers out of her. I was taking the kettle toward the little lavatory at the back of my flat when she said, "You shouldn't keep it there, miss. It doesn't look right."

"What?" I turned around.

"You shouldn't keep it there," Eleanor insisted, "right out on the bookshelf like that. It doesn't look——" She groped for the word. "Professional."

I thought about this for a moment. She had a point. "I don't know where else to keep it," I said. "If I put it down two shelves I can hardly reach it."

Eleanor Morgan looked at me incredulously. I had to be at least five inches shorter than she was. Then she smiled. "Bad back, is it, Miss?"

I was having a little trouble taking in air. Bad *back,* for God's sake. I was only twenty-five years old. I stared at the kettle in my hands and then at Eleanor Morgan. "Look," I said. "I—oh, never mind. Let me put some water on. Sit down."

She didn't sit down, but she did give me a break. "It was Sister Jane Desbry," she said. "Over at Saint Elizabeth's? She saw the ad and said it was yours. She said you do some work for them sometimes . . ."

Sister Jane Desbry. Saint Elizabeth's. *Nuns.* I looked down at the kettle I was holding and tried to clear my mind. It was worse than the cliché about the newly learned words. It was something out of the Twilight Zone. And Eleanor Morgan was wrong. I didn't "do work" for Saint Elizabeth's. I gave them money. Sister Tom or no Sister Tom, I find it impossible to go near places like Saint Elizabeth's. They give me the creeps. The children's homes in London are all stone and Gothic arches. The children's homes in California are all shiny modern brick and plate glass. It doesn't matter a damn. They always look alike.

I got a firmer grip on the kettle and said, "Just a minute." Then I hurried into the back and filled the thing with water.

On a rational level, I knew this was not as outrageous as it seemed. I *had* told Sister Jane Desbry I was looking for a receptionist. I had told her to send someone over if she knew anyone suitable. I should have known that Sister Jane Desbry's idea of suitable would be very different from mine. I filled the kettle and headed back into the office.

Eleanor Morgan had taken a seat, but she jumped up as soon as I came in. Then she said, "Excuse me, miss."

I waved a hand at her. "Sit," I said. I sat down on the edge of the reception desk (or what would be the reception desk when I finally got a receptionist) and started pouring water over the tea bags I'd dropped into my only two white ceramic mugs. Eleanor Morgan looked at me uncertainly and then sat down again. The panic and the feralness had been joined by something else, and I thought I knew what it was. Miss Eleanor Morgan was running. I wondered what her name had been. You do not use the name you were born with when you're trying to escape institutional solicitude.

"Now," I said. "Sister Jane Desbry sent you?"

"That's right, miss." Eleanor Morgan nodded.

"And your name is Eleanor Morgan?"

"That's right."

"And you're fifteen years old?"

Eleanor Morgan went into a kind of living rigor. I could have used her body for a floorboard. "Excuse me," she said, all traces of the cockney accent gone. "Excuse me, miss, but I'm twenty. I was twenty last—"

"Bullshit," I said pleasantly.

The feral look was all there was now. She was sitting on a couch placed exactly against the middle of a flat wall. She had no protection at all. As I watched her, the room seemed to expand, grow larger, as if she were willing it to.

I sighed. "Look," I said. "Why do you think Jane Desbry sent you here? Do you think my name started out to be Avra Mahon? Do you think anybody's name ever started out to be Avra Mahon?"

"I'm sure I don't know what you mean, miss."

"I'm sure you do. I was in foster homes and institutions from the time I was three to the time I was fifteen. My name was Linda Lee Jackman. And then one day I was fifteen, and it was—"

"Time," Eleanor Morgan said solemnly.

"Exactly."

She looked around the office, biting her lips. She had white lipstick on them, and now she was eating it off. There were a few jagged patches of it left, making her mouth look like the early-winter ground where snow has fallen fitfully.

"You really were—in homes?"

"In America, they tend to foster families."

"It sounds better."

"It was worse," I said.

"But it was all right," Eleanor Morgan insisted. "You— ran away. And it was all right."

"It usually isn't," I said.

"That's what she was always telling me," Eleanor Morgan said. I let the "she" pass. I knew she wasn't talking about Sister Jane Desbry. "She said I'd get out and all I'd be was a tramp. I'd have to sell myself. But I haven't—"

"No," I said, "you haven't."

She sat up very straight. "You don't have to take pity on me, you know. I don't need pity."

I thought, *Like hell you don't.* But I didn't say it.

"I can do things, I can," she said. "I can answer the phone. I can even talk proper. And I can type—"

"How fast?"

"Thirty." She blushed.

"Well, that's faster than I can," I said.

"And I'm *reliable,*" she said.

I was sure she would be. England has the dole, and most American communities have some form of welfare, but children like Eleanor do not take money from them. They can't. To do that, they would have to register with an agency. To register with an agency, they would have to reveal themselves. You can find out how to fake an identity from any Robert Ludlum novel, but these children do not read Robert Ludlum novels. Or much of anything else. To walk into a welfare office will always be, for them, to risk exposure, and exposure would mean being sent *back.* I wondered where Eleanor Morgan had been sleeping. The streets of Camden Town, probably. Or under the eaves of one of the shuttered and empty booths at the Camden Town Market.

"My name really is Eleanor," she said suddenly. She blushed. *"She* always called me Nell." (That "she" again.) *"She* said Eleanor was too fancy a name for *me.* But my name really is Eleanor. That's what my mother called me."

"What about the Morgan?" I said.

She turned away.

"Never mind," I said. "We're going to have to fake work papers for you, you know. That's tricky. You may have to be someone else for the Value Added Tax. We—"

The phone went off on my desk. Eleanor leaped for it. She got it out of its cradle, stuck it between her shoulder and her ear, and said, in a voice that, I swear to God, sounded just like Princess Di's, "Avra Mahon Tours."

I gaped at her. She was listening intently, but she was grinning at me.

"Just a moment, please. I'll see if Miss Mahon is in." She pressed the hold button and started swinging her legs like a child who has just got away with a terribly good trick on the teacher. "Good joke," she said, "i'n'it?"

"How did you do that?" I said. "You sounded like—"

"Like I'd been to tea with the Queen?"

"At least."

She shrugged. "Always have been able to do it," she said. "Keep it up for days at a time, I can, if I have to. People make such a *fuss* about the way you talk."

The English do not make a "fuss" about the way people talk. They make a religion out of it. "You ought to stick to Buckingham Palace," I said. "It'll get you a lot farther than cockney."

"Anything, as long as it's not this." Her accent now was a thick, solid, gutteral Yorkshire: native tongue. She waved at the phone. "That's someone named Jasmyn Cole. She said it was important, miss."

"Don't call me 'miss,' " I said absently. "Just call me Avra. Everyone else does."

"In the office?" Eleanor was scandalized.

"In the office you can call me the Grand High Poobah if you want to. I'll take that in the inner office."

Eleanor punched the hold button again and said, "I'm very sorry to have kept you waiting. Miss Mahon will pick up shortly."

I stopped in the doorway between the outer and inner offices, watching Eleanor Morgan: the Ghost of Christmas —and every other day—Past.

I was getting a headache.

Avra Mahon Country Tours came into being because I had a snit. That sounds childish and irresponsible, I know, but it happens to be the truth. Maybe I'm just getting old. When I first started working, I would put up with practically anything but an assault on my virtue. I lived with bosses who went through my desks, bosses who screamed at me, bosses who seemed to be Mrs. Catherine Hobart and Miss Anne Durbin rolled into one. Nothing mattered, as long as I got paid. In the beginning, nothing had mattered with Amelia Mortimer-Jones, either. I'd come to England after answering an ad she'd put in *The New York Times.* I was twenty and wanted to see something of the world. Miss Mortimer-Jones owned a tour business with a mostly American clientele, and she had a problem: She didn't really like Americans. Actually, Amelia didn't really like the twentieth century. She called her operation Empire Tours, and it wasn't from lack of imagination. If she had had her way, Victoria would be back on the throne, the coloreds would be back in Africa and India, and there wouldn't be all this nonsense about the falling pound. She was entirely consistent. She didn't like the Labour Party, but she didn't like the Conservative Party, either. What she wanted was Disraeli, at least, though she might have preferred Oliver Cromwell. She was a huge, brassy, obnoxious woman, and I hated her on sight.

I had my snit because she had one of hers. I had been given the responsibility of showing Salisbury to a party from Illinois, and I had done what I considered to be the only sensible thing. I had booked them into the most outrageously American hotels I could find, and when I couldn't find those I'd booked them into the most expensive English ones. The most expensive English hotels have serious plumbing. Amelia Mortimer-Jones was furious. The way these tours work is this: The client pays a flat fee, the hotel and transportation costs are taken out of that, and what is left over is profit. As far as Amelia was concerned, the Americans could have, or at least should have, been satisfied with bed-and-breakfasts. The fact that the men all had first-class jobs with large corporations and probably spent a lot of their time on company jets made no difference to her. Neither did the fact that most of the women had houses larger than the bed-and-breakfasts Amelia wanted to stash them in. They were Americans, for the dear Lord's sake. Americans had to be kept in their place.

It was just too much. I'd spent over three and a half years listening to that fat cow blather on about the vulgarity of Americans. She ate with her fingers and she hawked spit into a spittoon, and her accent would have made Eleanor Morgan's cockney sound refined. She was stupid, coarse, and loud, and somewhere in the middle of our argument, I lost all sense of proportion. Quitting would not have been such a bad thing. People quit Amelia Mortimer-Jones regularly. With the exception of Jasmyn Cole, who had been with Amelia forever, I was Empire Tours' senior employee. What was stupid was the way I quit. I told her exactly what I was going to do. I let her know what I thought of the way she ran her business. I proclaimed, in tones a Pope would have been embarrassed to use for dogma delivered *ex cathedra,* that in less than two years I was going to run her in to the ground. I rose up righteous, as some of the people I used to know back in California used to say, but I was beginning to think the only person I'd managed to smite down was myself. Needless to say, Amelia Mortimer-Jones wasn't talking to me. On her orders, Jasmyn Cole wasn't supposed to be talking to me either. Fortunately, Jasmyn never listened much to Amelia. I'd already had three calls from her since opening the office last January, and all three of them had been about sabotage attempts. Amelia had called a hotel I'd booked in Edinburgh and pretended to be me and cancelled the reservations. Amelia had called up a tour-bus company that I had decided not to use and signed me up for sixteen buses for a trip to the Pyrenees. Amelia had walked into the Connaught Hotel, complained that her purse had been stolen in the ladies' room, given a description of the thief, and nearly got me arrested. I was in the Connaught meeting a prospective client for tea. Amelia was out to have my ass any way she could get it.

Now I stared at the phone and wondered what this could be about. A phone call from Jasmyn Cole during business hours always meant trouble. I had no idea what the trouble could be. It's fairly difficult to sabotage someone with neither clients nor the immediate prospect of clients.

I picked up, punched in, and said, "Jasmyn?"

"Well, *there* you are," Jasmyn said. "What did you do, hire a distressed debutante?"

"I hired a receptionist," I said. "That's just her phone voice."

"Thought I ought to get up and curtsy, I did," Jasmyn said. "Listen, I've sent you over some business."

"You've sent me over some business? You mean somebody Amelia doesn't want?"

"Well, somebody she doesn't think she wants, anyway," Jasmyn said. "Do you think you could do with three thousand pounds plus expenses for a trip up to Yorkshire?"

I stared at the phone as if it had grown tentacles. Part of my mind registered the fact that Eleanor was from Yorkshire, but that didn't stick long. *Three thousand pounds?*

"You can't tell me Amelia doesn't want a client with three thousand pounds," I said. "Never mind the *plus expenses.* She'd take that if it was Hitler."

"Well, she doesn't *know* the client has three thousand pounds, now does she?" Jasmyn said. "The lady walked in here—well, you should see this lady, you really should. She should be there in a minute. I sent her right over. She walked in here, you see, and she was wearing this frumpy little coat and this frumpy little hairdo. She didn't look anything at all like the Americans Amelia's used to dealing with—"

"She's American?"

"Oh, yes. She's lived in London for years and years, but she's American. Never got rid of the accent, you know. Amelia took one look at this person and got her out of here without listening to a word she said, but *I'd* been listening, you see, in the outer office while we waited, and—"

"And she's got three thousand pounds," I repeated.

"Gave me a proper scolding for letting the poor woman in at all," Jasmyn said. "Said I should know better than to waste her time. If the fat pig ever read a book she'd have known better herself."

"Jasmyn, where is Amelia?"

"Down at the Regent having coffee with Lord What's-His-Name, the one with the courtesy title and the big nose. She has to come right by me when she gets in."

"Well, that's a relief, anyway."

"Don't worry yourself. I take care. This woman, her name is Mariliee Bonnard—"

"That sounds familiar."

"Of course it does. You read. This tour she wants, it's not just for herself. She has two friends coming from America. They have it all mapped out, and one of the American women—well, they're all Americans, aren't they?—one of the ones from America is paying for it. Caroline Matthews. Do you know that name, Caroline Matthews?"

As a matter of fact, I did, though I couldn't quite place it.

"The other one's named Belle March. The Caroline Matthews woman is from Boston. Belle March is from—I don't know—some kind of Carolina. North. South. Charleston, I think Miss Bonnard said."

"South," I said automatically.

"Whatever. They have it all mapped out. They know exactly what they want to do and the way they want to do it. Not like some of them. And I thought you'd like to be put on to three thousand pounds."

"Jasmyn, for three thousand pounds I'd climb the statue of Lord Nelson and do a handstand on his head."

"Then you should have no trouble at all with Yorkshire in October. *I* would have. I have to get off the phone. You-know-who's just coming in the door."

The phone went to dial tone and I stared at it, feeling a little dizzy. I'd have to do the guiding on this tour myself, if I really got a chance at it. Eleanor would type and file and answer the phone and probably sew my jeans for me if I asked her to, but I was fairly sure she wouldn't go near Yorkshire. Yorkshire in October. That was going to be a little like a trek to the arctic.

I got my cigarettes out of my purse and lit one. It was nine twenty-six in the morning, and the day had already been so unsettling, I was having a hard time making sense of it. Eleanor. Jasmyn. Sheila Ann Holme. Three *thousand* pounds.

31

My door opened, and Eleanor stepped in. She stood very straight and said, in her best Princess Di voice, "A Miss Mariliee Bonnard to see you, Miss Mahon."

I put my head in my hands. "Of course," I said. "Of course she's here, right now. Eleanor, have you ever had a day that felt like a chapter in a Martha Grimes novel?"

Eleanor looked blank.

"Send her in," I said. "Let's see what a woman with three thousand pounds looks like."

Eleanor went out with an expression on her face that said she finally knew what a crazy woman looked like.

She was four foot, eleven inches tall, and she looked like Mary Poppins. Not the Mary Poppins of the movie, mind you—not Julie Andrews—but the Mary Poppins of P. L. Travers's imagination. She was all pink and white and vague. She had on a coat in a princess cut that hadn't been popular for twenty years, and even then had only been popular for children. She wasn't wearing glasses but looked like she should have been. She squinted.

"Excuse me," she said. "Are you Miss Mahon?"

"I'm Avra Mahon, Miss Bonnard. Please sit down."

She felt around for my visitor's chair—she had to be nearly blind—and sat down on it. She put her pocketbook across her knees and smiled in the general direction of my face.

"I was over at Empire Tours this morning," she said.

I waved her quiet. "I just got a call from Jasmyn Cole. She said she'd recommended me to you—"

"Oh, that nice girl at reception. Yes, she did recommend you. It was quite a relief, let me tell you. I talked to Miss Mortimer-Jones—"

"I know Miss Mortimer-Jones," I said neutrally.

Mariliee Bonnard shot me a look that was anything but vague. "Silly snobbish bitch," she said.

I stifled a giggle. "Well, yes, I suppose that's one way of putting it. Miss Mortimer-Jones and I—"

"Are nothing alike," Mariliee Bonnard said, "and probably don't like each other much. Which is to your credit." She changed the subject. "Do you know Yorkshire?"

"Someone from my staff is from Yorkshire," I said. At least, I thought she was.

"Well, in a way it doesn't matter," Mariliee Bonnard said. "We don't need the usual sort of tour. We—did Miss Cole tell you about us?"

"Only that there were going to be three of you, two coming from the States. And your names, of course."

"Well. Yes. You see, this is something in the nature of research. All three of us are writers, we have been for years. We've known each other for years, too. Caroline Mathews and I grew up together, and we met Belle March at Wells College in—never mind when—a long time ago. We all started writing about the same time, and I moved here." Her voice trailed off. "I don't suppose any of this is useful information."

"It's very interesting," I said. "What do you write about?"

"Crime."

I blinked. I had expected—well, romance or something. Harlequins. Didn't Mariliee Bonnard look exactly the way lesser Harlequin authors are supposed to look: little and pink and doddering? She seemed like the stereotypical romance writer as she appeared to people who did not read romances. I thought about that "crime" for a moment and decided it wasn't impossible, either. Nice little English country-house murders, complete with doddering earls.

"I don't write really bloody books," she said. "Only Belle writes really bloody books, with ghosts in them. Caroline and I are more interested in detection. And, of course, in scandal."

"Scandal?" I repeated.

"Well, all mystery novels are about scandal, aren't they? That's why well-situated people kill each other off. Scandal and money and sex. And sex is a kind of scandal, if it isn't done properly."

"Done properly?"

"Oh, I don't mean the missionary position, dear. I mean more than one person at a time, for instance. Or multiple households. Or bondage."

My cigarette was out. I reached for another one.

"I'm very interested in bondage," Mariliee Bonnard said cheerfully.

I restrained myself from buzzing Eleanor on the intercom and asking her to bring me a drink. It was, after all, not yet ten in the morning.

"Well," I said, "Yorkshire. I don't know how long you mean to go for—"

"Six weeks," Mariliee Bonnard said. "Maybe longer. We won't really know until we get there, you see, because of the—of the research. But it will be six weeks at the minimum. If for some reason we decide to come back early, we would make up the difference financially, of course."

"That wouldn't be necessary," I said. "I just—"

"We've worked it out," Mariliee went on, "and what we can pay—what Caroline can pay, actually, since this is her trip and she insists—is three thousand pounds in fees and expenses. I don't know what you usually charge."

"About a quarter of that," I said. "Miss Bonnard, we could do this much more cheaply—"

"No, no. Three thousand pounds. We—well, we don't want to be unfair, do we? This is going to be quite a lot of work."

"I thought you said you'd already decided where you wanted to go."

"Oh, definitely. The bed-and-breakfasts and everything."

"Then it isn't going to be any work at all. That's what I normally do, you know. Establish itineraries. Scout out hotels. That kind of thing."

"Well, this time all you have to do is make the reservations and see to things like being sure we get on the train and, of course, coming on the train with us yourself, because none of us know our way around Yorkshire. We can be quite a lot of bother, really."

"Why do I doubt it?"

"I haven't the faintest idea." She said this in a flat, dry voice, the counterpart to the look she'd given me earlier, another indication that she was not quite as fluffy and defenseless as she liked to appear. I suddenly wondered what all this was really about. Three thousand pounds for the kind of trip she was talking about was outrageous. Caroline Matthews might be well-heeled; Mariliee Bonnard definitely was not. If her dear friend wanted to throw her money around, she should have bought Mariliee a better winter coat.

I sat back and looked out the window, at the windows of offices just like mine on the far side of the street. Mariliee Bonnard was on her uppers. So was I. I could use that three thousand pounds—the after-tax would get both Eleanor and me through the winter. The trip would be a hardship mostly because of the weather, which is awful in the north of England at any time except for July and August, but I am one of those people who likes the cold. It might even be nice to get away from London for a while.

I turned back. "All right," I said to Mariliee Bonnard. "You tell me what you want to do and when you want to do it, and I'll set it up. And if you change your mind about the three thousand pounds, you come talk to me."

She looked almost unnaturally relieved. She went from looking like one of life's downtrodden to a cheery little grandmother without a worry in her life in thirty seconds flat. "That's wonderful," she said. "I'll call Caroline as soon as the telephone rates change. She'll be so pleased. I'm not really very good at arranging things, you know."

I took that the way I'd taken Eleanor's saying she didn't need my pity.

Mariliee Bonnard rooted around in her oversize pocketbook and came up with a sheet of paper. "We want to leave on October fifth," she said. "Belle and Caroline are coming in on the fourth and we want to get started right away. We want to go to St. Edmund Cavateur. We—"

"Miss Bonnard, there isn't anything *in* St. Edmund Cavateur."

"Well, that's the point, isn't it? The real essence of Yorkshire. We wouldn't want to go to a tourist place. Now, I've written down a name of a bed-and-breakfast . . ."

The bed-and-breakfast named on her sheet belonged to one Mrs. Henry Copplewhite, and I'd heard of it. Everyone in the trade had heard of it. It was a hole.

"I think," I said, "you ought to apply some of that three thousand pounds to accommodations. This place—"

"Oh, no, no, no. It has to be there. I know it's not the best, but it's—"

"What?"

"Caroline's book takes place there," she said firmly. It was a lie. I knew it. She knew I knew it. She got to her feet and started gathering up her things. Bits and pieces of her belongings seemed to have fallen around her chair like dandruff. I sat in *my* chair and stared at her. The feeling I'd had before, that something strange was going on here, was now a full-fledged conviction. I didn't know why these women wanted to go to Yorkshire, but I knew it had nothing to do with what Mariliee Bonnard had been telling me.

She tried to lodge a misplaced packet of tissues into that bag of hers. It should have been easy, but she had grown very nervous in the last few minutes, and her hands weren't working right. She knocked the bag the wrong way and upended it, spilling things all over my worn industrial carpet.

I got up to help her automatically. I was on my hands and knees, picking at mysterious articles whose functions I couldn't have guessed in a hundred years, when I stumbled over the thing that had been making her bag so awkwardly full. To be precise, I put the flat of my hand on it. Then I looked down and uncomprehendingly stared at it, minute after endless minute.

It was that morning's *Sun,* and it was opened to the article on Sheila Ann Holme.

I sat back, very slowly. When I looked up, I saw that Mariliee Bonnard had gone completely white.

"Oh, dear," she said, getting down on her hands and knees to pick up the paper. "Terrible thing. Such a terrible thing. Please—"

"I read about it this morning," I said. "I hate the idea of even touching the thing."

"Well, of course you do, dear, of course you do. Somebody so young. Somebody with such—" She got the paper folded up and stuffed it out of sight. Its disappearance seemed to make her feel better.

"Well," she said. "I have to get along. I've got errands to do. I've got—well, I'm sure you have work to do yourself. Let me leave you my card." She got a tiny card case out of her pocket and put a square visiting card on my desk.

"There. Now you'll know how to get in touch with me. We can stay on top of this."

"Yes, of course," I said.

"Don't let that—that incident upset you too much. It's—well, things like that happen, don't they?"

She didn't sound convincing, and apparently she didn't expect to. She gave me a strained little smile, and whirled around. A moment later she was out the door.

I sat down behind my desk and lit another cigarette. God, I hated even thinking about Sheila Ann Holme and what had happened to her. Just then, I didn't like thinking of Mariliee Bonnard, either. I don't like mysteries. I don't like scary movies or private-eye novels or things that go bump in the night. I've had enough *real* trouble in my life.

A few minutes later Eleanor came in to ask how I was, and I didn't have an answer for her.

——— THREE ———

I am not a sentimental woman. That is partly because I have never had time to be. Mostly, it is because I know better. If I have given the impression that I divide the world between the villains of social services and the angels of foster children, let me correct that. I see social services in shades of black—I have damn good reason to. On the other hand, I have known a lot of foster children. Or ex–foster children. I have known a lot of other people, too. I have learned that many of those who do evil have not been the victim of abuse or neglect. I have also learned that, no matter what someone has as an excuse, they just cannot be allowed to do damage. There are people out there who are shocked at the mere existence of someone who would commit the kind of murder that had been visited on Sheila Ann Holme. There are other people who would look upon her murder as an opportunity for charity. I could do neither. Murders like Sheila Ann's happen all the time. They happen to rich people and to poor people and to women, children, and men. They happen in every country in the world. They *have* happened: Look back far enough, in history books and in old newspapers and in the kind of "contemporary-account" diaries the university presses are so fond of publishing, and there will be the equivalents of Ted Bundy and Jack the Ripper. The others will be there, too—the people who do what Sheila Ann Holme's murderer did, but to souls instead of bodies.

I was thinking about all this, of course, because of

Eleanor. England is much farther north than most people realize. It's on the same lattitude as Edmonton, Alberta, and it would have been uninhabitable without the help of the Gulf Stream. There are days in the middle of July when you need a good wool sweater to keep the chill off. By early fall, nights are best spent wrapped up in blankets with the heat on. The wind comes up from the Thames in a low slithering stream that permeates stone. There is no way to sleep on the ground anywhere in London at any time of the year without half-freezing to death.

The easy thing to do would have been to simply march into my outer office and tell Eleanor she was coming home with me. She could sleep on the floor of my living room until she found a place of her own. Unfortunately, I knew it wasn't going to work. Somewhere out in Camden Town, Elephant and Castle, or Shepherd's Bush—which are the places where London's homeless hide themselves so the tourists think they don't exist—Eleanor undoubtedly had a hiding place for the few things she owned. *That* was the place that defined her. *That* was the place she was "from." *That* was the point of reference without which any one of us would feel adrift and just a little crazy. The fact that it was probably a hole in the ground or a gap in the side of a market stall made no difference at all.

Add to that the pity factor and the fear factor. She didn't want charity. She would reject it if I offered it. She had heard enough stories, about girls taken home by "kind" strangers and turned out onto the streets as prostitutes two days later, to be wary of any invitation to a private house, even from me. I don't think it had ever occurred to me how complicated all this was, how difficult to penetrate.

I told myself this should be easier for me than it was for other people. I had been there. The truth is, however, that a life like Eleanor's is comprehensible only while it is being lived. Once you are away from that terrifying existence, once you exist in the world the way most people do, the other way seems blatantly impossible. The attitude that carried you through seems stupid and hostile and inconsiderate. I was twenty-five years old. I had left foster care at fifteen and the streets a year later. It had been over nine years since I had had to define myself by a hole in the ground. In my case, it had literally been a hole in the ground, dug under the turf in Central Park just inside the West 81st Street entrance. I did not remember what people had said to me to try to turn me around. I did not know what to say to Eleanor.

It was five o'clock. It would soon be getting dark. Somewhere out there was a person, probably a man, who had gone after Sheila Ann Holme's face with a blade, stuck four knives in her chest, severed an artery, and let her bleed to death. I had spent all day trying not to think about it, and I had not succeeded.

I had gone down to the Sea Shell for lunch, and everybody in the place had had a paper with the story in it. They'd been talking about it, too. I sat alone in my corner, listening to the whispers coming from the other tables, the scandal and the gossip and the fear. That was when something *else* had occured to me: It couldn't have been easy. Even with a severed artery, people don't just bleed to death. Blood clots. If you cut and ran, you risked the possibility that the blood would clot in time. To be absolutely sure—and for some reason I knew the murderer had wanted to be absolutely sure—you would have to stand over her and watch her die.

I hadn't even been able to convince Eleanor to let me buy her lunch, and I'd had a good excuse for that. It was, after all, *de rigeur* in many places in England for bosses to buy lunch for their new secretaries. Standard operating procedure, so to speak. Eleanor was having none of it. I went to the Sea Shell and she disappeared—probably just staying out of sight so I wouldn't notice she couldn't afford to buy anything to eat.

I sat at my desk, drumming my fingers on a pile of papers that outlined the tour I'd be taking to Stratford in March if I managed to stay in business that long. I couldn't let Eleanor go off on her own, I really couldn't. I couldn't think of how to stop her, either.

The buzzer went off on my desk and I flipped in automatically, willing myself to *think*.

"Good afternoon, miss. I was wondering if I could come in."

I sighed. Eleanor seemed to be determined to play this like something in a situation comedy. She was behaving just the way she'd seen the secretaries behave on "Sharon and Elsie."

"Eleanor," I said, "if I'm alone in here and you want to come in, you should just come in."

"Yes, miss."

I winced. Eleanor had a good ear for accents, but she wasn't much of an actress. When she thought you were a lunatic, she *sounded* as if she thought you were a lunatic.

There was a knock on my door. I sat back and said, "come in." I was beaten into playing it Eleanor's way whether I wanted to or not. Then I smiled to myself. One thing you had to give Eleanor: She was not a wimp. She was far less of a wimp than I had been. I was getting the feeling that if Eleanor got a chance, she was going to take over the world.

My door opened and Eleanor walked in, her rainbow hair covered with a thick scarf. I hadn't seen her since lunch. I'd heard her voice on the intercom—we'd had a lot of calls to make, getting the ladies up to Yorkshire—but I hadn't actually laid eyes on her. She'd come back to the office after I'd come in from the Sea Shell. I wondered what the scarf was about.

Eleanor grinned. "Wanted to show you something, miss," she said. "Went out and started making myself look proper, I did." Eleanor was back to Cockney.

"What do you mean?" I asked her. "You look fine."

Eleanor jerked the scarf off her head. I gaped. It was gone—the spiked rainbow hair—all gone. In its place was a smooth helmet of rich chestnut brown, dyed, certainly, but *normal* looking. I reached for my cigarettes. There was another difference: She had changed her makeup. She still had something on her eyelashes, but her eyebrows were no longer winged (when she'd first walked in, they'd looked like miniature bats) and the eye shadow was gone. From the neck down, she was still a punk. From the neck up, she could have been a middle-class career girl from Wapping. Jesus *Christ*.

I wasn't giving her the reaction she wanted or the one she'd expected, either. Her face fell.

"I'm sorry, miss," she said. "I thought you'd like it. I thought it would be more—in keeping."

"It is," I said. "And I do like it." *Like* it? Dear sweet Lord. Look at it this way: A lot of the rapes in England have a nasty tinge of class and caste to them. There were men on the streets of London who were looking to rough up the women who belonged to the men they thought of as their "betters." Eleanor as she had appeared in my office that morning would have been of no interest to these men whatsoever. She had just turned herself into a prime target.

She thought I was trying to keep her down. Of course she did. What else could she think? She drew herself up to her full height—which was probably five nine—and went as stiff and prickly as a bed of nails.

"*I* don't want to spend all my life knocking about like a tramp, *I* don't," she said. "*I* want to get on in the world. *I*—"

"Eleanor," I said.

"*I* know how it is," Eleanor said. "Don't think I don't. It matters, what you wear and how you look and how you talk. It isn't just working hard and doing right. I—"

"*Eleanor.*" I practically screamed it. I didn't know what else to do. I took a deep breath and tried again. "Look," I said. "I think it looks fine. You need some clothes. When you get it all put together, you'll look like you were born this way. It's just that, when you walked in, I had my mind on other things—"

"What other things?" She sounded suspicious.

She had a right to be. What other things? Think, think, *think.*

Usually, when I tell myself to think, all I do is come up blank. This time, thank God, it worked. Light dawned like the morning, as my landlady would say.

"Mariliee Bonnard," I said hastily. "And Caroline Matthews and Belle March. We've got to go out and read all their books."

"What are you talking about?"

"Well," I said, "we agreed, didn't we? We agreed there was something funny about the whole setup. I've been thinking about it all afternoon. They're writers. Maybe we can figure it out from their books. What they're really interested in, I mean."

"I think that's daft."

"It may be daft, Eleanor, but it's the only thing we've got."

"So where do we get these books? And what do we *do* with them?"

"We get them at Foyle's," I said. "And what we do with them is read them and make notes."

"Notes?"

"About—oh, well, you know. Themes. Obsessions, maybe."

"You think the old ladies are batty?"

"That, Eleanor, I really wouldn't know."

Eleanor smirked. "Well, I would," she said.

"Good," I said. "Then you're with me. We'll pack up and go right out to Foyle's, and then we'll go back to my flat—"

"Tonight?"

"Of course tonight. We don't have all that much time to work on this. And we can't do it during working hours. We have other things to do."

"Why can't we bring the books back here? Tonight, I mean?"

I made an educated guess and lost my temper. "For Christ's *sake*," I said. "It's after five. I've been in here all day. I'm going crazy looking at these four walls. And quite frankly, if I'm going to have to wade through a lot of scary books, I'd rather do it in my own living room, with a cup of tea in my hand."

"All right, miss," Eleanor said stubbornly. "I'll come out to Foyle's with you and take a few home with me, too."

"You'll come to Foyle's with me and then you'll come back to my flat," I said. "Don't be an ass. We have to discuss the damn things. If you're going to have a job, you're going to have to realize—"

"All right," Eleanor said.

We stared at each other. We did not smile, although we both wanted to. We both knew what had just happened here. I had wanted to bring Eleanor back to my flat. And Eleanor had wanted to come.

I had a friend when I was living in New York, one of those pale young men who wanted desperately to write in the tradition of Raymond Chandler, who always characterized women mystery writers as "little old ladies who do one book every five years." He should have seen the sections given over to the works of Mariliee Bonnard, Caroline Matthews and Belle March in Foyle's, London's largest and most confusing bookstore. Foyle's is confusing to Americans, because Americans are used to looking for books by title and author. In Foyle's, you have to look for books by publisher. This is not generally true in London—Hatchard's, London's best, would have made an habitué of Scribner's feel right at home—but it is true with a vengeance at Foyle's. There is an entire room given over to Penguin paperbacks, but that is as sane as it gets. The other paperback publishers —Pan, Fontana, NEL—are scattered through the twisting, overstocked rooms on a bookshelf-by-bookshelf basis, and if you don't happen to know who publishes the book you are looking for, you can spend six hours in the place without finding anything you want.

We had a little good luck with our ladies. Mariliee Bonnard, though American, was published as an English writer, which made her books easier to find than they could have been. Caroline Matthews and Belle March had both had remarkably loyal publishers or remarkably dim agents. We kept finding their books in clumps, six here, nine there. We might have missed one or two, but we couldn't have missed many. After being in Foyle's for half an hour, we had towering stacks of the things. Our ladies had been very prolific.

"Haunted houses," Eleanor said, turning over one of Pan's silver-foil packaged productions for Belle March. "All this lady does is write about haunted houses. Do you think she believes in ghosts, then?"

"I don't know."

"It doesn't actually *say* ghosts on the cover." Eleanor turned the book over one more time. "Perhaps the characters just think there are ghosts, but there aren't any really." Eleanor shrugged. "You'll like these better, maybe. Caroline Matthews. Hers are all about little towns in America with murders going on in them."

I took the books out of Eleanor's hands and put them down at the first cage. At Foyle's you hand your books to the person in the first cage (there are three or four of these throughout the store). She tots up the bill, hands you a slip with a figure on it, and then you take the slip to the second cage. You pay at the second cage. Your books are handed to you there, all done up in wrapping paper.

The woman at the first cage looked at the immense piles I had put down in front of her and said, "Going to get a little reading done, love?"

"Just a little," I said.

"I've read some of *these.*" She pointed to a Belle March. "Very good, I thought they were. Scared me into staying up all night."

"*Are* the houses haunted?" Eleanor said.

"Some of them are," the woman said, "but in the best ones they're not. In the best ones, what you have is a tall, mysterious man."

I took the slip she handed me and passed on to the second cage, but Eleanor stayed behind. There weren't many customers in the store, and no one was waiting behind us, and Eleanor and the clerk were getting on just fine. I waited for the man in the second cage to ring up my change and tried not to listen to all the talk about "that poor girl" and "that maniac" that Eleanor and the clerk were handing around.

The woman in the second cage brought my packages up—there were three of them; there wasn't a paper bag in the store big enough to wrap all that into one big bundle—and I motioned to Eleanor. She said goodbye to the clerk at the first cage and came up next to me, reaching for a parcel.

"That clerk said something very interesting," she said. "She said Belle March comes to London often, once or twice a year, and goes on the telly."

"What for?"

"Well, she's famous. She's very popular here. So last year, maybe it was this past January, I don't remember, she was on Terry Wogan. You know Terry Wogan?"

Terry Wogan is a talk-show host. Everyone in England knows Terry Wogan.

"Well, it seems she went on Terry Wogan and talked about murders. Not the kind she writes about, the kind that happen. Anyway, this lady said the way it looked, it seemed to her like someone this Belle March knew was murdered."

"Someone she knew?"

" 'The relative of a friend.' That's what the lady said."

We had come out onto the street. The bus stop for Putney was only half a block down. I headed for it, thinking about Belle March. What the lady said didn't sound as absurd as it should have—you should see the covers of Belle March's books—and I didn't like that at all. The difference between where I started and where I had brought myself to can be defined very easily in terms of violence. The people who spend their time working with battered wives and abused children are always talking about how that sort of thing happens "on every social and economic level." In a way, they're right. In another way, they're absolutely wrong. It happens *much more often* among the poor and displaced and dispossessed, and so does every other form of violence. Murder, assault, torture, kidnapping, rape: You are much more likely to be the victim of any one of them if you don't happen to have much money, or if you are forced to live in projects or council flats instead of a proper middle-class house. Violence was one of the things I had been running away from, when I had started running.

The bus pulled up to the stop and we got on. I led the way to the upper level. I'd started sitting there, originally, because that was where you were allowed to smoke. I still sat there because I was used to it, and I liked the view. We each took an empty seat and put the packages on the floor. London buses have conductors, and their fares are calculated by mileage. Someone comes around with a money belt and a ticket machine, asks you where you are going, tells you what you owe, and prints out a ticket.

I looked out the window at London going by and sighed. "You know," I said, "the only thing I've ever wanted in my life is peace and quiet. A nice flat, a little business of my own, a glass of wine before dinner, a big fat trashy novel every couple of months to blow off steam. No big deal, as we say in the States. And what do I get? I get *this.*"

"This?"

"Mariliee Bonnard. Belle March, and somebody she knew who was murdered. All those awful stories in the papers. Christ only knows what."

Eleanor went back to my earlier statement. "Don't you want a man, then?" she said. "You know, a—a husband?" She brought the word out as if it were something in a foreign language. In Eleanor's world, getting a man to turn himself into a husband was undoubtedly less likely than getting a frog to turn itself into a prince.

"I've never really thought about it," I told her. "Marriage, I mean. Maybe I've just had too much to do."

"Maybe," Eleanor suggested, "you don't trust the bastards an inch."

I smiled. "Maybe I don't," I said.

Eleanor turned her face toward the aisle. "Well, I don't trust them at all, I don't. Pick you up and wring you dry and toss you out, that's what most of them are like. But I *think* about it."

"Think about what?"

"Being married. Having kids. Having a house that's like one of those ones on the telly—the American programs. You watch the American programs?"

"Sometimes."

"I'm going to get myself a Yank, I am," Eleanor said. "Yanks are different. They don't care if you weren't born in a bloody palace."

"Some of them don't."

"Well, everybody here *does*."

I was about to say, "not everybody," but I gave it up. When I was Eleanor's age, I'd had the most perfect vision of life as I was going to live it when I grew up. It had included a man from New York, because I knew, I just *knew*, men from New York were different. California had the crazies and the flakes and the people who tagged and filed you based on how much money you'd spent for your sunglasses. New York had the intellectuals and the poets and the philosophers who were interested in your soul. Dear sweet Lord.

The bus was pulling into a stop located halfway up the Putney Bridge. I leaned over and got a pair of parcels.

"Come on," I said. "I want to stop at Sainsbury's."

"Sainsbury's?"

"We have to eat, you know."

Eleanor shrugged and got a parcel herself. We ran into the aisle and down the curving steps to the lower level. We got to the door and jumped to the pavement.

Which, of course, was when I saw him.

The man who had been in Foyle's.

47

If I didn't mention a man in Foyle's before, it's because I didn't really notice him, not consciously, not then. He was a very ordinary-looking man, thin and undeveloped, almost slight. He was wearing an inexpensive brown suit, a white shirt, and a subdued tie. He could have been any one of a million low-level government clerks. The fact that I'd noticed him at all was a fluke. There hadn't been very many people in Foyle's. I'd passed him two or three times. Once I'd even wondered if he was trying to block my path, although I hadn't given that serious consideration or entertained the idea for long. The only thing that distinguished him from the general population was, well, a sort of *tic*.

I say a "sort of" tic, because I was convinced then—and am half-convinced now—that it was not physically possible for a face to do what this man's did. The little jerky rippling movements shuddered through the right side of it, from the base of his very high cheekbone to halfway up his high forehead. The line of it was very fine and very jagged. It looked like those thunderbolts from God you see in old Warner Brothers cartoons. It pulsed like some low-rent motel's flashing neon sign, and it never stopped. It changed his face entirely. In full pulse, it made him look craggy and mean and crazy. In the intervals between, he looked like that government clerk I described, the kind of eternal wimp who secretly reads Nick Carter paperbacks at night in bed.

He had been sitting right next to the door leading outside, in the seat across from the conductor's seat. He had been watching the stairs when we came down, and when I saw his face staring up at me my stomach did a lurch and turned right over. I had not noticed him getting on the bus outside Foyle's, but he must have, because there wasn't any other way he could have gotten on it. What was more important, I had never seen him in Putney, and I would have. The television stars from up the hill might go to Knightsbridge to do their shopping, or send their housekeepers, but the less wealthy—like this man and myself—shopped on the Putney High Street. I knew almost everyone who lived in the area, by sight if not by name. I'd never seen this person until I'd walked into Foyle's that evening.

I had turned my face away from him and just kept moving, scolding myself. He could be coming out to Putney to visit friends. He could have just moved into the neighborhood. There were a hundred reasons for him to have been on that bus, not one of which had anything to do with me. I might even have been imagining his staring. He could have been looking into space, vegging out, as they used to say back in California. He could be worrying about a pile of final reminders back on his dining room table.

Eleanor had been behind me, and she tended to move like a cannonball rolling downhill, so we were out on the pavement before I knew it. A second later, the man was, too. And *that* was strange. There is an etiquette to life on the London omnibuses. The people on the bottom tier always get off first. He had waited.

Sainsbury's was on a side street off the High Street, way up at the other end. If I'd remembered I needed food, I'd have taken the other bus, the one that went all the way up that end. Instead, I'd got on the one that made the turn to the Lower Richmond Road and brought me close to home. Now I pulled Eleanor along toward the crossing, changing all my plans as we went. He was behind us. I had checked.

"Listen," I said, when Eleanor came up next to me at the light. "I'm not going all the way to Sainsbury's. It's too far to walk. Let's just go to the little market and get some take-out."

"There's Wimpy's," Eleanor said.

I winced. Wimpy's is an English fast-food hamburger chain which makes McDonald's look like gourmet food. Eleanor, of course, pointed out that there was also a McDonald's.

"They've got black-currant milk shakes there," she said. "I love black-currant milk shakes."

"All right," I said. "We'll get you a black-currant milk shake. But first let's get something normal. They've got taramosalata in this place."

"That's normal? I don't even know what it is."

"Eleanor."

"I'm moving. Aren't I moving?"

She was, indeed, moving. I looked over my shoulder, saw the man was still there. I headed straight on up to the crest of the hill. We went past the Marks and Sparks branch and the large empty storefront that had been a Woolworth's when I first moved in. I looked longingly across the street at the Spotted Horse, our local pub. It has really excellent pub food in vast quantities for cheap, and I could have used a dinner in its back room, hot and made up for me and accompanied by a pint of beer, with no washing up after. What I could not use was a long walk home, with that man still behind us.

We went into the little market, and Eleanor picked up a copy of the *Evening Standard* at the door, London's only afternoon newspaper. I went to the deli counter and got taramosalata and hummus and taboli and three kinds of meat spreads, and then I went over to the cheese counter and got four kinds of cheese. I got bread, too, and sliced smoked turkey, and both English and American mustard. I just knew Eleanor was going to be the kind of girl who can eat her way through half a dozen of Henry the Eighth's major feasts and still stay thin.

The man stayed outside, on the pavement, in the shadows to the side of the market's one door. I never took my eyes off him, and I stopped feeling silly. There was no way to mistake the fact that he was waiting.

To get from the Putney High Street to the Roskell Road, you have to leave the commercial district for the residential. Except for the crowded areas at the very center of town, all London neighborhoods are like this. There is a High Street, with a few short blocks running off it, on which stores and lights and people predominate. There are the quiet back roads, with nothing but houses on them. London may be an international city, but it is definitely not a city that never sleeps. The pubs close, by law, at eleven-fifteen. Most Londoners are home long before then. They closet themselves behind curtains and watch the telly, they read murder mysteries and historical romances, or they talk about what a mess the Greater London Council has made of everything.

I had two choices in routes. One of them was the Cwalior Road, a back route. Though shorter, it posed a few problems in the present circumstances. After the High Street, the first block or two was almost cheery. There was a fishmonger's there, a super-fashionable Upwardly Mobile Young People's pub, and a clutch of little restaurants that catered to people who watched their weight. After that, there was nothing, just trees and hedges and narrow sidewalks, with waist-high walls built right up against them. Behind those walls were houses, but you couldn't see them. There were never any lights in the windows that faced the street.

The other choice was the Lower Richmond Road. It was a wide street, technically a main thoroughfare, that ran with the curve of the Thames, about a block in from the water. There are pubs on the Lower Richmond Road, and even a few small businesses that stay open late, like the Chinese take-out and the newsstand the Indian couple runs. Unfortunately, English businesses are like English houses. Privacy is the key word. Even when these places are lit up, there never seems to be anyone in them—or at least not anyone you can see—and they provide nothing of the kind of protection the same sort of places provide in New York. You never get the feeling that you are being watched, and that, in turn, your potential mugger is being watched.

I turned us toward the Lower Richmond Road anyway, mostly because I couldn't stand the thought of all those drooping trees and trailing bramble bushes on the Cwalior Road. I was so spooked by then it wouldn't have mattered if the man had stopped following us, which he hadn't. He was right behind us, staying about a quarter of a New York City block away, keeping pace. I came around the curve past the little bookstore and sped up.

"The more you read about it, the worse it gets," Eleanor was saying. She had the *Evening Standard* open to the inside page where the story about Sheila Ann Holme had been continued. The beginning of that story was, of course, on the front. There were arc lights on the Lower Richmond Road, but they were far above us. I doubted if she could see anything in her paper, aside from the headlines and the pictures. She kept the paper open anyway. "Do you know what it says here? She was *moved*. She wasn't killed in the park at all."

I looked behind me again, saw the man again, faced front again. My chest was so tight, I could barely breathe.

"It makes sense she was moved," I said. "Look at what

51

she was. Girls like that don't frequent the Kensington Gardens."

"I'm what she was," Eleanor said.

"How often have you been in the Kensington Gardens?" Eleanor looked away.

"Oh, don't make so much of it," I said. "I wasn't implying anything about her morals. I was just saying it wasn't her turf. So either somebody talked her into going there or somebody found her someplace else and moved her. Moving her was more intelligent."

"You think the kind of person who does this sort of thing is *intelligent?"*

"Maybe the word is clever," I said. "Look, he moved her. He killed her someplace else. The police can't place her now, don't you see? They don't know where he's operating."

"What do you think he killed her for?" Eleanor said. "It says in the paper she wasn't known to the police. She hadn't been—"

"Walking the streets?"

"Or selling drugs," Eleanor pointed out.

"All right," I said. "Maybe he was in love with her. Or maybe it was a woman who was in love with somebody who was in love with her. Or maybe—"

"Maybe it's a new Ripper," Eleanor said.

"Eleanor, please." I looked over my shoulder again. He was still there. He had sped up when we did, but he hadn't tried to catch us. He was still the same distance behind.

Eleanor folded the paper under her arm and said, "I wonder if they know anything about it. Our ladies, I mean. Do you think they have to do a lot of research to write those books?"

"I think they'd get by quite well with morbid imaginations."

"Yes, well. But if they do research, they could be of some help to the police. They could—volunteer their services."

"At the moment, I wish they'd volunteer their services to us," I said. "There it is. We cross at the zebra and make the next left turn."

Eleanor peered into the darkness and said, "Quite out of the way here, isn't it? Dead as a farmhouse in Kent."

And it was, of course. That's why my flat cost a hundred pounds a week. This part of Putney was private, residential, and quiet. It was also half a block from the newsagent's, right off the Lower Richmond Road itself. I got Eleanor across the zebra, watched him cross behind us, and then turned onto the Roskell Road.

I don't know what I was expecting. Probably that he'd wait until we were surrounded by nothing but blank-faced little houses, then leap out at us. All the way down that block, I was drawing breath like a dying motor having trouble turnings its wheels. I knew the absolute worst thing would be to start running—that's what street criminals look for, fear and panic—but I was having a hard time keeping my speed under control. I blessed Eleanor. She was completely unaware of the man behind us. She was titillated and fascinated and shocked by the story of Sheila Ann Holme, but she did not empathize.

My flat was in a little narrow house with a wrought-iron gate around it. I got the gate open and pushed Eleanor through it, nearly jumping a foot in the air when I felt something brush against my leg—the cat, our neighborhood stray. I always keep my flat keys in my pocket, and I had them out, ready to unlock my door. My arms were shaking and my hair stood up as straight and stiff as the nap of a polyester carpet. I was sure the next thing I felt was going to be a hand on my arm.

I got us into the vestibule, got us to my door, got my key in the lock and turned around. Nothing. Nothing, nothing, nothing.

"Are you all right?" Eleanor said.

"I'm fine." I pushed my front door in and snaked my hand around the wall to turn on the light. My small square living room looked bleak and a little messy, but it was definitely empty.

"You seem all shook up," Eleanor said. "Did I say something?"

"Talking about that murder gets me a little upset."

"Well, I don't wonder," Eleanor said. Then she threw herself down on my couch and picked up the cat. It must have come in with us. It looked very smug.

I locked the front door and went to the windows that looked out at the street. This time, I expected to see nothing. Obviously, I had been exaggerating the whole thing. He was just some poor beleaguered man who had recently moved to the street. He was just someone whose face I would learn to know, and disregard, over time.

I was wrong here, too. I pressed my face to the glass, and there he was, standing right outside my gate. He saw me looking at him. I know he did, because he looked right into my eyes and smiled.

I backed away from the window and nearly fell over a needlepoint ottoman. Then I turned around to find Eleanor excitedly waving her *Evening Standard* in the air.

"Look," she said. "Here's another one."

"Another one what?"

"Another American mystery writer." She shoved the paper in my face. "Very different from our ladies, isn't he? The paper says he came to England to write a novel."

I looked down at the face in the newspaper picture and saw a large man with bushy dark hair, an athletic build, and that oddly open, outdoorsy face that Europeans have come to identify as "typically American." He looked nothing like the ratty-faced little wimp waiting outside my gate. I found him almost comforting.

"Benjamin Grade," Eleanor said.

"I think I've had enough of American mystery writers for one night," I said.

Eleanor shrugged. "I think he's cute. You would too, if you had any sense. He looks just your type."

I gave her a look that said that was enough of that—what could she possibly know about my "type" after only eight hours?—and she shrugged again and started carrying grocery bags toward the back of the flat.

I waited until she was out of sight and then went over to the window again. He was still there. He was still smiling.

Over the course of the next nine hours, I went to that window at least a dozen times. He was always there. And he was always smiling.

He left at exactly six in the morning, just as I was getting up my nerve to call the police. That was a residue of running, of course. Threatened, even by something as concrete as a man who'd followed me home and spent the night in the bitter cold outside my window, I was reluctant to deal with the authorities.

When he left he walked briskly toward the river. His topcoat was shabby and thin, but he didn't look cold.

——— FOUR ———

One week later, on the day Belle March and Caroline Matthews arrived in London and on the day before I was to meet them for the first time, the body of a girl named Margaret Jane Willeford was found in Green Park, under a clump of bushes, easily within shouting distance of Buckingham Palace. She was found by a stout, no-nonsense woman named Emily Hawse, a woman who made her living as a professional dog walker. It was six o'clock in the morning and there was a frost. The body of Margaret Jane Willeford was covered with a thin shell of ice.

The stories in the papers were predictable. The *Sun* was still walking the line, but only barely. Margaret Jane Willeford had been mutilated. Her face had been torn up. Her chest had been stuck through with knives. Her carotid artery had been cut and she had been allowed to bleed to death. Even the white rose was there, the *Times* having broken ground the last time without getting hauled into court for it. It seemed there was a Ripper on the loose after all.

What interested me most, however, was what I knew without having to be told. Margaret Jane Willeford had been placed "in care," as the British put it, at the age of six months. There was a suggestion that she had been left in a basket on the orphanage steps, although I didn't know if I believed people did that anymore. She had been a homely young woman, and apparently an even homelier child. Even in the midst of the adoption shortage, no one had wanted

56

her. Things had come out about her predecessor, Sheila Ann Holme—mostly that Sheila Ann had had a penchant for late nights and punk boyfriends—but nothing was going to come out about Margaret Jane. Nobody knew where she'd lived (probably because she hadn't lived anywhere, in the ordinary meaning of the phrase), but she'd been a regular at the Saint Thomas á Becket Church in Shepherd's Bush. She had been quiet, studious, shy, and perhaps a little stupid. One or two people described her as "backward."

She had not been killed where she was left, but everyone expected that.

I read all the newspaper stories twice and then threw the papers away. I didn't want to think about it.

PART TWO

─── FIVE ───

When I was a very small child—before the foster homes, I think, although I can't be sure—I had a toy camera that seemed to take real pictures. Of course, it didn't really. Toys were not so elaborate in those days, and if something like that had existed, it would have been prohibitively expensive. The little I remember about home before the change has nothing in it to indicate secret family wealth. A tiny room with a worn green ottoman in it; a tiny woman with hair as red as mine is now and bones so fragile they always looked bruised: home as I knew it when I still had one. Everything else I remember about that time is a kind of emotional recall. I loved the fragile red-haired woman with a fierceness very close to violence. Even now, the feeling comes over me sometimes in my dreams. It shocks me awake. Maybe that's why I want to think the camera came from her and not from some later, passing stranger. Maybe it's just that I don't remember my foster parents being big on giving me toys.

The camera worked like this: At the very front of it was a sponge, which you saturated with water. Then you took stiff plastic "plates" and pushed them in under the sponge. When you pushed the shutter button, the plates came out again. Going in, they were covered with eggshell-like white. Coming out, they showed a picture. It had something to do with the water. Once the plates dried, they turned white again.

One of those pictures was of a family: mother, father,

older child, baby. It fascinated me endlessly, so much so that I could probably draw it today in every detail of line and color. I remember precisely my waiting impatiently while the plate was in the camera and my anxiety as the plate dried and white covered the picture again. My feeling at the time was that I never really caught the picture. It was always coming or going or gone.

It was like that, in a way, with the business of the white roses. The detail had stopped me when I first read about it in the *Times,* and stopped me again when I saw it in the stories about Margaret Jane Willeford. Still, it seemed to keep going past me. Every time I tried to concentrate on it, it faded out of sight.

I don't know if I just had too much on my mind, or if I was deliberately repressing any mental image of it. I had a lot to do, not only for the Yorkshire trip but for two other clients-to-be recommended to my office by Jasmyn Cole. London on the day after Margaret Jane Willeford's murder hit the papers was a cold and fearful place. Two girls had died within a week of each other, both horribly mutilated. Even without the white roses it would have been obvious that a maniac was on the loose. Just because he was obsessed with slaughtering waifs now didn't mean he wouldn't become obsessed with murdering little old ladies tomorrow. That was very unsound psychological reasoning, but I didn't know enough about psychology to talk myself out of it. Neither did anyone else, it seemed. The cheerful young woman who rang up sales in the sweet shop on the first floor of my office building wasn't as cheerful as she used to be, and the normally pleasant middle-aged woman who kept the antique store half a block down had taken to locking the shop door and making her customers buzz. It gave Lisson Grove, which had always impressed me as being a particularly optimistic and energetic place, a pinched and suspicious air.

I turned into my office that day without the paper—I was no more eager to keep Margaret Jane Willeford with me than I had been to keep Sheila Ann Holme—without stopping at the newsagent's to say hello to Mrs. Parmaden. I could see her in there, biting at her nails and shuffling and reshuffling papers, looking frightened and thoroughly miserable. When there's a serial killer on the loose, there's always a lot of talk about the terrible things he does to the people he kills. There's almost never any talk about the terrible things he does to the city he lives in. "London Gripped In Fear," as the *Sun* put it, doesn't begin to describe it. Under the pressure of panic and suspicion, Londoners were becoming different people, people I didn't like as well as the ones we had been before.

I let myself into the office—Eleanor had come on ahead of me, as she always did; she thought it was more "proper" for a receptionist to be in ahead of her boss, even when the receptionist lived with her boss—and immediately heard the sound of the telly. Like everyone else in England, I rented my television. I had rented this one in my early days to keep myself from going crazy with silence. When you start a business, and sit for hour after hour in an empty office with nothing but the muffled sound of traffic to prove you are alive, you can go crazy very quickly. Fortunately, some time before I went out on my own, the British government had relaxed its regulations and allowed the telly stations to start broadcasting at six instead of noon, so the telly gave me something to listen to all of the day.

I was surprised to hear it because watching telly in the office was exactly the kind of thing Eleanor considered "unprofessional." She had, in fact, mentioned more than once that we should get rid of the thing altogether. I hesitated, afraid of jinxing everything. When I got rid of that television, I would be telling myself, and the rest of the world, that I was wholeheartedly serious about this tour business.

I put my bag down on a chair and looked over Eleanor's shoulder. She was watching a talk show I'd never heard of—the Brits say "chat show"—and one of the guests on the podium looked vaguely familiar: tall man, broad shoulders, black hair, obviously American. I tried to think of where I'd seen him before and couldn't.

I tapped Eleanor's hand and said, "I thought you didn't approve of watching telly during business hours?"

"This is business," Eleanor said, pointing at the screen. "The woman on the end there is Belle March."

She was small and round and cheerful looking. She looked

enough like Mariliee Bonnard to be her sister. She was not, however, in any way fluffy or vague. My private opinion had always been that Mariliee Bonnard adopted fuzziness to hide her intelligence. Belle March apparently didn't want to hide hers. She was a sharp old lady.

"Reminds me of a teacher I had for English once," I said. "If everybody hadn't been a chauvinist when she was growing up she'd have ruled the world."

"I like her." Eleanor pointed to the screen again. "The big man with the black hair is Benjamin Grade."

"Who?"

"Benjamin Grade, don't you remember? He had his picture in the paper the first night I worked here. He's—"

"I remember," I said. "American mystery writer. Private-eye novels."

"Also, due to show up in about fifteen minutes." Eleanor picked up our massive, and mostly empty, appointment book and handed it to me. "Nine-thirty," she said. "He called just a little while ago and I plugged him right in."

"How could he have called if he was on a chat show?"

"The chat show," Eleanor said witheringly, "is *taped.*"

I let that one go. I hadn't been as stupid as I sounded. Many British chat shows are not taped, and proud of it.

I picked up my purse again and headed toward the inner office. "I wonder how he got our number," I said. "Do you think Mariliee Bonnard or one of the other two gave it to him?"

"No," Eleanor said.

"No?"

"I've been watching this for half an hour. I think Belle March hates the man."

I let that one go, too. Eleanor would have put the mail on my desk, and I thought I'd get to it before Mr. Benjamin Grade showed up at my door. Benjamin Grade in the morning and the ladies for lunch—I privately promised myself that once this was over I'd refuse to hear a single word about American mystery writers again for at least a year.

He showed up at exactly nine forty-five—very punctual, very admirable, and probably a very good thing. The mail had been singularly depressing: two bills and a letter from the wife of the couple who'd signed up for a tour of Scotland in June. The wife was now a widow. The tour would not come off. I made a note to have Eleanor return the woman's deposit. Then I started thinking about those white roses. Like I said, my relationship with those roses was always on a kind of time delay. They were there and not there. That morning something kept reminding me of them. Every time I bent over the trip sheets for Yorkshire, there they'd be.

By the time Eleanor sailed through my door, wearing her very best posture and her very thickest Princess Di accent, I was exasperated and apprehensive. In this business, concentration is everything, especially if you can't afford a computer. I kept losing scheduled departure times and tourism tax rates in mental movies of white roses.

When Eleanor came in, I sat up in my chair and tried to look brisk and professional. I did all right, as long as it was only Eleanor at my door. The appearance of Benjamin Grade deflated me completely. I had seen him twice before, of course—once in the paper and once on television—but he was one of those people whom secondary images diminish. I'd had no warning of how *big* he was. He had to top out at six five, and his body was in proportion to his height. Broad shoulders, broad hands, a great thick mass of black hair: Looking at him was a lot like looking at one of those larger-than-life-size posters they did of Christopher Reeve for the first *Superman* movie. He looked like an ambassador of a race of giants.

If that had been all, I might have recovered very quickly, but it wasn't. The most distinctive thing about Benjamin Grade was not his size but his manner. It left me temporarily speechless. I know what The Look looks like in its male as well as its female form, and Mr. Benjamin Grade didn't have it. Whatever his history was, it had not included foster homes and juvenile centers. It had included *something* that corresponded to all that, some tragedy, some agony, some deprivation that left him angry. This is the kind of thing I ordinarily dismiss as melodramatic and silly, but I couldn't dismiss it with Benjamin Grade. The connection between us was alive and electric, and it wasn't just sexual, although that feeling was there, too. Eleanor had been more perceptive about that newspaper photograph than I had been. Benjamin Grade was a remarkably good-looking man.

I felt as if I had been standing there staring at him forever, but it must have been only a few seconds. He moved—shifted on his feet, I think—and the spell was broken. I'd picked up his aura but not his mood. His aura must have been very, very strong, because his mood was explosive. The man was in the grip of a royal, first-class, world-champion piss-off.

I had stood up when he came in, and now I sat down again, very carefully. I was afraid any sudden movement might set him off.

"Mr. Grade," I said. "I'm Avra Mahon. Won't you come in?"

He looked at my visitor's chair and frowned. Next to him, the piece seemed rickety and insubstantial. I thought wildly of alternatives. Go down to the antique place and buy something Victorian? Send Eleanor back to the flat to bring in my living-room armchair? Conduct the entire interview with both of us standing?

None of those things were necessary. Benjamin Grade strode into my office, and I realized he must have faced this problem a hundred times before. I'd often thought the world was not made for people as short as I am, but I'd never considered the possibility that the world might be equally uncomfortable for people on the other extreme. I almost felt sorry for the man. I had visions of him wandering endlessly with aching feet, looking for one single chair big enough to allow him to sit down.

I stopped feeling sorry for him a moment later. He did sit down—and the chair didn't break, thank God—and then he said, "I've come to talk to you about the fairy godmothers."

It was the first time I'd heard them called that, but I had no trouble at all knowing what Benjamin Grade was talking about. The fairy godmothers from *Sleeping Beauty,* of course: Flora, Fauna, and Merriweather. The pictures hit my brain in a rush. Marilee Bonnard, Caroline Matthews, Belle March—all small and short and round and bouncy, or bouncy on the surface, at least. I tried, and failed, to eject the image of them racing around with magic wands.

Benjamin Grade stretched out his feet—they went all the way under my desk—and said, "Just wait. Look at them the next time you see them together. The connection is inescapable."

"I haven't seen them together yet," I said, "but you're right. The connection *is* inescapable."

"In more ways than one, Miss Mahon. The fairy godmothers were always causing perfectly good-hearted trouble. The three of *them* are always causing perfectly well-meaning trouble. For me."

By now, the tension between us had eased somewhat. Benjamin Grade was no longer as angry as he'd been when he first walked in, and I was no longer as afraid of him. In the rush of release caused by the thaw, I got stupid.

"What's the matter?" I asked him. "Are they trying to marry you off to someone?"

He didn't even blink. "They think," he said, "I murdered someone."

My office is a small, square room without much ornamentation. Through the streaked, never-washed-often-enough panes of glass I could see the gray skies of a day heading toward rain and the dull brick of the building opposite. A slightly-less-narrow-than-usual street in a quiet part of London: not the setting of choice for significant events.

Even so, I could almost feel the entire situation—trip to Yorkshire, fairy godmothers and all—changing course. I must have sat there staring at Benjamin Grade for a good two minutes, absolutely silent. Bits and pieces kept floating through my head: Mariliee Bonnard's strangeness that first time she visited my office; the feeling I always got that she wasn't telling me everything and was sometimes even lying to me; all the peculiarities on the trip itinerary, the worse-than-cut-rate bed-and-breakfasts, the tiny and mostly uninteresting towns, the fanatical insistence on *just* this train at *just* that time.

Benjamin Grade started to relax again. He looked distinctly amused, as if my shock were the funniest thing he'd been presented with in ages. He took out a pack of cigarettes and held them up for permission to smoke. I took out my own pack and nodded.

He reached for the lighter I kept on my desk (an iron

replica of Godzilla) and said, "I take it they didn't tell you much about anything."

"They didn't tell me they thought you'd murdered someone," I said, "no."

"I take it they also didn't tell you they were following me."

"Following you," I repeated, stupefied. "What do you mean, following you?"

"Following me," Benjamin Grade said again. It was beginning to sound like a dialogue litany. He got his cigarette going and put the lighter back on my desk. "To be specific, when Caroline heard I was leaving the country, she took my secretary to lunch. She got my departure times, the names of the places I was staying at, my itinerary— everything. She and Belle would have come over on the same plane except it was booked. Fortunately for me, everything was booked for over a week. There was something about a royal something . . ."

"The honors reception," I said. "When they give people knighthoods for life or whatever. They make a big pageant out of it. You're right, everything would have been booked that week."

"Caroline and Belle," Benjamin said, "now have the room directly below mine at the Connaught."

The Connaught. I thought of Mrs. Henry Copplewhite's, the bed-and-breakfast in Yorkshire that Mariliee Bonnard had insisted I check the godmothers into. Presumably, the godmothers wanted to stay there because Mr. Benjamin Grade was going to stay there. Why would a man who could afford the Connaught want to stay in the gloom and doom and general unpleasantness of Mrs. Henry Copplewhite's?

Obviously, Benjamin Grade wasn't telling me everything, anymore than Mariliee Bonnard had. The difference between them was that I had some hope of getting the entire story out of Mariliee Bonnard. Benjamin Grade would not be so easy to crack.

I tapped cigarette ashes into my ashtray—a ceramic replica of a large green frog with its mouth gaping open that drove Eleanor *nuts*—and tried to work this out. Mariliee, Caroline, and Belle all thought Benjamin Grade had murdered someone. They were therefore following him.

I shifted in my chair, accidentally knocking against Benjamin Grade's foot. I pulled my own foot hastily back, knowing I wanted to stop touching him in a hurry without knowing why.

"Who," I asked him, "do they think you murdered?"

"My fiancée, Caroline Matthews' niece."

Bull's-eye. It was beginning to look more reasonable. The godmothers chasing after a man they suspected of any old murder did not make sense to me. The godmothers chasing after the suspected murderer of one of their own, did. At least, it did from what I'd seen of Mariliee Bonnard. I'd have to reappraise the situation after I'd met Belle March and Caroline Matthews.

I looked more closely (and, I hoped, more objectively) at Mr. Benjamin Grade. There was determination in him, too, of a harder kind than Mariliee Bonnard's. It had something cold in it, and something wild: an obsessiveness that broke through stubbornness into something not entirely healthy. Did I think him capable of murdering someone? Yes and no. Yes, if the murder in question was a reasoned, calculated, planned-through thing. I could easily see him plotting to assassinate a Hitler or a Stalin—or their local, petty equivalents—if he thought such a man was gaining dangerous power. No, if what had happened was a crime of passion. Benjamin Grade was a passionate man. That came out of every pore in him. It was, however, a controlled passion. He had his emotions under rein.

It was a startling way to think about a person. Did I really think he had *all* his emotions under control—lust, for instance, and love? I couldn't decide. He reminded me of the steel smelters I'd seen on an "industrial tour" of Yorkshire I'd conducted for one of Amelia Mortimer-Jones's American clients. There was all this pressure—steam pressure, air pressure, the pressure of molten metal—corked up and held in by a cap so thick it wouldn't crack even in the worst emergency.

On the other hand, caps like that did crack, sometimes, under peculiar conditions.

My cigarette was out. I couldn't remember smoking it. I dumped the butt into the frog's mouth and said the only thing I could think of, *"Did* you? Kill your fiancée, I mean."

69

"No."

"Well," I said, "that's straightforward enough."

"It's about the only thing in this mess that is." He put his hand through his hair and brushed the great mane of it off his forehead. "Look," he said, "I like Caroline. I always have liked Caroline. For a long time, she even liked me. But this has got to stop. It really does. For the last year, they've been hounding me, literally hounding me, from one end of the United States to the other. They show up at writers' conferences. They trailed me to Bimini on vacation. They almost got me arrested twice. And now they're *here.*"

"And on their way to Yorkshire," I said.

"Exactly."

"Mr. Grade," I said, "could you tell me something? Why are you going to Yorkshire?"

"Because I want to."

"Meaning," I said, "you don't think it's any of my business."

"Got it in one."

"All right," I said, "but look at it from my point of view. I've just started in business. I need clients any way I can get them. I have three very pleasant women who want to make a tour of Yorkshire and are willing to pay me to do it. And I've got you. You say they're following you. Have you tried to get a restraining order?"

"What?"

"A restraining order. Have you tried to get a judge to order them to *stop* following you?"

"Of course I haven't," he said. "I told you. I like Caroline. Hell, I like all of them. I don't want to get them into trouble. I just want them to stop trying to get me into trouble."

"Maybe," I said, "but the fact is, if you're the one who's responsible for this itinerary, you're the one who's living a very suspicious life. I don't know what you're up to, Mr. Grade, but I've got a lot more reason to think you're strange than I have to think my ladies are. And you're not paying me."

"Is that all that matters to you, the money?"

"No. But it's a start."

"Well, try to make *this* matter to you." His anger was back, in full flower. "Neither you, nor any of them, has the least idea what you're fooling around in. What's going on right now could be very dangerous. They could end up getting somebody hurt—maybe you. If you've got any sense at all, you'll talk them out of this. Now."

I sat back in my chair and took a deep breath. I thought I must be going crazy. My initial impression of him as a dangerous, passionate man was magnified. I still had no worries about his ability to control himself, but I was having second thoughts about his willingness to. In an odd way, it not only fascinated me, but excited me as well. Maybe that was why I pushed on in a direction I knew I didn't believe in, and kept pushing *him*.

"I think," I said, "you're making threats."

"I have not been making threats," Benjamin Grade said tightly. "I will now make a threat. If you don't get them to call this whole thing off, somebody's going to end up dead. And it's going to be entirely their fault."

Scrape of chair legs on wooden floor, creak of door hinges, smash of wooden door against wooden doorframe: He was out of my office before I'd had time to digest the fact that he'd stood up. I stared after him, all my self-possession dissolving. I had no idea why I'd done what I'd done, or said what I said. The rational part of me had been taking Mr. Benjamin Grade, and the danger he hinted at, very seriously. I wanted to drag Mariliee Bonnard out of bed—if that's where she was—and scream at her until she saw my particular brand of reason. And Mr. Benjamin Grade's.

I knew I wasn't going to do it. Not yet, anyway.

When the muscles in my arms started twitching, going spasmodic and out of control, I reached for the intercom and called Eleanor. Eleanor, like all good secretaries, had been listening. She walked in carrying an oversize cup of tea laced with "something medicinal I found in the file cabinet."

The "something medicinal" was a topped-up shot of Whittaker's Scotch Whiskey. I needed every bit of it, even if it was a quarter after ten in the morning.

——— SIX ———

The image came from private-eye novels, or maybe private-eye television programs. A terrible thing happens. Our hero, shaken, goes for the bottle under his desk. One good slug, maybe two, and he's all right again: calmed nerves, fires of anguish extinguished.

Putting the Whittaker's in a cup of tea was a nice feminine touch, but it didn't violate the principle. What happened after I finished, did. I am not much of a drinker. I like a glass or two of wine on occasion, sometimes sherry before bed. I have been known to try oversweet liqueurs with exotic-sounding names. I kept the Whittaker's as a courtesy to the one client who had followed me from Amelia Mortimer-Jones, a spaced-out octogenarian ex-colonial who called himself *Colonel* Debreham and went to the Edinburgh Festival every year. Colonel Debreham was probably an alcoholic—meaning he probably *had* to have his Whittaker's, appropriateness of time and place notwithstanding—but he was a very well-controlled one. He had never been, to my knowledge, drunk. On the other hand, I'd never seen him quite sober.

Whatever Colonel Debreham and the private eyes had that enabled them to drink at any time of day was something I lacked. I'd barely put the empty teacup back in its saucer before the headache started. Half an hour later, nausea came along to keep it company. Then the muscle aches kicked in—was that the liquor, or a delayed reaction to Benjamin Grade?—and I got up and went to my window.

The clock over the butcher's shop said eleven. People had begun to emerge on Lisson Grove in search of lunch.

I opened the window, looked out, and took a breath of what I thought would be clean air. There was a beer lorry in the street, and what I got was a combination of petrol fumes and ale gas. The smell was sweet and rancid. It poured into my throat and into my lungs and into my stomach in a rush, making me feel ready to faint.

I stepped away, slammed the window shut, and leaned against the outer wall. It was the only safe one. Mine is not an impressively constructed building. The inner partitions of my office are made of pasteboard with a tendency to punch through.

In the back of my mind, something was saying: *Get out of here, get some air, go for a walk.*

Good advice, I thought.

The intercom buzzer rang and I went for it, feeling just a little guilty. I knew what I wanted to do. It had been with me all morning. There were a hundred things wrong with it. Still: I *was* sick, I *could* use a walk.

I pressed the lever and said, "Eleanor?"

"I've got a man on the phone," Eleanor said. "Wants to know if we'll be in at three twenty-five."

"Three twenty-five?"

"Well, I pointed out three-thirty was more usual, but he said time—"

"That's all right." I stared at the papers on my desk, all the paraphernalia from Yorkshire. If "the man" on the phone had been Benjamin Grade, Eleanor would have said so. She would have recognized his voice. This had to be a client. I wondered where he had come from. "What time are the ladies due for lunch?" I asked.

"One," Eleanor said. "Do you think you'll be through talking to them?"

"In two and a half hours?"

"Well, these *are* our ladies."

"Point taken." Anyone who wrote as much as our ladies wrote had to talk a lot, too. "Set your man up," I told Eleanor. "I'll get rid of them by then if I have to kill them. I've only got a couple of things to say to them, anyway. And this time I'm going to make them listen."

Eleanor snorted.

"Don't get sarcastic," I said. "And listen, I'm feeling like hell. I'm going out for a walk. I think—"

"Out for a walk *where?*"

"No*where.*" I lied. "Just out to get some air."

The pause on Eleanor's side of the line was long. When her voice came back, it was entirely devoid of accent. It was also entirely devoid of emotion, but I thought that might be a ploy.

"There is," she said, "some sort of maniac killing women out there."

"As far as we know, Eleanor, he kills at night."

"All we know is he moves the bodies at night," Eleanor said. "Why don't you just open a window?"

"I tried. They're delivering beer to the Jack and Hammer. It smells like—"

"Never mind," Eleanor said.

I'd expected more of an argument. Maybe Eleanor was anxious to get back to the man on the other line. Maybe there was something in my voice that told her I wouldn't be talked out of this. Instead of logic dissolving into pleas dissolving into threats—Eleanor's usual method of trying to change my mind—all I got was "try to be back before ten to one" and a dead line.

I stared at my receiver. A little less than a week ago, I hadn't even met Eleanor. Now I was feeling like an abandoned child again, because she hadn't fussed and worried over me like a mother. Was it possible to get attached to someone that quickly?

I got my coat, feeling put-out and annoyed at the world: Benjamin Grade, the godmothers, Eleanor. Right at that moment, I wanted to wring each of their necks in turn, or maybe all of them all at once.

I took my purse off the desk and headed out the door.

I could have taken the tube, or even a cab. I probably should have. It was miles and miles between Lisson Grove and Green Park. Unlike other modern cities, London has been stretching out, not up, for most of its history. Acre after acre has been added to the municipal pile, built over by four- and five- and six-story buildings. There are a few skyscrapers in central London, but not many. Prince Charles is not the only person who hates them. Almost everybody but the developers do. That is why London always seems such a gracious city. They've solved the problem of "population density," as the people back in California would have called it, by never letting the population get too dense.

I took as direct a route as I could, straight south through Marble Arch. Unless I meant to get to Green Park and turn right around, I was going to have to catch a cab on the way back to be in time for lunch, but that early in the trip I wasn't worrying about it. The walk south took me right through the center of London, and it was much more relaxing than the liquor had been. There are things I admire greatly about the British, and their determined avoidance of ostentation is one of them. In New York and Paris, the center of town is full of women in clothes you know they paid too much for. In London, only Diana, Princess of Wales and Sarah Ferguson dress "in fashion," and maybe Princess Michael of Kent. Everybody else, duchesses and middle-class housewives alike, wears twin-sets. Some of this is just England's poverty relative to the rest of Europe, a poverty Americans—so used to thinking of England in terms of Empire—find hard to believe. Even after umpteen years of Maggie Thatcher and heroic economic recovery, England's national unemployment rate is still over ten percent, and five percent of the houses don't have refrigerators. Things Americans take for granted still look like luxuries to housewives in Glastonshire and Kent. Still, I have a feeling that if Maggie Thatcher gets everything she wants and England becomes once again the richest nation in the world, the duchesses will go on wearing twin-sets. Making yourself obvious, you see, just isn't *done.*

I was going to Green Park—on a mission, if only to exorcise my own demons—but as I walked my urgency evaporated. I took Upper Montague Street through Montague Square, then turned left at Portman Square and headed south on Orchard. These are lovely neighborhoods—Portman Square may be one of the loveliest in the world; it's certainly one of the most expensive—and they have kept their "Englishness," unlike South Kensington and The Strand. Great four-story private houses with stark white columns and overlong windows, graceful key-parks behind wrought-iron fences, the tiny Courthault Institute of Art with its Victorian-hospital facade.

Somewhere near the start of Park Lane, at the edge of Hyde Park, I must have slowed to a crawl. Hyde Park is vast and curving, green in all weather, and I took the park side of the street to walk on. My destination was very close, but all of a sudden I was in no hurry to get there. I stopped at Speaker's Corner to listen to a man who blamed mental retardation on "pheromes" in the air supply—he kept talking about the "air supply" instead of the air, as if the atmosphere was something manufactured and provided by the Tory government—and then I moved south again. Not much past Speaker's Corner, there is a path that leads to a tea kiosk. I thought I could use a cup of tea, having just begun to really feel the cold. My coat was not much better than Mariliee Bonnard's. I thought that by February, when the wind started to blow, it would be untenable. I drifted past trees and cultivated lawns, thinking about tea and coat sales at Selfridge's, thinking I'd use some of the three thousand pounds to get Eleanor and myself outfitted for Arctic weather.

Coats, tea, outposts of nature in the city: Those were the things I was thinking about. The anger and apprehension I'd felt earlier that morning had dissipated. I was a little spaced-out (California again) and totally calm. I was thinking of how good an idea the walk had been and how much of a better one turning back before Green Park would be.

Which, of course, was when it first hit me I was being followed.

It must have been there all along. I thought it through later and realized I'd had some sense of it even in Lisson Grove. Nothing fancy, nothing dramatic, just this growing conviction I was not alone. I didn't know why it hadn't bothered me before. I'd had my mind on other things when I left the office, and then I'd had my mind on nothing at all. In its way, the feeling had been almost pleasant, as if I had a guardian angel. Now it wasn't pleasant in the least. I turned and looked behind me down Park Lane. There was no one there but a bobby way down by Speaker's Corner. I looked down the street and then at some bushes. The street was full of traffic and the bushes were rustling in the wind.

I gave up the idea of the kiosk and started south again, hurrying this time. I told myself I was "projecting," good social-work word that it is. I had wanted to go down to Green Park to see for myself—what, I didn't know. I was getting morbidly and ridiculously obsessed with the Ripper case, identifying with those girls because they were what I had been, subconsciously visualizing myself as a victim. That was all this was, I was sure of it. Sheila Ann Holme and Margaret Jane Willeford had embedded themselves in my imagination. I was now recreating for myself what I thought they had been through.

As an argument, it was elegant. As a tranquilizer, it was useless. Like almost everyone else who has been on the run at a very early age and survived, I am almost preternaturally sensitive to danger. Every molecule in every nerve and muscle and bone was giving off shriek signals. I kept turning toward the park and turning away and turning toward the park again, peering into the bushes, looking for something that just didn't seem to be there. After a while, the park began to look haunted and hostile. The evergreens that had seemed so orderly and civilized only minutes before had now begun to look like traps. I couldn't shake the feeling that there was someone or something behind every one of them.

I started to get out a cigarette, remembered that "nice" girls didn't smoke on London streets, and stuffed my hands in my pockets instead. I was very short of breath. Fear had knocked the wind out of me. I could no more have inhaled a lungful of nicotine than I could have inhaled a lungful of anything else. I wanted the cigarette for protection. A lit cigarette can be a very effective weapon if someone comes at you. You can always go for their eyes.

Dear God, I thought. I'm losing my mind.

I was also running.

Up ahead, I could see the Wellington Arch and the flat

expanse of Green Park. When I'd come out, I'd expected to find it empty. The police, I was sure, would have done their work and gone.

The park wasn't empty. Two police vans were parked at the Piccadilly entrance, and bobbies were everywhere. Sightseers were three-deep on the sidewalk.

I whirled, one last attempt to prove I wasn't totally insane. Beside me, in Hyde Park, the bushes rippled in the wind one more time and then lay still. I looked up and down Park Lane, shaky and uncertain. Nothing. Nothing, nothing, nothing.

I rubbed the flat of my palm against my mouth, wiping away cold sweat. The feeling wasn't gone. I still felt watched, and I still felt followed, and I was sure that once I started moving again whatever was with me would start moving, too.

I had wanted to come to the Green Park to see for myself—that was the phrase I had used, in my head, while I was in the office trying not to think about it. I am not entirely sure just what I expected to see. The body would be gone. Thank God for that. I wanted to know what it had felt like, not just to anticipate something like that (I had spent my early life anticipating it), but to be caught in it. I was like someone who had narrowly escaped dying in a fall, who then becomes fascinated by defenestration. I had been so close, so many times. Margaret Jane Willeford had actually gone over the edge.

I pushed myself into the crowd at the gate and relaxed a little. I still felt followed, watched, but I no longer felt threatened. Certainly no one was going to try to kill me with a mess of police officers barely twenty feet away, and when I was ready to go back to the office I could get a cab right on Piccadilly.

I wormed myself as close to the police line as I could get—I didn't get to it; my way was blocked by a fat lady in a ragged maroon coat, who kept muttering over and over again, "They ought to take his balls"—and I looked at the small square of earth the police had staked out in the middle of the lawn. Unlike Hyde Park, Green Park is not densely populated by trees. It's more like the oversize front lawn of a manor house. I could see plywood stakes and string barriers and little crepe-paper bows marking off what must have been where the body had been found. Then I realized it couldn't have been. Margaret Jane Willeford had been found in the sparse shrubbery close to the palace.

The man beside me was middle-aged and stout and cheerful-looking. He looked like he'd been out for a while. His nose was beginning to blister in the cold. His hands were beginning to go a little blue. He must have been retired or on the dole or on vacation, and these possibilities provided a bit of interest.

I gave him my best nice-girl smile and said, "Do you know why they're still here? It's been hours."

He gave me a silent and suspicious appraisal—put off by my American accent, I suppose—and then decided I was all right. "They're looking for something," he said.

I swallowed my impulse to sarcasm. Of course they were looking for something. I could see that. "For what?" I asked.

The middle-aged man shrugged. "He's a sick one, this one is," he said. "One of those belongs up in Bedlam, much as in Dartmoor. Not that I think they should send him off to some nice hospital—"

"Of course not."

"Young people have a lot of faith in hospitals," he said. He looked across the park at the police. They were moving the plywood stakes and the string barriers a little farther north.

One of the youngest ones got down on his knees and started going over the new ground with something that looked like an oddly-designed vacuum cleaner. It had a long snout and almost no body.

"Whatever they're looking for must be very small," I said.

"Don't trust themselves to find it just by eyeing," the man agreed. "Well, they've been at it for hours. They haven't found it yet."

"What?"

"Don't know," the man said.

"*I* know," the fat lady in front of us said. She turned neatly in her place, not giving up a millimeter of territory. She had great bulging eyes and the sagging flesh of someone who had never done a thing to take care of herself. She also had the pinched, twisted mouth of the perpetually envious.

79

She gave me a nasty little smile that had just a suggestion of superiority in it. *"I* know," she said again.

I wanted to ignore her, but I couldn't. I was too curious. The middle-aged man had more strength of character; he turned away and pretended we weren't there.

I swallowed my dislike and said, "What is it? How do you know?"

"I know because I know," the lady said, indignant in the way people like that get when you challenge their unsubstantiated claims to omniscience. "You don't learn everything in school, you know. Just because you have the education don't mean you have the brains."

I should have told her I didn't even have the education. It would have been interesting to see her reaction.

She reached out and grabbed my arm and pulled me against her. Her breath was hot and foul in my face. This was the payoff, what she had stood in the cold for hours to get.

"She had a locket," she said, giggling a little. "The girl what died. She had a locket and now they can't find it."

"A locket?"

"One what you wear around your neck. With a picture of her mother in it. Her mother but not her father, if you get my meaning."

"Nobody wears lockets anymore," I said, not intending to get her meaning if I could help it. "It's old-fashioned."

"She wore one," the woman said. "She was wearing it the night she died. People saw her. They think he took it."

"What a godawful thing to do," I said, momentarily jolted out of my dislike. Lockets *were* old-fashioned, but from what I had read about Margaret Jane Willeford, a locket would not have been inconsistent. If I'd had a picture of my mother, I would have found a way to keep it with me, too. Even if it had meant doing something so blatantly unfashionable as wearing antique jewelry.

The woman pulled at my arm again. I looked down, feeling a little surprised. I had almost forgotten she was there.

"You know what I think?" she said. "I think she gave it to him."

"What?"

"I think she gave it to him," the woman persisted. Her voice had fallen to a rasping, carrying whisper, full of secrecy and malice. "Don't you believe what you read in the papers," she said. "All that about the church and how shy she was. They're all alike, they are, these girls. Not brought up proper. Not looked after. They've got bad blood, you know, their mothers are all whores—"

"Excuse me," I said, backing away.

"She gave it to him," the woman said again. "Just you wait and see if I'm not right. She gave it to him and she got it this time, that's all, got what they all get. What they all deserve. Whores, that's what they are. Their mothers were just like them. The papers try to make you feel sorry—"

She was getting louder and louder, but I seemed to be getting less and less able to hear her. My head was filled with a roaring like ocean water in a storm. The sound of her voice was perfectly clear, but her individual words were not. People in the crowd were turning to look at her and then turning away again. The ordinary mass was with me this time. It was a change from my childhood, when the people who passed me, all total strangers, had always seemed to be against me.

I had enough self-possession left to recognize the irony in that, but not enough to take any comfort in it. As I reached the edge of the crowd, her voice took on an added sharpness and her words came clear to me one last time: "They're all alike these girls they're all alike they're just like *you.*"

I turned all the way around and bolted for the wide, busy, frantic heart of Piccadilly.

Ten minutes later, I reached Piccadilly Circus, out of breath and out of gas. I must have been running. My lungs hurt and my muscles were twitching. My feet felt swollen and full of water, twice their normal size. I couldn't remember anything about what had happened since I left the park. People, places, weather, the sounds of a London gearing up for lunch—none of it had made an impression strong enough to stick.

Talking to that woman had been like wiping out time. The last ten years seemed not to have happened. I was fifteen again, and Miss Anne Durbin was sitting in her unsteady desk chair at Santa Clara Human Services, smiling her needle smile and telling me and telling me that I was nothing more than a *hole* men could stick themselves through and then walk away from.

There was a cabstand at the corner of Regent Street and Piccadilly. I walked to it as slowly as I could, calming myself down, bringing myself back to the present. I was not Linda Lee Jackman anymore; I was Avra Mahon, and Avra Mahon was a young career woman on the way up, nothing at all like Margaret Jane Willeford.

It was a crock, and I knew it, but I also knew it was what I had to believe if I was ever going to be in good enough shape to get back to the office. I had never wanted a cigarette so badly in my life, and I had never been so completely incapable of smoking one. I needed everything I had and everything I was and everything I'd done to convince myself that, "background" or not, I really was a nice girl.

There were two people waiting ahead of me for cabs. I stood at the back of the line and made myself still, made myself oblivious. I told myself that when I got into the cab I would let myself smoke and let myself feel. I told myself a lot of things, most of which I don't remember.

The cab that pulled up for me, when it came to be my turn, was one of the good ones, a great black Rolls-Royce with all its panels shined. I let the driver get out and open the door for me. I gave him one of my very best nice-girl smiles and got a smile in return. I was beginning to feel a little better.

We were pulling away from the curb when I saw him standing alone in the street, with a battered bowler hat on his head: the man who had been in Foyle's.

When he caught me looking at him, he smiled.

─── SEVEN ───

There was a simple explanation for it, of course, simple, logical, and straightforward: coincidence. The English are as fascinated by bloody murder as the Americans are, even if they don't like to admit it. Half of London had probably stopped by for a look at Green Park that day. Piccadilly Circus was the busiest traffic circle in the city. It was more likely than not I'd run into someone I'd seen before. Coincidence; not conspiracy, or obsession, or malicious intent.

I chain-smoked three cigarettes in a row between Piccadilly Circus and Lisson Grove, an exercise in self-destruction made possible only by the density of the traffic. The London streets at noon are even more hectic and clogged than New York's. The main thoroughfares were built for horse-and-carriage traffic. They are almost as wide as they need to be. The side streets were built for foot traffic. Cars jam into them and become stuck. They send up clouds of rust-red smoke, threatening to asphyxiate pedestrians.

My driver was British, London-born-and-bred—or so he told me—and smart about the London streets. We didn't take as long as we might have. Still, we took long enough. The farther we got from Piccadilly, the more clearly I saw the peculiarities of the problem. My mind wouldn't accept coincidence as an explanation, but the alternative was absurd. I'd felt followed. Did I mean to think that man had followed me all the way from Lisson Grove? If so, he must have followed me *to* Lisson Grove. If I wasn't going to accept coincidence in the case of a meeting in Piccadilly Circus, I could hardly accept it in the case of a meeting in Lisson Grove. Everybody passed through Piccadilly Circus once in a while. Almost no one came through Lisson Grove without a solid reason for being there. Lisson Grove—all Marylebone—had its shops, offices, restaurants, and pubs, but they were local affairs, small, and without importance to the rest of the city.

We were in Bloomsbury when I realized where this was going, and I had the grace to be embarrassed. Once I turned away from coincidence, I landed in a tangled mess of improbabilities. If he'd followed me *to* Lisson Grove, he must have followed me from my flat—which meant he must have come out to the flat at least once (this morning) since the first time I'd seen him. I knew he *hadn't* followed me the morning after that first night. I'd checked every day for four days straight and every night, too. I'd been that unnerved by the first incident. There'd been no sign of him.

Alternative: He hadn't followed me *to* Lisson Grove, because he'd started following me *in* Lisson Grove. That meant he'd followed me from the office to Foyle's, where I'd first seen him. As an explanation, that left something to be desired. What had he been doing in Lisson Grove to begin with? Like Putney, Lisson Grove is a section with a stable population. I knew most of the regulars at least by sight. Nor did this man seem the type to patronize the businesses that are there. He wasn't an American, or at least I had no reason to think he was one, which made him an unlikely client for me. He was too shabbily dressed to afford the antique stores. Everything else the neighborhood had—except, perhaps, the Sea Shell, which does the best fish and chips in London —could be duplicated anywhere in the city. London has many distinctive, even unique sections, places like Bloomsbury and Chelsea, that are out of the way but worth an extra effort to get to. Lisson Grove is not one of them. It's just a pleasant little neighborhood, comfortable and quiet, of no interest to anyone who does not have business there.

The sticking point was this: There was only one reason for him to be following me—meaning he was our Ripper—but nothing in the newspaper reports, nothing in the BBC commentary on the crimes, nothing in the cautionary pronouncements of the police, indicated that the Ripper had followed his victims for weeks before doing them in. In fact, a great deal contradicted it. Sheila Ann Holme would have been difficult to follow. Her life was as peripatetic and disorganized as a renegade flea's. Margaret Jane Willeford would have been easier to follow, but not by much. She slept in the back of the church she'd given so much of her energy to—without the knowledge of the priest—and sometimes hid so well she wasn't seen by anybody for days at a time.

There was another objection. I had been what Sheila Ann Holme and Margaret Jane Willeford were. I was not, any longer. Here was a man with a demonstrated penchant for ruining teenagers. What would he want from me?

As we approached Marylebone, freed at last from the center city's insane post-noon jams, I thought of the very worst thing: There wasn't a person in the world I could discuss this with. I couldn't go to the police; I didn't have enough hard information, and what I did have would make me sound like just another overemotional woman-with-the-Ripper heebie-jeebies. There were a hundred or more of them already scattered through the city. They'd be calling up their local bobbies with stories of moving shadows and strange noises and things that went bump in the night, always at the most inconvenient hours.

There was Jasmyn Cole, but I didn't know her well enough to be sure she'd believe me in a case like this.

There was Eleanor, but what would be the point? I would only frighten her, and she was frightened enough already. If she got any shakier, she might take off. That was the last thing in the world I wanted. If Eleanor bolted now, it would be signing her own death sentence—and she wouldn't need a Ripper to carry it out.

The cab pulled up to the curb in front of my building. I got my wallet out of my purse, paid, and then climbed down onto the street, looking both ways as I did. After the cab pulled away, there was nothing—not a person on foot, not even a beer lorry.

I felt like a goddamned fool.

"You," Eleanor said as I came through the door. "I'm glad it's you. They got here twenty minutes early."

I looked around the empty reception room and then glanced pointedly at the inner office door. Eleanor nodded, looking a little wild.

"I got them in there a minute ago. I'm supposed to be making them tea. They'd hardly come in the door when they started arranging my whole life for me. Schools—do you know what they've decided I'm to do? I'm to go to LSE. LSE, for Lord's sake. I'd have to have three A-levels and I don't even have one. So I tried to explain that, and the one with the shawls—Belle March, I think—said if the British universities were too stuffy I should come to America, because I'd make a wonderful lawyer. A *lawyer*. A solicitor, she means. And then—"

"Whoa," I said, "count your blessings. At least they weren't trying to marry you off."

"I don't think they approve of marriage," Eleanor said. "Maybe that's why they write bloody stories instead of romances. When they weren't trying to make me a lawyer, they were telling me I shouldn't count on a man to pay my way. Not even a nice man, one of them said."

"Sound advice," I said.

"Miss March and Miss Matthews offered me places to stay, if I went to university near them." Eleanor shook her head. "Lord God. *University.*"

In England, getting to university—for people without family connections at Oxford or Cambridge, at any rate—is about as easy as getting knighted. I understood Eleanor's stupefaction. On the other hand, I understood Miss Bonnard, Miss March, and Miss Matthews, too. Besides, I liked the idea of Eleanor as a college girl. Maybe it satisfied a secret ambition I had not had the money or time to achieve for myself.

"I'll admit we ought to get you through high school first," I said, "but think about it anyway. It's not such a bad idea. You might like university."

"Snobs," Eleanor said.

"Some places. There are some places in the States, though, where nobody has much money and everybody's working their way through and you're all in it together. Good places, too."

"*You* want me to be a lawyer?"

"I want you to get an education. It would be good for you."

"Said by somebody who never got one herself," Eleanor said. "You'd better get in there and take care of them before they come back out here and start trying to take care of me again. You going to bring them to the Sea Shell?"

"In about ten minutes."

"Could you bring me some plaice and chips in a bag? I've got some typing to do."

Plaice and chips from the Sea Shell comes in a quantity sufficient for four. I knew Eleanor would eat it all.

"You just don't want to be anywhere near where they can lecture you again," I said. "I'll bring you plaice. You never eat enough anyway."

"I eat like a horse," Eleanor said, "and you know it. Go *do* something about them."

I said I would, and then I stood for a moment before the inner door and gathered strength, force, and determination. In all that weirdness with the woman at Green Park and the man I thought might be following me, the particulars of my morning had slipped my mind. Now they were coming back in vivid technicolor. I had a bone to pick with my godmothers.

I grabbed the knob, pulled the door back with the force of a nineteenth-century aristocrat who expects to find his daughter on the couch with a groom, and strode into the office.

"Ladies," I said, "I want to tell you about a visit I got this morning from a Mr. Benjamin Grade."

Benjamin Grade had put the image in my mind, but I would have come to it myself eventually. Sitting all together like that, they really did look like the fairy godmothers from Disney's *Sleeping Beauty:* Flora, Fauna, and Merriweather. They were all just barely five feet tall, if that. They were all very pink and healthy looking. Mariliee Bonnard, as I have mentioned before, wore Mary Poppins–like princess cuts. One of the others (Belle March, as I would learn later) wore lacy shawls and a comb in her hair. The third was more determinedly sensible: good wool suit (albeit pink), just-slightly-stack-heeled shoes, hard leather handbag. The sensible one was perched on the edge of my desk, swinging her legs.

There were discrepancies, of course. For one thing, the one in the shawls was smoking a small brown cigar. Maybe they had been too deep in discussion to hear me talking to Eleanor in the outer office. Whatever the reason, they weren't expecting me. None of them looked in the least bit fluffy. Belle March—the shawls, the cigar—looked positively fierce.

I gave them a few minutes to get used to the sight of me and then came in and shut the door. There was no place for me to sit, but I didn't want to sit. Standing, according to the books I read on management, gives one an advantage over those sitting. I wanted all the advantages I could get. Even Mariliee Bonnard could be as relentless and irresistible as tide against rock. The three of them were going to be quite a challenge.

I leaned against the window frame and stared down at them.

"Don't just gape at me," I said, "tell me things. Like, are you really following Benjamin Grade?"

The shawls stirred. The lit end of the cigar flashed briefly. The shawl-lady put out her hand and said, "I'm Belle March."

It was a calculated attempt to put me in my place, and I wasn't having any of that. I took Belle March's hand, and then Mariliee's, and then Caroline Matthews's (the sensible-looking one). I even murmured a "good afternoon." I did not give ground. I knew that once I gave a little, I'd give the whole estate.

I'd stood up to Benjamin Grade when he was where the godmothers were now, but I didn't tell them that. I'd stood up to him because I didn't like his attitude. I didn't think his point was necessarily illegitimate. They shouldn't be following the man and making accusations against him unless they had something solid to go on. If they had, Benjamin Grade would not be out walking the streets.

From the pit of my visitor's chair, Mariliee Bonnard sent up a sigh. "It isn't going to work," she said. "I told you it wasn't going to work."

"Nothing's ruined *yet,*" Belle March snapped.

"I think we all ought to get some lunch," Caroline Matthews said. "We'll feel better when we've had something to eat."

I started to protest. What was this, after all, but another attempt to get control of the situation? Caroline Matthews stopped me with a glance.

"I'm not trying to weasel out of it, Miss Mahon," she said. "I'll tell you everything you want to know. More than he did. I'll tell you just what we're going to do, too. Because he did kill my niece, Miss Mahon. He killed her, and I can almost prove it."

I looked at each one of them—three small, older women working hard to look solemn and even penitent—and something in me melted. They looked brave, even noble, and very vulnerable.

Reality, of course, was somewhat less sentimental. Push had come to shove. I folded.

I hadn't known about the Sea Shell when I rented my office in Lisson Grove, but if I had it would have been a point in its favor. The Sea Shell really does have the best fish and chips in London, maybe in England. They use first-class fish and not too much oil—some of the hole-in-the-wall places give you stuff so deep-fried you could use what comes off on your hand to fry something else altogether—and they serve in quantity. Almost everybody in the neighborhood eats there, which means the place acts as a kind of barometer of acceptance. Once you've established a regular workday table, you're in.

My regular table was upstairs, in the back room, in a corner. I liked it because it was quiet and out of the way of waitress traffic. The tables in the Sea Shell are pushed very close together. Rents are high in London, and salaries are low, which means quantity is the only way to survive as a lunch place. The Sea Shell has managed to maintain that quantity. The place is always packed.

I said hello to the girl from the sweet shop and exchanged *isn't-it-awful?*s (about the murders) with Mrs. Parmaden on the way through. Fortunately, Mrs. Crail, the only really unpleasant person on the block, and the woman who owned the most elaborate of the antique stores, ate downstairs, so I didn't have to deal with her. I explained to three people that no, these were not my aunts. I waved away the waitress's suggestion of an ale. Belle March did not. Rearranging coats and purses, ordering, being served: It didn't take long for the little rituals of sitting down in a restaurant to get me crazy. I wanted to get on with it. The godmothers were in no hurry at all.

I had to wait until we actually had fish in front of us before I heard anything. The Sea Shell is fast—it has to be, to serve so many people who can spare only a half hour for lunch—but that day it wasn't fast enough. I was beginning to feel not only crazy but defeated. The godmothers had much better control over themselves than I did.

When the waitress had put down three orders of plaice and one of fried shrimp and finally moved out of the way, Caroline Matthews picked up her handbag. She rummaged around for a while and came out with a small, undersize manila envelope.

"Here," she said, handing it across the table to me. "Start with that."

The envelope was stiff. Caroline had put cardboard in it to keep whatever she had from being accidentally folded and damaged. It took a little while for me to get the little sheaf of papers out where I could see them. They were newspaper clippings, stiff and brittle and beginning to go yellow with age.

What I had in front of me was not what I had expected to see, so it took a while to sink in. I had anticipated a run-of-the-mill account of an ordinary murder and a picture of Caroline Matthews's niece that would show her to be what I was sure she was: the pampered object of affection of a famous relative. Part of me thought—because I knew Caroline Matthews came from Boston—that whatever had happened had happened on a city street somewhere, probably at night. A mugging, a robbery, an eruption of mindless violence Caroline Matthews could not accept.

What I had in front of me was a newspaper photograph of a girl with The Look.

That and a banner headline from the Boston *Globe,* saying: KILLER STABBED VICTIM THROUGH ROSE.

I dropped the clippings on the blue linen tablecloth, next

to my plate. My mouth felt very dry, painfully so. I was dizzier than I had been when the Whittaker's wore off. I was also numb. The real fear would come later.

"What the *hell* is this?" I said.

Caroline took the clippings and the envelope away from me and started putting the package back in order.

"The rose-Ripper murders started just after he got here," she said, quietly but somehow implacably. "It's much too much of a coincidence. It isn't the kind of thing just anyone would think of, just like that."

"No," I said. "It's not. And I read the London tabloids. If there'd been any publicity about it here, I'd have heard about it. When——"

"About a year ago," Belle said. "Last November."

"They were engaged to be married," Belle said. "My niece Julie and Benjamin Grade. She was in college at Wellesley, and she——"

"She'd been in foster homes," I said. "Don't try to pretend she wasn't. *I* was in foster homes. I can pick them out every time."

"I told you she reminded me a little of Julie," Mariliee Bonnard said.

"My sister Penny," Caroline said wryly, "was not exactly the most stable of women——"

"She was a twit," said Belle March.

"She probably was a twit." Caroline sighed. "She was also a great deal younger than I am and very dear to me. When she got pregnant out of wedlock, in her thirties, mind you, when women usually know better, I wasn't in a financial position to help her much. So she took off. I don't know where. Took off with the baby, and by the time I tracked them down, Penny was dead and Julie was fifteen."

"In jail for drugs," Belle March said. "Be honest, Caroline."

"It was only possession of marijuana," Caroline said. "If she'd been living with me, she wouldn't have gone to jail on a charge like that at all. Well, if she'd been living with me a lot of things wouldn't have happened. Anyway, I took her to Boston, and I sent her to Miss Haverham's, and I sent her to Wellesley. Unfortunately, I also introduced her to Mr. Benjamin Grade."

"At an Edgar dinner," Belle March put in. "Caroline brought Julie to the Edgar Awards dinner—that's an award the Mystery Writers of America give every year for the best mystery books—anyway, two years ago, Caroline brought Julie and Benjamin Grade was seated at their table—"

"We didn't expect anything like this new business," Mariliee Bonnard broke in. "I mean, we didn't think he was a homicidal maniac. We just knew he'd killed Julie, and he was going to get away with it. And we thought—I don't know what we thought."

"No," I said. "I don't expect you do."

"Of course we do," Belle March said. "We wanted to get the evidence on him. We wanted to make it right."

"That would be possible," Caroline said, "because he was never tried for Julie's murder. He was never tried for anything. If he had been, there would have been double jeopardy."

"But what did you expect to find?" I asked. "It's been a year. You said you had no idea there was going to be a—a series of these. What could you have possibly—"

"We didn't know," Belle said. "We just knew something strange was going on. Caroline had a private detective on him—"

"Good Lord," I said.

"—and she'd cultivated his secretary," Belle went on. "Everything went along very routinely for months, and then all of a sudden he started behaving very oddly. This trip to England, for instance. We know Benjamin Grade. He's a planner. There was no planning for this trip at all. Usually, his secretary gets instructions months before he wants to leave. This time, she had days. And Mrs. Henry Copplewhite's bed-and-breakfast. I've been to England forty times, Miss Mahon. I've never been out of London except to Stratford and Oxford, that kind of thing, but I have heard of Mrs. Henry Copplewhite's. It's supposed to be a hole. Can you imagine a man who sells a million books a year—a man who doesn't know there's a hotel in Boston besides the Copley Plaza—staying in a hole?"

"We thought he had evidence," Mariliee said. "Something incriminating him. We thought he was going to come over here and get rid of it."

"You thought," Belle March said. "I never saw much sense in that explanation."

"The fact is," Caroline said, "almost as soon as he got here, there was another murder with a rose, another stabbing death just like Julie's. And he's still in London and there's been another one."

"And now he's going to go to Yorkshire and do some more?" I said.

"I don't know," Caroline said.

I hadn't touched my food, and it was growing cold and congealing on my plate. I pushed it away and tried to make sense of what the godmothers were telling me. The pieces didn't lend themselves to sense.

"Look," I said. "Let me start out by granting you that the circumstances are suspicious. No, this isn't the usual kind of thing. The fact is, the man has booked himself into Mrs. Henry Copplewhite's, all the way up in Yorkshire right at the beginning of bad weather. Why? If all he wanted in England was the chance to do in some more girls, he could manage that from the Connaught and be more comfortable while he was doing it. Why all the extra bother?"

"Maybe," Mariliee said, not sounding as if she had much hope, "that's part of his being a maniac."

"I've told you and told you," Belle said, "maniacs are not illogical. Irrational, yes, but not illogical. What they do has a reason, no matter how bizarre."

"All right," I said, "we are now agreed you have to find a reason for his going to Yorkshire that fits in with his being the killer"—I stuck a little at the words, but went on—"if your following him is going to do any good. We can't find any such reason—"

"We can't find any reason at all," Belle pointed out.

"True," I said, "but—"

"I'm not going to give this up," Caroline said. "He did kill Julie. He was with her—seen with her, by reliable witnesses—only hours before she died. They had a terrible fight—"

"It seems," Belle said, "she was throwing him out on his ear."

"She *had* thrown him out on his ear," said Caroline. "He was furious at her. And jealous. And he got back—"

"Whoa," I said. "Pick one. Either he killed her with a

motive, or he killed her because he's a homicidal maniac. I don't think people do both."

"Maybe her throwing him out set him off," Caroline said stubbornly.

I let it go. Obviously, for these three women, the particulars didn't matter as much as the central conviction: that Benjamin Grade had indeed killed Julie Matthews. They would hold to that single premise no matter what I did. I could take each of their theories and explode them in turn, but nothing—not even an alibi from the Oval Office—would convince them he had not killed her.

I sat back, took out my cigarettes, and lit up. "Has it occurred to you," I said, "that what you're doing is even crazier if he *did* kill her?"

"I don't see what you mean," Caroline said.

I saw Ben Grade making threats in my office. "You tell me you think this man is a murderer," I said. "You tell me you more than half-suspect he's a serial murderer. If you go chasing after him like this, what's to stop him from killing you?"

Caroline opened her mouth, shut it again, opened it again, shut it again. Impossible as it was to believe, it appeared she'd never thought of this. The other two had. While Caroline was going definitely green around the gills, as the cliché goes, the other two looked sheepish.

"We're really not as fragile as we look," Belle March said. "We can take care of ourselves."

"Against a man who stabs women dozens of times and . . . and impales things on them?"

"Young women," Belle pointed out. "None of them even twenty."

"Most young women will have a lot more strength than the three of you," I said, "and they'd be faster, too. It hasn't helped them any."

"If you don't want to be involved in this," Mariliee Bonnard said, "we'll understand. That's why—"

"Why you didn't tell me when you hired me?"

"Something like that," Mariliee said.

"*Everything* like that," Belle said, disgusted. "Who'd have expected him to have the nerve—"

"If anything at all of what you think of him is true," I said, "he's obviously got a lot of nerve. Actually, from what I saw of him in my office, I think he's got a lot of nerve, period."

"We'll do the right thing," Caroline Matthews said, suddenly brisk. "You made the arrangements. You did the work. We'll pay your fee, of course. You've earned it. It was very wrong of us not to tell you from the beginning. If you'll just turn the itinerary and reservations receipts over to us—"

"No," I said.

Caroline Matthews blinked.

"Tsk, tsk," said Belle March. "You should know us by now. It won't stop us if you don't. We'll just—"

"I'm not trying to stop you," I said. "I'm saying I'll go with you. I won't quit the tour."

I'd surprised them. I don't think they thought themselves capable of being surprised. It was a very satisfying moment. Even Belle March gaped.

"We will leave for Yorkshire from Euston Station," I said, "at ten o'clock, on the morning of October ninth, one week from today. Take a cab. And don't be late. It's an express train. Now—"

"Why?" Marilee demanded. *"Why?"*

I had a hundred reasons to give them. I really did need the full three thousand pounds. I might easily go bankrupt without it. I was growing fond of them. I hated to see them put themselves in danger with no help from a younger person. I was, oddly, almost inexplicably for me, intrigued. I had been drawn into a story, and now I wanted to see how it would come out.

I gave them the reason that superseded all others. "I'm going," I said, "because although I couldn't tell you right now if I think Benjamin Grade killed Julie Matthews, I can tell you I don't think he's running around London killing others. I think he's up to something. I don't think murder is it."

"You mean you're going to come with us because you think we're going to fail?" Marilee said.

"If I thought you were going to succeed," I said, "I'd be on the first train for Kent." I picked up a candy. "Sweet, ladies?"

They all wanted a sweet. So did I.

——— EIGHT ———

Half an hour later, I walked them to the street and put the godmothers in a cab for the Connaught. I was feeling a little giddy. All my reasons made perfect sense and no sense at all. Part of me was appalled at what I'd agreed to do. Even if Benjamin Grade wasn't a murderer—and at the time I couldn't make myself believe he was—he could cause us all a lot of trouble if the ladies kept pushing him. He had *promised* to cause us trouble. Another part of me, though, wouldn't have given up this trip for the world.

I watched the cab disappear up Rossmore toward Regent's Park and Queen Mary's Gardens, and tried to shake off my tendency to self-analysis. This was a sound business decision. I'd score brownie points with the godmothers and they'd give me good reviews when they returned to America. I needed those desperately if the business were to survive.

I turned around and headed back to the office. The clock on the butcher's shop said *3:36,* and that bothered me a little, though I couldn't think why. I stopped to look in the window of Mrs. Crail's antique store and decided I'd never seen such an ugly piece of furniture; it wasn't entirely obvious what said piece of furniture was supposed to do. I stopped in the sweet shop and bought half a pound of candied ginger.

I was having one of those conversations with the sweet-shop girl—one of the ones everybody in London was having that day, about what an awful thing the murders were and how we were afraid to go out at night—when I remembered:

the *appointment*. Eleanor had set up an appointment for me at three twenty-five, with a man who apparently had some *reason* for the odd choice of time. I was missing it. I, possessed of hardly enough clients to count as a legitimate tour company, was standing in a sweet shop talking about blood and candied ginger while a source of revenue was cooling his heels in my office, probably developing a very negative impression of my reliability.

I dumped twenty-five pence down on the counter and ran. The door to my office wasn't very far, hardly ten feet, but I was anxious enough so the run felt as if it took forever. I went flying through the door and headed for the stairs. I bolted up the stairs without stopping for breath on the landing. The building was Victorian and the stairs were steep and long. By the time I reached my office door, my lungs felt as if they'd been attacked by nails.

I stopped, took three deep breaths, fixed my clothes, and ran a hand through my hair. Racing in out of breath and dishevelled wouldn't change a negative impression to a positive one. I cursed my cigarette habit—bad for me, even though I smoke American low-tars that Englishmen hardly count as cigarettes at all—and counted to ten. Control. Contrition. Professionalism.

I grabbed the knob, pushed open the door, and ran straight into Eleanor.

She looked wilder than I'd ever seen her, wilder even than she had been on that first day. Then, she'd looked frightened but ready. Now she looked frightened to death.

I thought our man with the appointment had turned out to be some kind of nut. I thought we'd been burglarized. I thought a lot of things. Mostly, I thought I should get in there and protect Eleanor from whatever was making her look like that.

I shoved her aside and ran into the office.

And stopped.

The way anyone would have stopped.

Because the office was filled, flooded, *drowning* in roses, dozens and dozens of them, every last one of them white.

Eleanor's voice came from behind me, high and panicked. "I don't know who they're from," she said. "I don't know, I don't know. They came at three twenty-five exactly, a man brought them and left them, they were all wrapped up in paper. And I read the card and I thought they were from our ladies—"

"What card?" I said.

"I dropped it."

"Okay," I said. My voice sounded odd, as if I were speaking underwater. "Calm down. Go find the card."

"It was for you," Eleanor said.

"I'm sure it was."

"Your appointment never showed up," she said.

"That's all right. I have a strange idea that maybe this is it."

She was calmer now. She walked away from me toward her desk, sat down, and started to search the floor near her feet. I stood in the center of the office, feeling unnaturally calm. The scent of roses was thick, sweet, and heavy in the air around me, making it difficult to breathe.

He must, I thought, have brought them here himself. An order for white roses would have caused suspicion in any florist's shop in London, especially an order as big as this.

"Eleanor," I said, still in that overcalm voice, "did you see the man who brought them? Would you recognize him?"

"No," Eleanor said slowly. "I never saw his face. He had a hat—"

"Pulled down over it," I finished for her. "I suppose he would have."

"I found the card," she said.

I thanked God for Eleanor's monumental self-possession. Anyone less self-controlled, or less intelligent, would have asked all the obvious questions: *Was that really him? Was he really in here with me?* I couldn't have stood that. I didn't have the answers. I didn't know if I wanted to have them.

I took the card out of her hand, a plain white square florist card like millions of florist cards all over the world.

Eleanor said, "The white rose is a kind of symbol of Yorkshire, you know. From the Wars of the Roses. I forgot about that."

"So did I."

I turned the card over in my hand. It said: "Looking forward EAGERLY to our trip north. Love."

PART THREE

── NINE ──

Yorkshire is a wild and erratic country, a solid contradiction—a bloody contradiction, too, politically and every other way. In 1399, the nobility of York took up the badge of the white rose in opposition to Lancaster's red. Parliament had just deposed the king they favored— Richard II—and installed a king they didn't. That was Henry IV, a strong man with good sense and not much of a tendency toward greed. His son was much the same. His grandson was a horror story: Only nine months old when he ascended the throne, spoiled and pampered into weakness and venality by cabals of intriguers looking to tie him and use him when he reached his majority, he was the paradigm of the kind of aristocrat whose rule ends in revolution. In the case of Henry VI, rule ended in civil war. In 1455, York, having had enough, took up arms and raised its white-rose banner against the crown and against the south, in favor of its own duke. The war that resulted went on for thirty years, fought as much with plunder, savagery, and vandalism as on the field of battle. Monasteries and convents were sacked by first one side and then by the other. Crops were burned into stubble and then burned again, until the memory of the time when England had fed its people well and without difficulty was so faint it seemed mythical. Like all civil wars, this one divided families, father against son, brother against brother, wife against husband. Like many, it would never be completely over. York lost a decisive battle at Bosworth Field in 1485. Lancaster's champion, knowing nothing was decisive as long as York had a grievance and time to recoup, tried to head off further disruption by marrying Richard's daughter, Elizabeth, joining the two warring houses and making them one. In a way, it worked. The battles stopped. The sacking and pillaging stopped. Elizabeth was lovely and of good reputation. No one in York, knowing her cult among the common people, wanted to move against her. Henry VII came to his marriage an absolute monarch, the nobility weakened and depleted by so many years of fighting. England was united and remained united. And yet, these things never end. The American Civil War is over a hundred years dead, but there are people in Alabama and Mississippi and Georgia who speak as if it happened yesterday, or maybe is still going on today. There are secret and not-so-secret rebels in Mobile and Biloxi and Macon who still hold their grudges close. The Wars of the Roses are five hundred years dead, but York is a riot of white-rose loyalty. There is a White Rose Walk, a White Rose Highway. There are White Rose inns and White Rose manors without number. There are white roses, too, in florists' shops and cottage gardens and men's lapels.

I had forgotten about the white rose of York until Eleanor reminded me—unsurprising in someone who's had as little formal education as I have—but I hadn't forgotten the rest of it, and the rest of it was hardly comforting. Yorkshire, someone said once, is split down the middle between the moors and the mines. That's untrue geographically, but very true psychologically. The moors gave birth to *Jane Eyre* and *Wuthering Heights*. The mines gave birth to bitter poverty and labor battles so bloody they made Pinkerton's men firing into a crowd of Rockefeller workers in Colorado look like hostesses at a tea party. The mines and moors together give birth to violence of a more modern kind: murderers, singular and serial. The Yorkshire Ripper, who killed twelve people in the late seventies, was only the most recent of them.

There are still people in Yorkshire who refer to the Ripper of the seventies as "our Peter."

None of this was the kind of thing I told clients who wanted to go to Yorkshire—even when I was still with Amelia Mortimer-Jones and not very happy with her. None of this was the kind of thing I ever really thought of, partially because there would have been no point (I am, by necessity, a very practical woman), and partially because not that many clients wanted to go to Yorkshire. People on romance-writer tours travel to the moors to see the landscape that inspired the Brontës. College students hike the Pennines because the trails are good and the country is unspoiled. The people I deal with want to see Queen Elizabeth I's bed and the meticulously restored country palace of Anne Boleyn. Neither of these are in Yorkshire.

I thought about the nasty side of Yorkshire—or the romantic side, if you happen to be the sort of person who can find romance in insanity and hauntings and sudden death (which Eleanor is)—almost incessantly in the days after I got the roses, but I did not back out of the tour, although I certainly thought about it. I spent three solid days locked away in my office, telling myself I was a perfect little fool. I didn't like this sort of thing. I didn't even like to watch it on television. And here I was, checking lists, packing bags, confirming reservations, going about the minutiae of putting myself in what just might be danger as if I were taking an afternoon outing to Kent.

It was the best-planned tour I would ever run in my life. I planned everything five or six times. I could do that because there wasn't much planning to do. Most tours require reams and reams of paperwork: getting all the sights lined up so the client can see them without being exhausted and footsore at the end of every day; getting different bed-and-breakfasts and hotels lined up for every day or two; working out the transportation schedule so you don't end up dashing from one end of the country to the other in no particular order and wasting all your time on trains. The godmothers had no interest in sights, except for the sight of Mr. Benjamin Grade. The only accommodations they were after were to be provided by Mrs. Henry Copplewhite. All I had to do was make sure we all got on and off the train together, with luggage intact. After that, I could sit around reading Barbara Cartland novels for the next six weeks.

"I've got enough to do," Eleanor said, when I complained to her I hadn't. "And I'll be glad to have you all out of here. Then I'll be able to do it."

It was a brave statement, true enough even though she didn't mean it. We had a few major arguments after the delivery of the roses. Eleanor was sure the Ripper had staked me out and was going to follow me to Yorkshire. ("He'll get you up there where there's nothing and nobody. You don't know what it's like.") I was unsure as to whether she was right or wrong. Logic argued against Eleanor's views, and in this case it argued so strongly against them, it was impossible to ignore. We had called the police after the delivery, and their reasoning confirmed my own. If it was the Ripper who had sent the flowers, he was behaving distinctly out of character.

"Look at it this way," I told Eleanor, on one of the days the godmothers had gone off on their own. (This was unusual. Mostly, they hung around the office, trying to "help." If they'd been domestic sorts, which they weren't, they'd have cooked and cleaned and mended clothes, which might not have been so bad. Being what they were, they did the books, organized the files, and plied Eleanor with American college catalogues they had prevailed on friends to ship Federal Express from the States.) "The girls he's killed were strays—they didn't live anywhere, they didn't have connections or family or anything. He couldn't have sent them eight dozen roses before he killed them. He wouldn't have had any place to send them to. And if they'd arrived on the streets of Camden Town, somebody would have noticed."

"He's crazy," Eleanor said, "he might do anything."

"Maybe," I agreed, "but I've been reading up on serial killers. They establish patterns. Patterns they stick to, Eleanor. According to the books I've read, the patterns are almost as important to them as the killings. And a lot of these people aren't crazy in the way you're using the word."

"They'd have to be crazy," Eleanor said. "Why else would they do that sort of thing?"

"Nobody's sure." I rummaged through the books on my desk. "The kind of person you're talking about is incompetent. He goes into frenzies, he barely knows what he's doing. Like David Berkowitz, the Son of Sam killer in New York. He went around killing young women with long, straight brown hair. The very last one was blond, but she was sort of the same type. Anyway, in all probability he hardly remembered what he'd done when he'd done it. His brain was all compartmentalized. His normal life went in one place. His killing life went in another. With people like this, there are serious questions about whether they're competent to stand trial—the courts usually decide they are, because there's no other way to get them off the street for good. Then there are serial killers like Theodore Robert Bundy—"

"I read a book about him," Eleanor said. "He was crazy, too. He heard voices. It *said* so."

"Eleanor, he only started saying he'd heard voices after he'd racked up two death penalties in Florida."

"Are you trying to tell me he *didn't* hear voices?"

"I'm trying to tell you I think it finally occurred to him they were going to fry him if he didn't do something fast, and this is what he thought of to do. Up to then, they gave him psychological test after psychological test. No psychiatrist who didn't know beforehand what he'd been accused of doing ever pronounced him anything but sane. Adolescent, yes. Unstable, yes. Not very nice, often. But never crazy."

"Then why did he do it?"

"I have a terrible feeling the answer to that is very simple," I said. "I think he liked it."

"And you don't call that crazy?"

I shot her my most significant look. "Eleanor, you and I have both had vast experience with people who hurt children. Sometimes physically, more often mentally. That 'she' you're always talking about, the one who called you 'Nell.' She did it because she liked it. Didn't she?"

"That's different," Eleanor said.

"No, it's not. It's just easier to get away with."

"That's worse, then," she said stubbornly. "If he's a person like that, he'd have sent the roses if he could have. Now he wants to get you and you're not like the others. He can *play* with you."

I shook my head. "Not that simple. Remember the pattern."

"Oh, *hang* the bloody pattern."

I shook my head. "I can't. Eleanor, I've been over and

over these books. I've read every case study of every serial murderer since Jack the Ripper. The pattern matters. Even if the roses came from the Ripper, they weren't an announcement of my impending death. He doesn't do things that way."

"What *were* they an announcement of?"

"I don't know."

"So you're going to go up to Yorkshire and find out," Eleanor said. "Oh, that's bloody wonderful. That's bloody marvelous. That's the sanest thing I've ever heard."

"Eleanor—"

"Don't pay any attention to *me*," Eleanor said. *"I'm* not anybody. *I* don't have sense enough to be grateful for the charity the Crown of England is keeping me with. *I've* always known that."

"Eleanor—"

"Bugger," Eleanor said. She grabbed her copy of Belle March's *Shadows of Darkness* and locked herself in the bathroom.

I sat back and thought. The argument we'd just had had ended in my victory, but only because Eleanor didn't know how to argue. Her point—buried under emotionalism about maniacs, not clear even to herself—was well-taken: What did I think I was doing and why was I doing it? At some later point she accused me of "trying to be just like Nancy Drew," a statement that surprised me a little, because I didn't know they had Nancy Drew in England.

I did seem to like this mystery. The problem of that—of what was making me so fascinated, of what was making me so stubborn about seeing it through—occupied me more and more as the day of departure approached. Every time I thought I'd found an answer, I soon changed my mind.

We were due to leave London on October ninth. On October eighth, I came in late to the office after stopping at British Rail and the Home Tourist Office to clear up a few details. I'd intended to stop at Inland Revenue and do what I could to regularize Eleanor's position with the tax people, but getting my reservations confirmed at British Rail took so long it was after eleven by the time I had the papers in order. Inland Revenue was going to have to wait another day. It was going to take hours to get anything done there, too.

I took the tube to Marylebone station. It would take longer than a cab, but I wasn't worried. Eleanor had gone directly to the office that morning, and I was sure she was holding the fort with no difficulties whatsoever. The godmothers were, at least theoretically, out of town. Belle March wanted to make "a quick run to Stratford."

I hit Lisson Grove at a stroll, stopped at the sweet shop for candied ginger, stopped to talk to Mrs. Parmaden about the stupidity of the police (because they hadn't brought the Ripper in), stopped to talk to Mrs. Crail about this year's awful fashions. As far as I knew, Mrs. Crail had been expounding on the awfulness of this year's fashions every year since 1952. I walked up the stairs and down the hall to my office door with nothing more worrisome on my mind than a routine anxiety about the car I'd hired to take us from Ramsmoor to St. Edmund Cavateur. Provincial car-hire services in England are notoriously unreliable, but none of the multinationals, like Hertz, had offices in Ramsmoor. Hiring a car in the city of York would have been prohibitively expensive.

I had my hand out for the doorknob before I realized someone was waiting in the hall for me. I looked the woman up and down, more than once. She was an anorectically thin middle-aged woman dressed in ill-fitting tweeds, too heavy and too cheap to look good on anyone. She had a pair of glasses hung around her neck with a ribbon, and one of those hard-plastic pocketbooks that look like weapons. She wore makeup in a way that let me know she found painting her face an unpleasant duty. Her lipstick didn't quite cover her mouth. Her foundation was thin and flaking, bought cut-rate at a sale and applied with a miser's protest.

She was a type I recognized. I hated her on sight.

I opened my pocketbook and got out my keys. The door would be locked. Eleanor would have seen this woman coming and bolted. I sent up a prayer to Sister Tom or whoever her equivalent in Eleanor's life might be, whatever force had caused the act of providence that let Eleanor see before being seen.

Then I told myself to calm down. I was ready to kill this

woman on the spot, just as I'd have been ready to kill Miss Anne Durbin if she'd ever shown up in a place where we were alone.

The woman cleared her throat, whacked her pocketbook against her leg, and said, "Miss Mahon? I am Mrs. Charlotte Derme."

Mrs. Charlotte Derme. Lovely name. Have you ever noticed how people like this always use full name and title? It was always Mrs. Catherine Hobart, never "Cathy." It was always Miss Anne Durbin, never "Annie." I considered calling Mrs. Charlotte Derme "Charlie" and almost immediately gave it up.

"Sorry to keep you waiting," I said, in the most cheerful voice I could manage. "I had some errands to run. Being alone—"

"I'm from Child Services, Miss Mahon."

"Are you?" I said. "I don't have a child."

I had, by this time, got the door open. Mrs. Charlotte Derme pushed past me, strode into my outer office, and looked around. There was no sign of Eleanor—or no sign anyone who hadn't known me a long time would have noticed. The office was tidier than I'd kept it when I'd been by myself, and more professional-looking (as *professional* is defined by magazines for career girls), but Mrs. Charlotte Derme had no way of knowing what a slob I usually was.

She headed straight for the door to the inner office, as if she owned the place, as if she owned *me*.

I stood watching her, thinking I knew exactly how this scene would progress. Mrs. Charlotte Derme would march into my inner office, I would stop her, we would fight. That was the way things would have gone with Miss Anne Durbin. I didn't think there was much difference between the British and American versions. I closed the outer door behind me and willed myself to relax. I knew Eleanor had to be in the inner office. There was no back way out of the suite and none from the building, either. I was sure she wasn't in there sitting at my desk, exposed to whoever might walk in. She would have hidden herself in the supply closet, at least.

Mrs. Charlotte Derme faked me out, as we used to say back home. She stopped dead in the middle of the floor, turned around, and came back to the receptionist's desk.

Then she sat down in my client's chair and folded her hands in her lap.

It put me off balance. I had been ready, even eager, for a certain kind of confrontation. I think part of me had seen myself as a kind of caped crusader, a knight in navy-blue rayon. I was going to save Eleanor from the dragon. Mrs. Charlotte Derme wasn't a dragon. She might be a fox, or a weasal, or a rat, but she wasn't the full-blown, full-speed-ahead force-of-fury Miss Anne Durbin had been. I hadn't the faintest idea what I was going to do with her.

She said, "Excuse me. I know you don't have a child. I just need a few minutes of your time. I need to talk to you."

Politeness, apparently, was going to be the order of the day. I took a deep breath and sat in the chair behind Eleanor's desk. If Mrs. Charlotte Derme could be polite to me, I would be polite to her. For exactly as long as I absolutely had to.

She reached into her pocketbook, took out a small envelope, and laid it on the desk. "I am," she said, "as I told you, from the Child Services division of the Department of Health and Social Security. We were notified early last week by our children's home in York that one of our girls was missing. This girl." She opened the envelope, took out a pair of photographs, and passed them to me. "As you can see," she said, "the girl is very young. Just fifteen."

What I could see was that the girl was very miserable. The face in front of me was Eleanor, all right, just not the Eleanor I knew. This girl had neither the noble, reckless defiance of Eleanor as a punk nor the stubborn optimism of Eleanor the professional. If I'd seen this face on someone in the street, I would have wanted to call Suicide Watch as a preventive measure.

Had I looked like that? I didn't know. My memories of myself at that time are colored now by what came after. My escape was successful. I therefore think of myself as sturdier and feistier than the girls I knew at the time. I was probably just luckier. For all I knew, on the day I left Santa Clara on the bus for New York, I'd looked just as downtrodden, just as defeated, as Eleanor did in those pictures.

I pushed the pictures away from me back across the desk toward Mrs. Charlotte Derme.

"She looks miserable," I said.

Mrs. Charlotte Derme put the pictures back in the envelope and the envelope back in her purse. "I suppose she does," she said. "But you know, I can't be sentimental about this kind of thing. Most of these girls make themselves miserable. We provide them with food and clothing and shelter and education. Without us, they'd be living on the street, if they were living at all. They don't appreciate it. Sometimes I wonder what they want—to go back to the time of Victoria, when orphans starved or were sold to Fagins to be trained as thieves?"

"Maybe they just want not to be orphans," I said.

"Well, that's hardly something I can arrange, is it?"

True enough, I thought, the catch-22 of abandoned children. Only one thing could make it better, and science had yet to work out a way to resurrect the dead.

I shook my head, as if to clear it. I was letting Mrs. Charlotte Derme take me in. There were, after all, alternatives: Adoption, for one—although adopting parents wanted infants, not children three or four or ten years old; a foster-parent system more strictly regulated and more logically run, so children could stay with one set of foster-parents indefinitely, instead of being hauled away to a new environment every time the administration thought they were getting too attached; an end to the bureaucratic ivory-tower nonsense that took children away from good people who were "too old" or the "wrong" religion or single and then put them with people who were the right age, religion, and marital status but who hated children. There were a *million* alternatives. If they ever put me in charge of a child-welfare service, I'd use every one of them.

". . . and with the situation the way it is in London," Mrs. Charlotte Derme was saying.

I looked up. I'd been so busy reforming the world, I'd missed what she was saying.

"I'm sorry," I said. "I'm a little tired. I'm afraid I drifted off for a minute."

She shot me a look that was anything but sweet reasonableness. The mask came off for just a second, letting through the dragon beneath.

"I said, with the situation in London the way it is—the Ripper, I mean—we're very anxious to make sure none of our girls is out wandering around the streets. We don't want a ward of the Crown stabbed to death in Green Park. Of course, once these girls run, it's almost impossible to find them. Most of them, anyway. They go to Camden Town or East Liverpool and dye their hair purple and make themselves up, and they're unrecognizable. That's what we thought had happened to Eleanor. That's this girl's name. Eleanor—I think she usually calls herself Nell—Pratt."

"Eleanor Pratt," I repeated, just to have something to say. That cleared one thing up, anyway. In America, we tend to lump surnames from the United Kingdom together and call them "English." The English have a much more precise sense of place. Pratt was an English name—Anglo-Saxon, to be exact. Morgan, the name Eleanor had been using, was Welsh. I had wondered about that. The Welsh are notoriously proud of being Welsh.

Mrs. Charlotte Derme went on. "From what I was given to understand by Miss Denbar, the headmistress of our St. Thomas's School in York, the most likely place for Eleanor Pratt to have headed for was Camden Town. Miss Denbar said it would suit her. I'm afraid Eleanor does not have a very good reputation at her school. There have been some charges of petty theft and one or two of breaking and entering. There's been some minor trouble with the police."

"Drugs?" I asked.

"Not that I've heard," Mrs. Charlotte Derme said, frowning a little. "Of course, she just might have been lucky in that. Never caught. There usually are drugs with girls like these, aren't there?"

"Maybe there are," I said.

"Well, I put the circulars out anyway," Mrs. Charlotte Derme said. "I didn't have much hope, but I had to try. We really *can't* let these girls wander around on their own. Without proper supervision they backslide. They go to drink and drugs and prostitution. You're an American, so I suppose you don't believe in bad blood, but *I* do. I've been at this thirty years, and I can't find any other explanation for it. It doesn't matter what we do to them. They have no sense of morality, no sense of responsibility—I suppose they're mostly not very intelligent, either. You don't get the heredity for genius in a children's home. And as for gratitude—"

"They don't have any," I said blandly.

"Not the least bit."

I took my cigarettes out of my pocket and lit one, willing my hand to stay steady. I had once thought women like this had an extrasensory organ that let them know when you were afraid. Either I'd been wrong about that, or I'd developed better camouflage in my adulthood. I was afraid—afraid for Eleanor, afraid for myself, a hundred times more afraid than I'd been about getting eight dozen white roses delivered to my office—and I was sick, too, but Mrs. Charlotte Derme didn't know it yet. How long I could go on without her knowing it, I had no idea. My stomach felt as if I had swallowed poisoned sand.

I moved the things on the desk around fitfully, including Eleanor's blue-glass flower vase, one fresh, perky, out-of-season mum sticking out of its narrow neck; her square mosaic ashtray, brought in for clients and to make the desk look brighter; Eleanor's thumbnail reproduction of the famous Madonna-and-Child icon from Hagia Sophia in Istanbul. They were all small things, not very valuable in a monetary sense, but I knew they were all desperately important to Eleanor. They were among the first things Eleanor had ever been able to call her own.

If I kept thinking like this, I was going to start crying, and I couldn't let myself do that. Never let them smell your fear.

"All this is very interesting," I said, "but I don't see what it has to do with *me.*"

"But I thought I'd made that clear. She's been seen."

"Seen?"

"In Lisson Grove," Mrs. Charlotte Derme said. "At least, she's been reported seen. We got a call from a Mrs. Robert Crail—"

It figures, I thought.

"—that Eleanor Pratt was regularly in the neighborhood."

There were a number of people on the street who wanted to strangle Mrs. Robert Crail, for her bad temper, her miserliness, her way with gossip. I joined the club.

I took the only tack I could think of. "Are reports like that usually accurate?"

"Usually? I don't know. Sometimes they are. Sometimes—" She gave me a hard, speculative look. "The public is very sentimental, you know, Miss Mahon. These girls make up the most fantastic stories, and people believe them. People *hide* them."

"Is that what you think is happening here? Someone is hiding this—Nell Pratt?"

"I don't know."

I gave her my best shrug. "I don't know either. I'm not hiding her, and I haven't seen her. Maybe I wouldn't have noticed her if I had."

"She's not very noticeable, is she? Not pretty or even striking in that way some of them have."

"In the picture you showed me, she hardly looked alive."

"Well, I'm told she's very lively. Too lively, if you know what I mean. Miss Denbar said she was very popular with boys."

My private opinion was that that was just what Miss Denbar *would* say, but I didn't let it out. Mrs. Derme was suspicious of me. She was probably suspicious of everyone else on the street, too. She looked horribly frustrated. I wondered what the rest of them had told her—the girl in the sweet shop, Mrs. Parmaden, the waitresses at the Sea Shell. My guess was: not much.

My cigarette was burned down to the filter, smokeless and cold. I made the expected motions of putting it out.

"This has all been very interesting, as I said," I told her, "but as I also said, I really can't see what it has to do with me. I haven't seen her. I don't think I'm likely to. And at the moment, I have a lot of work."

"This is a tour bureau?"

"A tour service, yes. For Americans, mostly."

"You must get around the country quite a bit."

"Actually, I hardly ever get out of the office except to go to British Rail."

"One of the ironies of life," Mrs. Charlotte Derme said. "Foreign-service desk officers who've never been farther than Surrey. Rocket scientists who won't even fly in ordinary airplanes. Tour directors who never go on tour."

"Mrs. Derme—"

"Excuse me. You did say you were busy." She stood up, pulling her pocketbook across her stomach like a shield. "I'll be checking back again, in a day or two. With a maniac on the loose, we really can't let this go. If you see her, you'll call and tell us?"

"Of course."

We both knew I was lying, but neither one of us wanted to make an issue of it.

She went to the outer door, put her hand on the knob, and turned back, looking toward the door to the inner office. I tensed, surprised I could get any tenser than I already was. My muscles were pulled so tight they felt ready to crack. Mrs. Charlotte Derme went on looking at my inner door. After a while, she started to smile, very slightly, very slyly, in a way that chilled me to the bone.

"You know," she said, "in emergency situations, we sometimes get search orders. If there's danger to the life of the ward, for instance, and if we think someone is *colluding* in her disappearance. I think a homicidal maniac killing girls who've been in care constitutes an emergency, don't you?"

She didn't give me a chance to answer. She didn't even give me a chance to think. One second, she was standing there. The next, I was alone in the office, listening to her heavy shoes pound against the carpet in the hall.

—— TEN ——

I sat at my desk for a long time after the woman from Child Services left, partly from necessity, partly from common sense. I needed her to be well out of the building and away before I routed out Eleanor. I wouldn't have put it past her to go to the stairwell, wait a few minutes, and then come right back, hoping to catch us. That was unlikely in the extreme, and I knew it, but better safe than sorry, as Mrs. Catherine Hobart used to say, mostly about me. Eleanor and I were in enough hot water without actually getting caught in the act.

The other reason I sat so long was purely physical. I had only been half aware of it while Mrs. Charlotte Derme' had been in my office, but during that interview I'd been wound so tight it was almost beyond endurance. I couldn't have moved right then if the building had been on fire. My arms and legs were twitching and shuddering out of control, and the situation in my stomach had gone beyond anything the poisoned-sand metaphor could cover. I put my forehead down on the green felt blotter Eleanor had bought at the stationer's back in Putney and closed my eyes. I counted to ten. I took deep, ragged, painful breaths without number. I sat there for a good five minutes, expecting to let loose all over the desk and the carpet in one great outpouring of fear and relief.

I didn't. The counting took my mind off my body. The deep breaths steadied me. I sat up and watched the second hand move around the face of the wall clock one or two times. Then I got up, crossed the reception room, and locked the outer door.

Was she out there waiting for us to make a wrong move? No, of course she wasn't. She was gone for the day. She had, however, promised to come back.

I went to the inner door, opened it, and peered into my office. It was late in the day, already dark outside, and only the lights in the reception room were on. My office was a black hole sucking in energy and giving none back. Still, I could hear sounds in there: Eleanor breathing.

"It's okay," I said. "She's gone. You can come out."

"Maybe I don't *want* to come out," Eleanor said.

I stood back and held the door open. "I know how you feel, but you've got to come out. We've got to talk. We've got to make plans."

There were rustling movements in the dark, and then Eleanor appeared in the doorway. She looked green, and I didn't think it was a trick of the light. She was shaking even more badly than I had been. The sweat must have been pouring off her the whole half hour Mrs. Charlotte Derme was in the office. Her hair was so thoroughly soaked it looked as if she'd just taken a dive into a pool. Her clothes were limp and soggy.

She threw herself onto our little two-person couch and said, "Shit."

"Don't use words like that," I said automatically. "In England it sounds—"

"I don't care about the way it sounds," she said. "Did you hear her? She knows I'm around here someplace. She'll keep looking and looking. She practically threatened to call the police in."

"Don't panic," I said. "She doesn't *know* you're here. She only *thinks* you are."

"I don't see why I can't panic if you can," Eleanor said.

I gave her a look that said she wasn't doing either of us much good and sat down behind the desk again. Eleanor rolled herself into a ball, hugging her knees to her chest.

"You know," she said, "I don't mind Mrs. Derme so much. I met her the last time I bolted. Got picked up in less than a week. I wasn't as smart about it then." She shrugged.

"Only thirteen then, you know. Looked it. But Mrs. Derme isn't bad. She doesn't really hate people. But that place up in York—"

"Is a hole?"

Eleanor made a face. "It's not really in York, you know. Not in the city, I mean. It's just outside, on the edge of the moors. And I don't think it's so bad for everybody as it was for me. I just—Miss Denbar just—"

"I know," I said. "It's all right. I had a Miss Denbar of my own. A couple of them."

Eleanor stuck her face into her thighs, hiding her tears. "It's not my fault, is it? It's not my fault. And I can't—I used to be able to remember my mam. I used to have the clearest picture. She was pretty, I know, and she had hair like mine. Dark brown. Sometimes, in the beginning, I used to lie in bed and call her up, like a ghost, I guess. And I kept thinking it was important. I had to grow up to be just like her. If I grew up to be just like her, everything would be all right. But Miss Denbar said—"

"Eleanor," I said firmly. "Miss Denbar couldn't possibly have known."

Eleanor looked up. "What do you mean?"

"I had someone who did that to me, too," I said. "Told me things about my mother, terrible things, filthy things. I didn't want to believe her, but I couldn't help myself. Then, after I grew up, I found out a few things about children's welfare. And one of the things I found out was that they don't tell the Miss Denbar's of this world anything about people's mothers."

"In America," Eleanor said cautiously. "Maybe it's different in England."

"Maybe," I agreed. "But I don't think so. From what I understand, the American system is modeled after the British one in a lot of ways. If your mother were alive, there'd be someone—a social worker, not the headmistress of your home—who had contact with her, because they'd be trying to bring the two of you together. If your mother is dead, the files are sealed unless they're needed for a psychiatric evaluation or something, like for proof of family history of schizophrenia."

"You think my mam was . . . was schizo?"

"Schizophrenic," I said. "No, I don't think that. I think she's probably dead. If she weren't, you'd have heard something about her by now. But it wouldn't have been from your Miss Denbar. Your Miss Denbar knows *nothing*, Eleanor. She was making it all up."

"Do you think really?"

"I *know* really."

"That's crazy, then, isn't it?" Eleanor said. "Sick in the head."

"Sick in the soul. That's always been my way of describing it. I've got a memory of my mother, too, Eleanor. You hold on to yours. You go right ahead trying to grow up just like her. She must have been a pip."

Eleanor swiped at her eyes with the heels of her hands, smiling just a little. "You know what I remember? I remember her telling the butcher he overcharged her on the meat. Not yelling or nothing, the way some women do, just *telling*. Sort of the way the history mistress tells you the Normans invaded in 1066, like there's nothing to argue about."

"Told you she must have been a pip."

"What do we do now?"

"A very nice woman I used to know always said, 'When in doubt, punt.'"

"What's that supposed to mean?"

"I'm not sure," I admitted, "but—"

We both heard it at the same time: the heavy tread of shoes in the hall, the rustle of a body coming to a stop outside our door. We both froze at the same time, too. Neither of us breathed for the next thirty seconds.

Then from just outside the door, Mariliee Bonnard said, "Avra? Eleanor? Let me in. The *oddest* thing just happened to me."

She came in in a rustle of rain poncho and Harrod's bags. I was so shaken that it didn't even occur to me to wonder how she managed to afford to shop at Harrod's. Her bright white hair was clean to the point of squeakiness and bouncy from a recent trip to the hairdresser's. Her dress was bouncy, too, made out of some quasi-diaphanous fabric which was bright green. She looked more like a fairy godmother than ever.

Eleanor and I shot simultaneous smiles at each other and

then sat back. After what we'd been through with Mrs. Charlotte Derme, Mariliee Bonnard was a welcome diversion, no matter what odd thing had just happened to her. Actually, I think that after Mrs. Charlotte Derme, Eleanor and I would have found a visit from the Ripper himself a welcome diversion.

Mariliee scattered her bags in a rough circle at her feet and looked pointedly at the teakettle. Eleanor got up to put it on.

"I thought you were in Stratford," I said. "That's what Belle told me."

"Belle is in Stratford," Mariliee said. "And so is Caroline. I've already been more times than I ever wanted to go. They ought to be back soon, though. They were supposed to meet me here at five."

"They'll be here at five-thirty," I said drily.

Mariliee gave me a reproving look. "You must never suggest that Belle is habitually late. She gets very snippy about it. Even though it's true."

I got the Earl Grey tea and the sugar and the non-dairy creamer out of the desk drawer Eleanor had grown accustomed to keeping them in, just to be ready when the kettle blew, and said, "So what happened to you that was so odd? And if it's that you found Benjamin Grade dead in the street, I don't want to hear about it."

"Benjamin? Oh, no, it had nothing to do with Benjamin Grade. It was—well—I took the tube to Marylebone—"

"With all those packages?" Eleanor said. "You must have been daft."

"I'm perfectly capable of carrying a few packages," Mariliee said. "Anyway, I got to Marylebone and then I walked here along Boston Place and Rossmore, and just as I got to the corner of Rossmore and the Grove—you know, where people wait for cabs—I met the strangest woman. Ugly as sin, though she didn't *have* to be. Bad with makeup, if you know what I mean. And stingy, not just with money but every other way. You could tell."

Next to the kettle, Eleanor had frozen in place. "Maybe," she said slowly, "I should lock the door again."

"Maybe you should," I said.

Mariliee looked from one of us to the other. "After I

119

talked to her, she got into a cab and told the driver to take her to Euston Place. I don't think she's coming here."

Eleanor and I relaxed. Mariliee looked back and forth between us again and shook her head.

"I knew there was going to be something to this," she said. "I just knew it. It had all the earmarks of a nasty situation."

"What was she doing when you saw her?" I asked.

"Doing?" Mariliee said. "Well, what she was doing was waiting for a cab, of course. It wasn't what she was doing. It was what she did. Just as I got up to the curb, she stopped me and asked me if I lived in the Grove, or worked here. And I said no, you know, because of course I don't. And then she asked me if I came here often, and I said I did lately, that I had business here. The whole thing was very strange, because English people don't ask those sort of questions of strangers on the street. I was beginning to wonder if she was a purse snatcher—"

Eleanor didn't quite manage to stifle a hoot. "Oh, *God,*" she said. "Mrs. Derme picked up for snatching—"

"Mrs. Derme," Mariliee said. "Is that her name?"

"Mrs. Charlotte Derme," I said. "Yes. I'm surprised she didn't tell you."

"Well, she didn't. She just opened her handbag and pulled out an envelope and showed me a couple of pictures—of someone named Nell Pratt."

"Nobody," Eleanor said angrily, "ever called me Nell but Child Welfare. My own mam—"

"Eleanor, hush," I said. "Mariliee, what did you *tell* her?"

Mariliee blinked, all fluffy innocence again. "Why, I told her the truth. I told her I'd never heard of such a person in my life. Or seen her, either."

I let myself fall back into my chair so hard that I nearly tipped the damn thing over.

We were halfway through explaining when Belle and Caroline walked in, and then we had to start over again. By the time we'd managed to get everyone caught up, it was after six o'clock. Outside our window, the streetlights on the Grove looked like incorporeal moons, buoyed by the mist. A fog was rolling in from the Thames, the first real pea-souper of the season.

It was Caroline who spoke first when we were finished, a

fiercer Caroline than I'd ever seen before, even more so than the Caroline who wanted to *get* Benjamin Grade.

"We'll just have to hide her, that's all," she said. "If we weren't going to Yorkshire tomorrow, I'd find a way to get her to the States. I don't suppose you could go to Yorkshire?" she asked Eleanor.

Eleanor shook her head. "All this started in Yorkshire," she said. "I'd be a sitting duck. Especially in a place as small as St. Edmund Cavateur."

"Try not to be foolish," Belle March said. "Of course the girl can't go to Yorkshire. That would be suicide. But we're going to have to find someplace to hide her."

"I thought you *approved* of child welfare," Caroline said reproachfully. "You were always telling me when I complained about what had happened to Julie—"

"I was always telling you child welfare was a good idea in theory," Belle said, "and often in practice. I believed that then and I still believe it. I did not, however, discount the possibility that there are bad apples in the system. Or that Julie ran afoul of them. Or that Eleanor has, too."

"At least you agree this Mrs. Derme person sounds like a bad apple," Caroline said.

"From what I've heard so far, this Mrs. Derme person sounds like the thing from the pit of hell. Our problem now is how to keep Eleanor safely away from her until we can get back from Yorkshire and do something permanent about this mess." Belle took out one of her small brown cigars and contemplated its tip. "Where," she said, "is someone like this Mrs. Derme going to be least likely to look?"

"I would have said here," I said. "Most runaways end up where Mrs. Derme thought Eleanor would be—places like Camden Town. Punk enclaves. Tenderloins. Every city's got a section like that. Lisson Grove certainly isn't it."

"Yes, yes," Belle said, "but that was before that awful busybody called in. Now your Mrs. Derme is going to be looking in places exactly like Lisson Grove. Which reminds me—I don't think it would be a good idea for Eleanor to go back to the flat tonight. For all we know, this Mrs. Derme will be checking."

"But where will I go?" Eleanor said. "I can't go back to—"

"I wouldn't let you go back to Camden Town," I snapped. "That's all I'd need, you wandering around there with a Ripper loose."

"I know where she could go," Mariliee broke in. "At least, I think I do."

We all turned to look at her. Mariliee on her own was a chatty and gregarious woman. Mariliee around Belle and Caroline tended to be silent, to step back and let them take center stage, as if she thought they were more interesting than she could ever be. I would have argued that point. In my book, Mariliee was one of the most singular people on earth.

"Well," Belle March said, "come on. Where could she stay?"

"At the Connaught," Mariliee said promptly. "In your suite. It's going to be vacant for the next six weeks anyway—"

"At the Connaught Hotel?" Eleanor's voice was a squeak. "You can't mean that. That's dafter than Mrs. Derme."

"Why?" Caroline asked.

Now Eleanor definitely had that look on her face, the one that said she was temporarily trapped in a lunatic asylum. "The Connaught," she explained patiently, "is a very expensive place. Earls stay there. Oil sheiks stay there."

"We're staying there," Caroline pointed out. "And we're going to have to pay for the suite anyway. That was the only way they'd hold it for us."

"She could look after our things," Belle said slowly. "And she could check in on the office phone if we got her one of those machines—"

"They only work with touch tones," Caroline said. "I don't think they have touch tones in England."

"We could disguise her," Mariliee said eagerly. "Change her hair. Buy her some clothes. Harrod's is open till seven-thirty."

"Harrod's," Eleanor said faintly.

"Selfridge's is open until eight," Belle March said.

"We could say she was my daughter," Caroline said.

"Wait," I said. "You couldn't say she was your daughter. She doesn't look anything like you. Never mind the accent."

"I can do accents," Eleanor said defensively.

"I wouldn't want to bank on you doing one for six weeks," I said.

"We'll say she's some kind of relative, anyway," Caroline said. "We'll work something out. But it's almost six-thirty. If we're going to get this all done, we're going to have to get started now. And then there's dinner—"

"That's why we came," Mariliee said. "We wanted to take you to dinner."

"At a very nice place," Caroline said. "Your Mrs. Derme wouldn't be able to afford it for a minute. Do you think we should call in for a cab, just to be sure?"

"Probably," Belle March said.

"Don't I have anything to say about this?" Eleanor said.

I patted her affectionately on the head and said, "No, dear."

──── ELEVEN ────

In the end, it was the cat that made us late. Not the absurdity of taking Eleanor out the back window into the courtyard and through Mrs. Sherman's to Gateforth Street. Caroline Matthews thought that up, and at the time I was still so shaken it made some kind of sense. Caroline's worries that Mrs. Derme might have come back to watch our door—or sent someone to watch it—fed my paranoia. I imagined dark figures in the street, lying in wait. It never occurred to me to wonder if the dark figure of my fantasies might be the Ripper. The Ripper had become, for me—much like wars in foreign countries are for many people—something awful that happened in a place I didn't know to people I'd never met.

I had no trouble taking Eleanor's situation seriously, or believing that it happened, all the time. I had been there myself—been caught and brought back, been found out but not apprehended—and the sight of Eleanor's pale round face under the diffuse light of London streetlamps wrenched at me. She looked like someone who had narrowly escaped being killed by a hit-and-run driver. She talked and laughed and admired the things the godmothers wanted to buy her, but part of her was always somewhere else, reliving what had happened. She drifted through Harrod's and Selfridge's and the tiny back-street specialty boutiques where the godmothers had connections, and could therefore get us in after closing time, like a wraith. Sometimes, her distraction frightened me nearly out of my mind.

We were standing on Regent Street, trying to hail a cab, when she remembered the cat. By then, she didn't look anything like the Eleanor I knew, in any of her incarnations. Her hair was scraped back off her face and held back with a raw-silk scarf—eighty pounds at Anabelle Lee's. Her body was covered in a long black suede skirt and an oversize pink sweater that fell down past her hips: high style in London that season. She looked expensive and forbidding and at least twenty-two years old. It made me sad. I liked Eleanor's innocence. It was rare.

It was after eight and bitterly cold. A harsh wind was coming up the Thames. Eleanor was spared the worst of it because of the length of her skirt. I got more than I wanted because my skirt was shorter and lighter and not as well-made. Regent Street was lit up and busy, but I knew the rest of the city wouldn't be.

Eleanor's new things were packed into a black canvas suitcase Caroline Matthews had insisted on buying in Selfridge's, her theory being that a visiting relative would most naturally arrive with luggage, not just shopping bags. Especially a well-heeled relative, which Eleanor was supposed to be. I forget what the cover story was, exactly—it was complicated—but it had something to do with a horse farm, because Eleanor (surprisingly to me) knew a great deal about horses. Maybe I was just being hopelessly, provincially American. Maybe almost everybody in rural England knew a lot about horses. Having grown up in the States, I always had thought that that sort of thing was restricted to debutantes.

Belle March was standing in the street when Eleanor brought up the cat. We'd sent Belle out there because, in contrast to New York, "little old ladies" have a very easy time finding cabs in London, not that Belle would have allowed anyone to call her a "little old lady." She accepted the wisdom of this particular plan of operation. She looked like somebody's mother, and London cab drivers like to pick up women who remind them of their mothers. I was standing at the very edge of the sidewalk because Belle was a reckless cab-hailer. I'm not sure she actually *saw* traffic. She just marched right out there into the middle of a lane and expected speeding minis to make their way around her.

I was thinking: *Thank God for the suitcase. At least we aren't weighted down with bags.*

Eleanor said, "We've got to go back and get the cat. If we leave him alone, he'll starve."

Four pairs of eyes turned to stare at me, three of them murderous. Even Belle March had heard what Eleanor said, screaming horns and squealing tires notwithstanding. Eleanor looked anxious. The godmothers looked as if they thought I was a monster. Here I was, setting off for six weeks out of town, stashing Eleanor in a hotel, leaving my apartment empty, and *I hadn't even considered my cat.*

I could feel that headache coming on, the one I always got when I had to deal with the godmothers for any protracted period of time.

"For God's sake," I said, "the cat isn't going to starve. He isn't even our cat."

"He is now," Eleanor said stubbornly. "I adopted him."

"Eleanor, that cat's been living off the people on Roskell Road the whole five years I've been there. He's ten pounds overweight and he always looks brushed up fresh. I've never seen him wet, dirty, or cold. The only time I ever saw him miserable was when he tried to kill a jay and got his nose pecked in the process."

"It's different now," Eleanor said. "He counts on us."

Belle March came back from the street. "I think Eleanor has a point," she said. "Of course, the cat won't starve unless you've locked him in the apartment without food—"

"There's an open window in the bathroom," I said. "He gets in and out that way. And yes, I know it's open, because the damn thing's stuck and I can't *close* it."

"He won't starve, then," Belle said. "But he will be lonely, and probably angry. Animals are very sensitive to slights."

"Cats are very intelligent," Caroline Matthews said.

"Oh, rot," Mariliee Bonnard said. "I don't like to see a dumb animal abused, but I'm *not* going to listen to any of that *nonsense* about how bright they are."

"It's not nonsense," Caroline Matthews said. "My Ashtavara—"

"Let's not talk about Ashtavara," Belle said hastily. "I don't want to go into *that* again."

126

"All I know," Eleanor said, "is that we have to do something about the cat."

I looked from one to the other of them, exasperated. The usual sticking point didn't apply here. In America, most hotels are reluctant to accept animals. In England, the best ones are used to animals and the eccentricities of their patrons. Cats are the great folk passion of the British common people. Dogs are the equivalent for the aristocracy. First-class London hotels almost always have accommodations for both. If Eleanor wanted to bring the cat to the Connaught, the Connaught would probably let her.

The sticking point, as I saw it, was in matters of time and place. We were on Regent Street, way up at the north of London. The Connaught, where we had to deposit Eleanor's suitcase before we did anything else, was in the West End, to the south of us, not *too* far away. The restaurant, however, was to the southeast of us, all the way down in Westminster, and the apartment was even farther south*west*. We had a reservation at the restaurant for nine and formalities to clear up at the hotel. The logistics were impossible.

I crossed my fingers behind my back and told myself to rely on reason. These were very reasonable women, most of the time. Even Eleanor did her best.

"Look," I told them, "I'll feed the cat when I go home tonight. Then I'll bring it with me tomorrow morning. I'll leave early and stop at the hotel to drop it off. We don't have to go back now—"

"Yes, we do," Eleanor said. "We're already late. He's not used to us being this late."

"Eleanor, he's a cat. He can't tell time."

"Not in the conventional sense," Caroline Matthews said, "but—"

"What I'd worry about," Mariliee said, "is the furniture. They do tend to shred the furniture when they get angry."

My furniture belonged to my landlord and was probably worth about five pounds. Eleanor knew that. I'd seen her eyebrows go up when Mariliee mentioned the shredding. My furniture could have used shredding.

I turned to her, appealing.

"It really does make more sense if I bring him tomorrow,"

127

I said. "We'll miss our reservation if we tramp out there now. Besides, you probably shouldn't go back to the apartment. That—that woman may suspect you're staying there."

"I hadn't thought of that," Belle March said. "My God, she probably does suspect Eleanor's staying there."

"Well, I just hope she's standing out there on the street, *freezing,*" Caroline Matthews said.

Eleanor turned luminous close-to-tears eyes on me, and said, "Avra, *I adopted him.*"

There are hundreds of thousands of words in the English language, and those were the only three that could have got me out to Putney on a freezing-cold night just to pick up a cat. I knew the kind of transference Eleanor was making. I didn't blame her. I had once poured out my affection on rag dolls and hand-me-down daydreams. Mrs. Catherine Hobart would never have allowed me a cat.

She hadn't been too keen on dolls, either.

I am exaggerating, of course. Logically, I know I must be. Mrs. Catherine Hobart was a hateful woman, but her style didn't run to nineteenth-century melodramatic gestures. Still, the emotional tone is right. Maybe emotional landscapes are truer than the physical kind.

By the time the cab got me to Putney, it was raining, a hard, steady assault that was almost like sleet. Drops *pinged* rapidly against the windshield, leaving a faintly metallic echo. Putney had gone in for the night. There were lights on in the windows of the houses we passed, but only faint ones, as if what lamps had been lit were tucked away in back rooms.

Roskell Road was even darker. Being a side street, it didn't have streetlamps of the high intensity—or in the same frequency—as the Lower Richmond, and for some reason none of the people who lived on it seemed to be home. All the houses up and down the two-block stretch were blank: no lights, no sounds, no signs of movement. It was as if the street had been evacuated while I had been away.

The cab pulled to a stop in front of my gate, and I started to put the cigarette I was smoking out in the ashtray. I stopped myself in midreach. A cigarette can be a weapon, as I have said, and I found myself suddenly desperate for a weapon. Like the houses on most London residential streets, those on Roskell Road had tiny front lawns thickly planted with "garden." Thorny, misshapen bushes pushed against the edges of the lawns and hung out over the sidewalks. In the eerie, somehow unnatural, blackness, they made the neighborhood into a haunted grove.

Silly, I told myself. You're spooking yourself.

It is customary to get out of London taxicabs before you pay the driver. Often, the driver comes out and opens the door for you. This one might have if I had given him time, but I didn't. I was too jumpy to sit still. I popped open the door and climbed out onto the sidewalk, reaching into my purse for my wallet. Then I did something I used to do often in New York and Buffalo but hadn't done once since coming to London. I not only got out my wallet, I got out my keys. With my left hand, I handed the driver a ten-pound note. I kept the key to my front door in my right hand, ready for instantaneous use.

Idiot, I thought. You're being a complete and utter idiot.

I turned around and looked up at the house. I'd never noticed before how Victorian it was, how Victorian *all* the houses on the street were. They weren't the impressive stone hulks of Kensington, but they were turreted and ornate and topped by round ornamental windows. The sight of all those round windows chilled me: blind cyclopic eye after blind cyclopic eye.

Behind me, the cabbie shifted into gear and took off, toward the turn to the Upper Richmond and the lights of Putney's High Street.

I stood longer than I should have on the sidewalk, working up the nerve to open my own gate. I kept glancing up and down the street, not knowing what I was expecting to see. The man from Foyle's? Maybe. But the street was deserted, silent, unmoving. Even the neighborhood cats had gone into hiding.

Eleanor's cat, our local stray, was also missing.

I pushed the gate open harder than I needed to—maybe to show it who was boss—and hurried up the short cement walk to my porch. The most recent upstairs tenants had been prone to wild parties and long nights of heavy-metal music, but they'd moved out around the time Eleanor moved in. For the first time, I wished them back.

I stood at the door and looked carefully around the porch. The cat was black. It could be hiding in the shadows. Eventually I walked from one end of the porch to the other, finding nothing, not even the nests of winter birds that usually hung above the side rail.

I went back to the door, reached for the keyhole with the key, hesitated. My cigarette was out, unsmoked. I considered lighting another one, but realized I was being ridiculous, behaving like the heroine in a novel by one of Belle March's less intelligent imitators. I wasn't making any sense and I was growing steadily more frightened—of nothing.

I put my key in the lock, opened the door, and walked into the hall. I reached out for light and got it on almost immediately. I was presented with a perfectly ordinary hallway and a perfectly ordinary staircase, both in need of a little paint, neither sinister.

I unlocked the inner door that led to my flat and snaked my hand around the wall to flip on the light switch. The four little square-based lamps that occupied the corners of the room glowed to life, showing me the red-and-green comforter Eleanor had folded so neatly that morning and a pile of *Sun* tabloids in an untidy stack on the coffee table. I came in and shut the door behind me, feeling like a prime ninny.

With the dissipation of my fear, I also began to feel a little put-upon. The cat hadn't come out to greet me on my arrival, which meant he wasn't in the flat. That cat can hear a door open two hundred yards away through half a dozen six-inch-thick walls. He knows it means food, the meaning of that animal's life. I dropped into the ugly yellow wing chair and contemplated going out to the restaurant without the beast, just saying he was gone and not to be found. I knew it wouldn't work. If I did that, Eleanor would just insist on coming back here after we'd finished eating.

Obviously, I was going to have to go chasing all over the neighborhood. The most sensible thing to do, then, would be to change out of my work clothes into warmer things. A pair of slacks, a heavy sweater, a poncho: I couldn't go to the restaurant like that, but I could always change back into something respectable after I got Eleanor's cat in hand. Exasperation rose and twisted in me. This project was getting positively baroque.

I hauled myself out of my chair and wandered into the back hall, feeling like a martyr. The bathroom door was closed, and that pricked at me, feeding my annoyance. I like my bathroom door open when somebody isn't using it. That way, I know it's available. I only have the one. I told myself I'd do something about it before I left and then headed into the bedroom.

I got as far as the door. That, too, was closed, and I knew I hadn't been the one who closed it. I knew Eleanor hadn't been there either. We'd left together that morning.

The bedroom door opened half an inch and then thudded to a stop against something heavy and immovable.

My head jerked up and around, until I was looking again at the closed *bathroom* door. It had been open that morning. I was sure of it.

Then I felt a breath like wind against my neck and I was turning, whirling around with such force and lack of thought, I almost fell.

Standing behind me in my hallway was Benjamin Grade.

——— TWELVE ———

The first thing I thought was that Caroline Matthews had been right about everything. He *had* killed Julie. He *was* the Ripper. Now he was going to kill me. Then he stepped back, far enough for me to see his face in the hall light, and I realized he wasn't looking at me. His attention was focused on the door of my bedroom. His gray eyes were unblinking. I stepped away, out of reach.

When I had my back to the open escape hatch of the living-room doorway, I started to relax a little. God only knew the man looked murderous, but the murderousness was not directed at me. In the dim light—all the lights in my apartment are dim; my landlord doesn't like to waste electricity—he reminded me of all the stories I had heard of the Black Prince, whose ferocity in victory was tempered only by his love for his wife. *The twelfth century,* I thought irrelevantly. *Chaucer knew that prince. The wife's name was Blanche.*

There was a strangled, angry cry at my feet, and I looked down to see the cat—drenched, cold, and indignant.

It broke the spell. I almost shook my head to clear it a little. My God, what had I been doing, hypnotizing myself? On reappraisal, I decided Benjamin Grade looked nothing at all like the Black Prince. He looked like what he was, a big, outdoorsy man, an American of the self-made variety. Good-looking, yes. Impressive, certainly. Nothing in the world is as impressive as an American who has made a

132

fortune from nothing and is doing something he respects himself for doing. The Europeans who are so quick to criticize American egalitarianism always drop that last part. They want to believe all self-made men are cheats, like Ivan Boesky. They don't want to know about men like Benjamin Grade.

I was doing it again. Standing close to this man worked on me like a drug. I kept getting tangled in irrelevancies.

I leaned down, picked up the sopping-wet cat, and said, "Do you want to tell me what you're doing here?"

Benjamin Grade dragged his attention away from my bedroom door. "Excuse me. I mean, I'm sorry. I called your office, but you'd already gone. I called here, but you weren't in yet. I thought I'd just come out and see if I could catch you."

I raised my eyebrows skeptically.

"What if I hadn't come back until late?" I said. "What if I'd had a date? Coming all the way out here from the center of London in the *hope* you might catch me—"

"You wouldn't have a date," Benjamin Grade said patiently, "the night before you were leaving on a six-week tour."

Logic, I thought. I really hate people who use logic on me. I took the hem of my jacket and started to rub it absently at the cat's head, drying her off. Benjamin Grade gestured at the bedroom door.

"You want me to go in and find out what's blocking it?"

I hesitated. In the shock of seeing him, I'd forgotten how frightened I'd been by those closed doors and by the thought of what might be behind them. Now that fear came back to me. Somebody had been in the flat while I was away, moved through my rooms, touched my things, left evidence— accidentally or deliberately—of his passage. What if that person had been Benjamin Grade? Had he been hiding? He'd come through the living room into the hall, and I knew he hadn't been in the living room. That room is tiny and has no secret corners.

He turned to consider me. "What's wrong with you?" he said. "Can't you answer a simple question?"

I screwed up my courage and went on the offensive. "I

want to know how you got in here," I said. "I want to know *now*."

"How do you think I got in here? I walked in through the front door."

"It was locked," I said.

"It was standing wide open," he corrected me. "The hallway was dark as sin. Hell, the whole street looks like it's had a blackout, but your door was open."

"I *remember* closing it," I said, "and it locks automatically."

"Well, then you remember wrong." He pushed tentatively against the bedroom door. "I think it's a pile of papers or something," he said. "I don't think it's anything awful. You can't spend your life in the hallway, for God's sake. You're going to have to go into the bedroom sometime."

"How do you know it's a bedroom?"

"What the hell *else* would it be?"

We glared at each other for a moment, and then I gave up. I was wet, cold, and exhausted emotionally, physically, and every other way.

"Go ahead," I told him, "as long as you understand I half-think you're responsible for this."

"Oh, I don't mind that," Benjamin Grade said. "I'm getting used to the idea that practically everybody thinks I'm responsible for practically everything. Except the *Telegram*. They don't even think I write my own books."

He waggled the door back and forth a few times and then gave it a good hard shove. It tremored, caught, and then yawned haltingly open, dragging something with it.

I put my hand in and found the wall switch for the overhead light.

Benjamin Grade and I stood looking down at a hundred paperback books; the books I had left that morning in a pile in the corner of the living room were now strewn all over my bedroom floor.

We tried the bathroom after that. There was nothing in there. It was as if someone had gone in there to use the loo, then closed the door on the way out—not thinking about it, a matter of habit. Fear and agitation and annoyance warred for primacy in my mind. The situation was creepy in the extreme, terrifying, but I knew I wasn't going to be able to *do* anything about it. The effect depended on the infinitesimal shifting of trivial things. I could imagine what the police would say if I called them in about it. Things like: Maybe you're mistaken about where you left the books, maybe you're mistaken about leaving the doors open, maybe you're just another nut spooked by Ripper stories. Of course, the London police would never call me a nut. They're much too polite for that. No matter how diplomatically they put it, though, the import would be the same.

Fear and agitation and annoyance began to give way to anger. How dare he do this to me? Who did he think he was? Then I remembered I had no idea who "he" might be. Was Benjamin Grade lying? I wasn't sure either way.

I still had the cat under my arm, tucked against my ribs the way I used to carry books when I was in elementary school. She was making mewling noises and scratching against my coat—probably hungry. I carried her into the kitchen.

My kitchen is oversize, the one large room in my flat. I got the lights on and looked around, but there was no sign anyone had been there. Even so, I assumed someone had been there. It wouldn't have made sense for whoever it was to have prowled around the rest of the flat and have left the kitchen unexamined.

I put the cat down and went to the back pantry to get some Nine Lives—rabbit, the cat's favorite dinner. I opened the can with an opener and dumped the contents into the cat's dish. Then I checked the pantry shelves. Nothing had been moved. Nothing was out of place. Why would it have been? Why would anybody want to move the cans in my pantry?

Why had someone moved the godmothers' books from the living room to my bedroom? To spook me, of course.

I heard a sound behind me and turned to find Benjamin Grade standing in the pantry archway. "Are you all right? Are you going to talk to me?"

"I don't know if I'm all right," I said, "and I don't have a lot of time to talk to you. As it turns out, I do have a date. I'm supposed to meet some people for dinner. I just came back to get the cat."

"I was lucky to catch you."

"You could put it that way."

"Oh, *Christ.*"

He stomped back into the kitchen. I heard the screech of boards that meant he'd taken a seat at the kitchen table. I could have kicked myself. If he was the person who'd moved things around in the flat, I'd have a much better chance of getting him to admit to it if I didn't antagonize him. Benjamin Grade in a conversational frame of mind was just what I needed. On the other hand, maybe I didn't really think he'd been my intruder. This conviction was totally irrational. I knew nothing about him but what I'd picked up from one short visit, which had ended in a very unproductive argument, and from what the godmothers had told me. There was enough in all that to make me suspicious of him. He hadn't been tried for Julie Matthews' murder, but he had been questioned in connection with it. He'd had motive, means and opportunity enough to fall under investigation. There was violence in him, too. That I'd seen that very first day.

There were also the coincidences. The white roses stabbed into the chests of each of the victims, both in Boston and London. The similar brutality of the crimes. The fact that all the victims, beginning with Julie Matthews, either were or had been foster children. If I had any sense, I'd call the police immediately—not about books being moved, but about Benjamin being with me.

The cat was slurping noisily and happily at her dish. I made a sour face at her and went out to the kitchen. Ben was still sitting at my table, his legs stretched out across the tile floor, his hands lying palms down against the laminated plastic tabletop. He looked frustrated and helpless and royally pissed off.

I leaned against the edge of the sink and said, "What did you come out here *for?*"

"What do you think I came out here for?" he said. "To try to talk sense to you one more time. We're all supposed to be leaving for Yorkshire in the morning."

"And you walked in the front door, which was standing wide open, only a few minutes ago."

"I should think that was obvious," he said.

136

"You weren't here before I got home," I went on. "You weren't in the apartment when I walked in."

"What are you talking about?"

"I'm talking about the fact that somebody was in this flat while I was out. And I've got every damn reason to think it was you."

Ben Grade looked at me admiringly. I don't think he thought I was capable of controlled anger, only the other kind.

"How do you know someone was in the flat?"

"Two of the doors I left open were closed," I said. "The books that are now on my bedroom floor were in the living room this morning."

"That's it?"

"Isn't that enough?"

"You could be mistaken about those things."

"I'm not," I said.

"All right." He nodded. "I'll give you that. I've written enough books where the hero comes in and finds some tiny little thing out of place and knows immediately he's been searched. But try this: You've got one very narrow hall between your living room and this kitchen. Nobody could have passed you in it without your knowledge. Hell, nobody could have passed you in it, period. There isn't room for two people side-by-side unless they both flatten themselves against the walls, and maybe not even then. I came in at you from the living-room end. If I was hiding in the flat, how did I get there?"

I'd been thinking about this. "You weren't hiding in the flat. You were hiding in the outer hall. Under the stairs."

"Was the inner door locked when you came in?" he asked.

"Of course it was. What difference does that make?"

"How did I get it locked again after I went out that way?"

"You—" I stopped, confused.

He smiled slightly. "That's a skeleton-key lock, Avra. They're easy to open. All you need is a pair of hairpins. They're impossible to lock up again. No matter what it was that did or didn't happen here, if someone was in this flat they neither came nor left by that door. Unless they had a key, of course. I've got no idea who you've given keys to."

"Just Eleanor," I said pensively. I took a seat across from

him and put my chin in my hands, almost as disturbed as I had been to find those doors closed and the books moved. One of the great problems with having been orphaned, or abandoned, or whatever it was I had been is that you know nothing at all of your history, social or genetic. It's always possible there's some kink in your physical makeup. Hereditary disease, hereditary madness: There was a chance those things were in me, and I didn't have the comforting memories of wonderfully-sane-old Aunt Hattie or hale-and-hearty-to-the-age-of-ninety-three Uncle Joe to ease my fears.

"Are you trying to tell me I'm imagining this?" I asked Benjamin Grade. "Because I'm really not. I did leave those doors open. I always do. And the books were in the living room. I put them there a week ago. They were cluttering up my life."

"They're certainly prolific, aren't they?" Ben said. "No, I'm not trying to tell you that you imagined it. I can think of ways—whoever it was could have come in and gone out a window, for instance. Are you sure you closed the outer door when you came in tonight?"

"I'm positive. Believe me."

"Yeah. The street spooked me, too. Why is it so dark? Anyway, if you shut the door and I found it open, someone must have gone out that way. Who lives upstairs?"

"Nobody at the moment."

"Is there a back entrance to the upstairs flat?"

"Fire stairs," I admitted. "In the garden. Although you can't really call it a garden. I mean, it's paved."

Benjamin waved this away. "He could have come into this flat by a window, gone out by the same window, then gone around to the garden, up the fire stairs, and into the upstairs flat by *another* window. Then he could have gone out the door of the upstairs flat and hidden in the stairwell when he heard you coming in. Once you were in the flat, he could have gone out the front door. In a hurry, maybe, so he didn't realize he left the outside door open. That's a little elaborate for my taste, but not implausible. Especially if what he's trying to do is make you think you're crazy."

"You're very good at this," I said quietly.

"It's what I do for a living. You want to go and check the door on the upstairs flat? If I've got the scenario right, it should be open. Like I said, no way to relock a skeleton-key lock once you've opened it."

"I'll wait," I said.

"Fine with me," Ben said. "If I'm wrong, I'm going to feel like an idiot."

We sat looking at each other, second after second, in a relaxed, almost congenial silence. As the seconds passed, I found myself feeling more and more grateful for his analysis. It was rational and balanced and depended not in the least on demons in the night. It put my fears of genetic disaster to rest, one more time.

"You know," I said, almost apologetically, "if you came here to talk me out of going to Yorkshire tomorrow, it really isn't going to work. I couldn't cancel everything at this late date. It would cost a fortune."

"Would you rather be dead?"

"I think I'd like you better if you weren't always threatening to kill me."

Benjamin snorted. "I'm not threatening to kill you, and you know it. Look, our godmothers told you a story, right? What exactly did they tell you?"

"You want the whole thing?" I asked. "It was a long story."

"Never mind. I know what they told you. I also know what they didn't tell you, which is that Julie had walked out on me nearly two months before her murder. And for two months before that, she'd been behaving very strangely. Not that behaving strangely was necessarily an odd thing with Julie Matthews."

"She'd had a rough life," I said.

"She'd had an appalling life," Ben said. "I didn't really mind the strangeness much. Sometimes it was a little hard to deal with, but I dealt with it. But the two months before she walked out—she'd met someone. I was sure she'd met someone. It's beyond belief she thought up all that stuff on her own."

"What stuff?"

"Occult stuff," Ben said, suddenly angry. "Ghosts and goblins and séances and God only knows what else. It was crazy, but it wasn't Julie's *kind* of crazy. She started disappearing for days at a time. She was supposed to be living at school, so I don't think Caroline noticed, but I did. Her dorm counselor did, too. One minute she'd be there, the next minute she'd be gone, the next minute she'd be there again. One time she disappeared for four straight days. When she turned up again, she was really flying. I would have suspected drugs, but I didn't know of any drug that would have that kind of effect."

"What kind of effect?"

Ben gave me a sideways look. "She said she'd seen her mother."

I blinked, confused. "I thought her mother was dead," I said. "I'm sure Caroline told me—"

"Avra, Julie's mother *was* dead. She'd been dead for twelve years, to be exact. And Julie hadn't forgotten that, either."

"You mean she thought she was communing with her mother's *ghost?*"

"That's right."

"But—" I stopped. As much as I hated to admit it, it made emotional sense. If I believed we could contact the spirits of the dead, would I try to contact my own mother? "You know," I said, "under the circumstances, that may not be as crazy as it sounds. She'd been deprived of her mother at a very early age. That's—that's hard. She probably found it very comforting to believe she could talk to the mother she'd lost. I would."

"Avra, *why* did she believe it? Julie wasn't a religious person. Caroline had a hard time just getting her to go to church on Sunday. I'd known her for over a year before that, and she'd never shown any signs of interest in the occult. She didn't even read horror novels, and I read horror novels. She thought all that sort of thing was rank nonsense."

"And then she changed her mind," I said.

"Exactly," Benjamin said. "Why? Somebody had to have been feeding her this stuff, Avra. If you'd known Julie, you'd realize it doesn't make sense any other way. And it wasn't just the occult business. She was odd all the way around. Like she was stoned out all the time, except not exactly. Maybe like she was in a trance."

"Hadn't she had drug problems?" I asked him. "Maybe she was on some drug you hadn't heard of. I don't keep up with the, uh, drug scene, but from what I understand from reading the papers, they invent something new all the time."

"That they do," Ben said, "but you know what I did before I started writing private-eye novels? I worked for the Federal Drug Enforcement Administration."

I said, "Oh."

"I've got a master's in chemistry and I know just about everything there is to know about recreational dope, most of which has nothing recreational about it. If Julie was on a drug, it wasn't just something I'd never heard of, it's something I haven't heard of since, either, and it must have been developed by some government's chemical-warfare division, besides. People get high to feel good, if only temporarily. Julie definitely did not feel good."

"Then what was it?" I asked him. "What could it possibly have been?"

"I don't know," he said. "I've spent the last year of my life trying to find out. Caroline's got one thing right, anyway. When Julie walked out on me, I didn't give up."

"That's admirable," I said truthfully. "I don't know too many people who can be that—committed to other people."

"Don't you mean bullheaded?"

I laughed. "I can't throw stones about bullheadedness," I said. "I probably take the prize myself. But Ben, I don't understand what you're doing here. What could you possibly find out after all this time? And in England? I know your being here has to have something to do with all this. Nothing else makes the parts make sense. Mrs. Henry Copplewhite's, for God's sake. But—"

"I said I thought at the time she was seeing somebody," Benjamin said. "Now I know she was. And two girls have died just like Julie died. Here. *Just* like Julie died."

"You couldn't have come over because of the Ripper stories," I said. "They didn't start until after you got here."

"I didn't say I came over because of the Ripper stories."

"You implied it."

"Maybe I did. But Avra, these girls—girls like Julie—most of them don't have a Caroline in the background. Most of them are just strays. You could kill them and hide them, and if you were smart enough about it, no one would have to know."

"Impossible," I said, everything in me instinctively antagonistic to the idea. "Of course they find them. They always find them."

"No, they don't. It's been ten years since they put Ted Bundy out of business. It's been fifteen since he started killing. There are still some girls they think he killed in Washington State whose bodies have never been found."

"You're trying to say you don't think Julie was the only one killed in Boston," I said.

"You're right." He nodded. "I don't think she was. You know, I've written four books with psycho-killer murderers. I've done a lot of research. These guys start out very smart. A lot of them do, anyway. They hide the victims, they hide the crimes, they cover their tracks perfectly. They also don't kill very often, in the beginning. Some of them start with murders spaced months and months apart. After a while, though, they lose control. The bodies start showing up. The killings start getting closer and closer together. In Boston, we had Julie and no one else we know of. Here, we've got two bodies left in public parks and slaughtered a week apart. I think this guy's beginning to lose it, Avra. And once he loses it, things could get very bloody."

"What does all this have to do with Julie's séances?"

"I think that's his method," Ben said. "At least it was in Boston. He gets these girls, these lost and abandoned girls, and he promises to get them in touch with the one thing they want most desperately. Since it was months with Julie, I'd have to say there was more involved than the killing. Sex, maybe. I don't know."

"That's the most godawful thing I've ever heard," I said. "That's the nastiest—the nastiest—"

"It isn't nice," Benjamin agreed. "These guys seldom are."

Something occurred to me that hadn't before, although it probably should have. "You know who it is," I said, shocked. "You *know*."

"I think I do," Benjamin corrected. "I couldn't prove it."

"I don't care if you couldn't prove it," I exploded. "You should go to the police. You have to go to the police. There are two people dead in London already."

"Avra, Avra. I *did* go to the police. What do you take me for? The police have got more sense than Caroline, Lord knows. They don't think I'm offing teenagers, or at least they don't think it out loud. They do tend to feel, however, that my accusations may be an attempt to throw suspicion away from myself."

"Because they secretly feel you're guilty?"

"Because they not-so-secretly feel I'm tired of being harassed," Ben said, "which, by the way, is the God's honest truth. I *am* sick to death of being harassed." He stood up. "I suppose we ought to get you out of here. You're going to be late for your dinner. I don't suppose you're now willing to give up this nonsense and stay away from Yorkshire?"

"Are you following this man?" I asked him. "Is he going to be in Yorkshire?"

"I sincerely hope not. Seriously, I'm going to Yorkshire to find something out. I've got no reason to think our friend is going to be along for the ride. It would be worse than a nuisance if he was. That doesn't mean it isn't going to be dangerous, Avra. More dangerous than I may have counted on."

"I think Yorkshire sounds a hell of a lot safer than here," I said. I grabbed the cat as she ran between my legs and folded her into my lap. "I think getting a couple of hundred miles away from where this guy's operating—and getting the godmothers away—sounds just fine."

"I knew you were going to say that. I'd kill to know how I could convince you you're wrong."

"Don't try."

"Stuff that animal in a carrier or something," Ben said. "I'll call us a cab."

I should have told him, of course: about the roses that had been delivered to my office, about the little man who had followed me from Foyle's, about everything. I don't know why I didn't. In some way, the subject just seemed closed.

Waiting for the cab, we talked about the godmothers and the success their books had had and the way the English always made us feel better about human nature, because they always held onto their manners and their common sense, no matter what the emergency.

——— THIRTEEN ———

I never went back to the apartment that night. When the godmothers heard what I had to say, they insisted I stay in their suite. I slept on a couch in the sitting room, with Eleanor and the cat stretched out on the floor beneath me.

The next morning we overslept—just a little, but enough. All of a sudden, we had a lot to do and not much time to do it in. We bid a nervous farewell to Eleanor and I got us all to Euston Station at the last possible minute. We came close to having to board the train at a flying leap.

Two hours later, just as we were getting into the hilly country, I found myself in a first-class smoking compartment with all of my company asleep. The godmothers had had their tea and dozed off in their chairs. I went rummaging through my tote bag for something to read, and came up with the morning papers. They'd been delivered to our door at the Connaught, but we hadn't had time to look at them.

Maybe that had been a blessing. The papers were full of news about murder number three: Emily Jemima Bald, fifteen years old, drugged-out and dragged under and wild, all rainbow hair and metal-studded clothes. She had been a runaway from The Thomas Morton School in Kent. The authorities had been looking for her for two weeks. All the elements were in place: She had been mutilated, she had been stabbed numerous times, she had

145

died from loss of blood after her carotid artery had been severed.

And she'd had a white rose impaled on her chest.

None of those things could shock me anymore, but this did: She had been found in the open in Putney Common Park, four blocks and less than a third of a mile from my flat.

PART FOUR

PART FOUR

──── FOURTEEN ────

St. Edmund Cavateur is like an Agatha Christie fantasy village. There is a stone church, dating back to the eleventh century, with a churchyard cemetery that dates back even further and is still in use. There is a cluster of two-story, open-beamed buildings arranged irregularly around an intersection: a grocer's, a butcher's, a chemist's, a newsagent's (where you pay your phone bill), a sweet shop (which is also the post office), and a pub called The Cock and Bull. The pub has been renovated. Its name is its new owner's idea of a joke, and indicative of something about St. Edmund Cavateur and the surrounding towns: A lot of people have recently moved up there from London. The thatched-roof cottages, impossible to cool in the summer or heat in the winter, still belong to locals. These cottages would take too much time and money to fix. The solid Elizabethan farm houses all belong to artists and writers, who come up on their vacations from points south. They're exactly the sort of places that look so perfectly "literary" when photographed for magazines. They're also tucked away against the moors in full view of the mountains, making them "quiet."

If I sound as if I don't have much respect for the artists and writers, it's true. I would have had the same sort of disrespect for an American writer who moved down to Appalachia because he thought the place was "picturesque." Yorkshire is desperately, frighteningly poor, as poor as any Third World country. Before Maggie Thatcher and her anti-socialist revolution, as much as twenty-five to thirty percent of the county was more or less permanently unemployed. Even after ten years of Maggie, fewer than fifty percent have regular central heating instead of shilling meters. The mines have been worked out. Labour Party law and Labour Party taxes made heavy industry untenable. The foundries and factories that were once Yorkshire's heart closed long before the Tories came to power. Nothing else has moved in.

I wouldn't have minded the artists and writers so much if they had stuck to mouthing idiocies about the wonders of going back to nature. Unfortunately, they tended to get very militant about keeping those wonders unspoiled. They opposed every form of development. They publicly objected to the establishment of any enterprise that might pollute the air, however slightly. None of this would have made much difference in some place like Cleveland, where the economy was in reasonably good shape and the population could afford to limit the amount of investment in the area without actually starving to death. It made a great deal of difference in Yorkshire, where large doses of development were needed in short order just to keep people eating. The answer, the people from London said, was "tourism." Tourism would bring in foreign money and, properly controlled, hurt the environment not at all.

It didn't work. The city of York got its share of visitors, but the rest of the county saw only a few students hiking in the Pennines or the Royal Birdwatcher's Society staking out a place on the moors. There just wasn't enough going on in Yorkshire to attract the kind of foreign money the literate back-to-nature types wanted. In my five years in the business, I'd booked rooms in Ramsmoor, the market town closest to St. Edmund Cavateur, exactly five times. I'd booked rooms in St. Edmund Cavateur once before Mariliee Bonnard showed up in my office. All these rooms were in run-of-the-mill, inexpensive bed-and-breakfasts, the kind of places people on limited budgets usually find on their own, without the hassle and expense of travel agents. I made not one dime on any of these transactions. I did them all as favors for the children of well-heeled clients.

I was thinking about all that as a way of not thinking about the Ripper murders—or as a way of not thinking of the coincidence of Benjamin Grade in my flat and a body in Putney Common Park. That coincidence nagged at me, made me chilled and apprehensive. I didn't think Ben had killed them, but everything I could think of was sinister in the extreme, and almost bizarrely elaborate. Maybe it was the Ripper who was sending me roses and who had searched my flat and, after leaving it without finding me there, took his hostility and frustration out on some passing runaway. Benjamin's talk about skeleton-key locks and open windows was convincing on the surface, and we *had* found the front door of the upstairs flat open, but I knew too little about the mechanics of those things not to believe there couldn't be another explanation yet: a method Benjamin didn't know about, perhaps. Then there was an even more bizarre possibility. Maybe the Ripper was following *Benjamin* around. Maybe the bodies were deliberately being left in places Benjamin would have been able to put them. Maybe the Ripper's point was not bloodlust or paranoid schizophrenia, but some wild compulsion to see Benjamin Grade destroyed.

Did people really behave that way? I didn't know. I did know I was probably losing it. I was making up plots Belle March would have been proud of. I have a wider view of what is possible in real life than most people do. Some of the places I've been and some of the things I've seen people do have been as unbelievable as the story lines on "Dark Shadows." A mass murderer who killed his victims for no other reason but to incriminate a man he hated was too much even for me.

I sat with my forehead pressed against the windowpane in that first-class compartment for mile after mile, smoking cigarette after cigarette and worrying. In the sky over the mountains, the clouds were massing for a terrific storm, all black water and sheet lightning.

We got to Mrs. Henry Copplewhite's just after five: too late for tea and too early for dinner. That was what Caroline Matthews said as the cab we'd hired in Ramsmoor pulled up to the Copplewhite gate. She'd been grumbling about food for most of the hour-long ride from the station. I had been thinking about the weather. The promised storm had broken just as our train pulled in to Ramsmoor Station. The violent pounding of water against the station's tin roof had made it sound as if the place were being invaded by Visigoths. It was impossible to hear anything anyone said, too, which meant it took fifteen minutes for me to find our cabbie and get the arrangements squared away. Then there'd been the run from station door to the cab—less than ten feet, but far enough in that rain to drench us all to the skin. The godmothers climbed into the back, I took the front seat beside the driver, and we set out along the rutted, half-paved road to St. Edmund Cavateur in mutual states of discomfort and depression.

I had heard a great deal about Mrs. Henry Copplewhite's, but always about the service, never about the house itself. I had expected the place to be like every other tenth-rate B-and-B: a small house crammed with tiny rooms, uninteresting architecturally and possibly unsound. When the cabbie stopped in front of that great Victorian pile, I just thought he'd mistaken the address. The house he'd brought us to was an anomaly in Yorkshire, a true product of Empire, three twenty-foot-tall stories high and girdled with gingerbread and filigree. It looked like the cover illustration for a paperback novel about The House That Wouldn't Die. It might have been frightening if it had been possible to take it seriously. Instead, it made me think of the stories children tell to give each other nightmares.

In the back seat, the godmothers shifted and turned and started to whisper among themselves. That wouldn't have been possible in a London cab—those big Rollses hold half a dozen people in back—but in this tiny Ford economy model, they were crammed in together and without me. Their whispering made me crazy. I hated even thinking of them plotting something without me. I hated imagining what they'd come up with next.

Belle March pushed up against the front seat and said, "Caroline says she can see the number and it's the right one. This is the place."

I took a second look at the house, a more careful one. I decided I liked it even less than I had expected.

"Well," I said, "there's one consolation. Unless she's turned the place into dormitories, we won't be cramped."

"There's Ella Jergens's place down the road," the cabbie said. "You'd probably like that better."

We probably would, but I knew there was no way to talk the godmothers out of their already-established plan. I thanked the cabbie for his advice and opened the car door.

"Don't bother getting out," I said. "You'll catch pneumonia."

"No worry about that," he said. "Never been sick a day in my life."

"You're *going* to be if you go on smoking like that," Mariliee Bonnard said. "Those things are very bad for you."

"Right," the cabbie said.

I ran around the back and got the door open on Mariliee's side. I was using a copy of *Radio Times* I'd bought on the train to cover my head, but it wasn't doing much good. The road was pocked and full of mud and water. By the time I'd hauled Mariliee out and onto the small patch of asphalt in front of the gate, my stockings were streaked with dirt and snagged with a hundred minute pebbles. I reached into my pocket and got the cabbie a tip, a nice big one.

"Thanks," I said. "You've been wonderful."

He stuffed the twenty-pound note in his shirt pocket. "Thank you, miss. You call me whenever you need the ride back to Ramsmoor. I'll come out."

The godmothers had climbed out onto the sidewalk, and now they stood in a huddle just outside the gate, getting drenched. Having finally arrived at the place they'd spent so much effort and expense to get to, they suddenly seemed reluctant to go in.

I didn't want to go in at all, but I thought I was going to have to if I wanted to avoid drowning.

Mrs. Henry Copplewhite was what used to be called a slattern. I don't think there's a twentieth-century word that covers it. She greeted us at the door in person, dressed in a fading lavender sprigged-print frock that had probably been bought in 1952 and washed only twice since. There were great black stains of dried perspiration under her arms and a smear of something brown across her breasts. Her smell overwhelmed me; the stench of dirty clothes and dirty flesh had been buried under a thick layer of heavy perfume. The perfume was as lavender as her frock and a little rancid, like sour milk.

I was standing closest to the door when she opened it, and I stepped back almost immediately. Distance and wind swept the smell away. My eyes focused again and I was able to see what the woman looked like: awful. She was thin in a way I wouldn't want to be, all bones and angles and jutting Adam's apple. Her face was a mass of pockmarks and congealing cosmetic foundations. Her eyes were piggy-small and bright with malice. She reminded me of the villainesses in Dickens. In another era, she might have run a sweatshop with orphaned children for labor or bought babies from girls pregnant out of wedlock to sell them as chimney sweeps. In this day and age, I thought, she was probably nothing more than the town bitch, a thoroughly nasty woman whom the rest of the village had as little to do with as possible.

My instant judgment of her character wasn't helped by the way she was looking at me, up and down, up and down, as if I were a piece of prime beef. I've gotten similar appraising looks from men, and never liked it, but the way Mrs. Copplewhite was staring at me made the sexual once-over seem innocent.

Stepping back, I had not only plowed into Mariliee Bonnard, but deserted the slight protection of the entry overhang. I was getting drenched again. I held my breath and stepped boldly forward, determined to get aggressive for once. We had to get in out of the rain.

"Mrs. Copplewhite?" I said. "I'm Avra Mahon. We have a reservation for this evening."

"I *thought* you were Avra Mahon," Mrs. Copplewhite said. She gave me a smile that revealed a shelf of teeth gone black with rot. "I *know* you have a reservation."

"Well," I said. She was standing directly in front of the door, blocking it. I could have pushed past her, but I didn't want to touch her. The idea of putting my hand against that filthy dress made my stomach roll.

Belle March saved us. She came right up to the front, pushed me out of the way, and said, "If you know we've got a reservation, let us in. Our luggage is being ruined in the rain."

Mrs. Henry Copplewhite gave Belle a cursory once-over, dismissed her as of no importance, and then said, in a voice that was almost pleasant, "Bitch, aren't you?"

She did, however, get out of the way.

It was one of the great tragedies of Victorian architecture that that house had fallen into the hands of Mrs. Henry Copplewhite. It had started out to be a beautiful thing. The entrance hall we finally made our way into was fifteen feet square and framed by the angled banisters of a pair of twin staircases. The wood had been carved and polished and stained to a dark brown. The hall floor was a mahogany parquet, a checkerboard in patterned wood. The great double doors that led to the interior were mahogany, too, and meticulously carved. They were framed by plaster molded to look like hanging curtains.

It was going to ruin. The flooring was pitted and eaten through in a few places, the way it will get if rock salt is tracked over it and not cleaned up. The long, narrow windows on either side of the door were cracked and pasted over with tape. The staircases looked as if they hadn't been dusted in months and hadn't been polished in years. There was dirt, and ruin, everywhere, and no carpet to catch the rain and mud we brought in. Mariliee Bonnard kept trying to shake herself off on her newspaper. Caroline Matthews planted herself just inside the door and refused to move. Only Belle seemed to have no compunctions about making the mess even worse than it already was.

She strode right into the middle of the floor and said, "Where did that woman *go?*"

I looked around. Belle was right. Mrs. Henry Copplewhite had disappeared. "Maybe we were supposed to follow her," I said, doubtful. "I can't think—"

"Old cow," Belle said. She swept her hand in an arc, taking in the staircases. "Can you believe what she's done to this place? You couldn't get hold of a house like this back in the States for love or money."

"If we were supposed to follow her," Mariliee said, "she'd probably leave us standing here forever rather than come back for us. Maybe we should—"

"I'll move when I want to," Belle said. "Don't push me."

"Don't get aggravated," Caroline said. "You know how testy you get when you're under stress."

I knew how considerably testy *I* got when I was under stress. At that moment I was feeling particularly out of sorts. I'd done my time in dirty rooms on dirty sheets. One of the advantages of having made it up and gone into business for myself—in a very genteel profession—was that I was supposed to be rid of all that. Now here I was in a flea bag as bad as any I'd ever seen, and it had just hit me that I was supposed to stay in it for *six entire weeks*.

"Look," I told them, "I know you want to be where Benjamin Grade is, but this is impossible. You've got to know this is impossible."

"I don't mind roughing it if I have to," Caroline said. "And you shouldn't either. You're young. You're strong."

"I also like hot baths and good food and clean sheets," I said. "There's nothing we can do about this tonight. The weather's awful and I wouldn't know how to go about looking for another place. But tomorrow—"

"We'll be fine," Caroline said. "We'll get used to it. Just wait."

"Oh," Mariliee said, "I suppose this place is a little—"

"Rank." I finished for her. Desperation made me creative. "For all you know, Benjamin Grade isn't even here. He was supposed to be on that train, but I never saw him. And I would have, if he'd been in a first-class compartment. And why wouldn't he have been?"

"He probably goes second-class for research," Belle said. "That's the kind of book he writes. Full of pimps and prostitutes."

"No, he had first-class tickets," Caroline said. "I talked to his—" She flushed.

"Maybe he missed the train," I said. "Maybe he changed his mind and decided not to come to Yorkshire. Then what do we do?"

Caroline seemed to be having a difficult time. Committed as she was to seeing justice done for the murder of her niece, she wasn't any happier with Mrs. Henry Copplewhite's than I was. Caroline Matthews was a meticulous woman. Her hair was always in place, her clothes always looked pressed, and her shoes were always polished to a high shine. I'd assumed she was hugging the door because she didn't want to track mud on the floor, but I might have been wrong. She might have been hugging the door because she couldn't force herself to walk into all that dirt.

"Look," I said, "I know how important this is to all of you. But this is extreme. We could watch Benjamin Grade just as well from Mrs. Jergens's down the road. Better, maybe, because we wouldn't be wasting our energy avoiding bugs."

Caroline shook her head firmly, making up her mind. "No. We've tried that. I even hired a private detective in Boston. If we're not right on top of him, it just won't work."

"And if he isn't here? And doesn't come?"

"We'll give him two days," Caroline said. "If he doesn't show up, we'll go looking for him."

Just then the great double doors to the interior opened, and Mrs. Henry Copplewhite returned, smiling and simpering and looking just plain nasty.

"Why don't you just come in and sit for a while," she said. "I've got all my guests assembled for a glass of sherry."

"I want to go to my room," Belle March said. "I have to freshen up."

Mrs. Henry Copplewhite caught the insult. I wouldn't have thought her capable of it, but she did. She turned her too-small eyes and her too-wide smile on Belle like she was delivering a dose of poison.

"Your room isn't *made up* yet," she said. "I haven't had time to turn the sheets."

Insult for insult, indignity for indignity. It was going to be a very long six weeks.

I wasn't ready to face Mrs. Henry Copplewhite's parlor, or her guests. Saying I was cold, wet, miserable, and tired didn't even begin to cover it. I'd been on edge so long; my nerves were shot and my temper was turning lousy. I needed a little breathing room.

"Excuse me," I told them. "I have to use the phone."

It is possible to make a collect call to a hotel room, it just isn't easy. I sat in Mrs. Henry Copplewhite's old-fashioned wood-paneled telephone room—what had probably started out to be a closet and was now the only cramped room in the house that hadn't been constructed for servants—and listened to the clicks and whirrs of machinery and the clucks and grumbles of the people who had to pass me on before I reached Eleanor. The idea of Eleanor sitting in the Connaught, with a massive circular tub in her bathroom and room service twenty hours a day, almost made me want to cry. I was sure no guest at the Connaught had ever been handed a dirty sheet, not in the entire hundred-odd-year history of the hotel. The Connaught was the kind of place where the maids check in four times a day to smooth the bed, wash the ashtrays, empty the wastebaskets and deliver fresh towels.

I passed the time looking over what Mrs. Henry Copplewhite thought of as decor. The walls of the room were hung with framed and glass-fronted photographs, black-and-whites mostly, of the type and size that used to be produced by Brownie cameras. The pictures weren't professional and their arrangements were even less so—there were four to six of them stuck within each frame, like little squared-off, unimaginative collages—but the framing was professional. Mrs. Henry Copplewhite had spent serious money on that, or at least what amounted to serious money for a woman in her circumstances. I wondered why. They didn't seem to be pictures of anything in particular: family scenes mostly, parents and children in the sort of poses that become all too familiar to people who work in print-processing plants. A little boy on a shingle beach, probably Brighton. The same little boy with a pail and shovel in what looked like a backyard, what the British would call a "back garden," even if nothing grew in it but grass. The same little boy again, standing next to a horse under the banner of a county church fair.

I idly went from frame to frame, holding the phone receiver in one hand and periodically reidentifying myself and my mission to someone I'd been passed on to without introduction. Something about those pictures made me distinctly uneasy, although I couldn't for the life of me understand what. They were ordinary enough. They showed no evidence of neglect or abandonment or abuse. I really could identify The Look any time I saw it, and this boy didn't have it. I stopped in front of the one studio portrait in the place, an eight-by-ten, badly colored print. The boy was older in this one than he'd been in the snapshots, maybe nine or ten instead of six or seven. He had on a shirt and a tie and a jacket, and very neatly combed hair. He looked the way all little boys look when they get their pictures taken for school.

And I didn't like him. I didn't like him *one bit.*

I stepped away from the wall, so shocked I missed the hotel operator telling me she was ringing Eleanor's room. She had to repeat herself, and even when she did I wasn't much more responsive than I'd been the first time. I *like* children. I like all children, almost all the time. The prickly ones don't bother me the way they do some people. I was a difficult child myself. I always assume children who behave badly have something going wrong in their lives. There are intangible losses as well as tangible ones. Some children who are meticulously well-cared-for in every other way lack the love and respect of their parents. Some children who are well-loved are also badly misunderstood—a truth, even if it has become a cliché. I'd never in my life disliked a child for his personality.

I didn't even know what this child's personality had been. All I had were badly taken pictures. Even so, the boy shook me. Then I thought: He reminds me of someone.

On the other end of the line, the hotel operator said, "Miss Morgan will take your call."

I turned away from the picture in grateful relief. Of course the boy didn't remind me of someone. He was probably Mrs. Copplewhite's son, or something, and no one I'd ever met or ever would meet. He didn't remind me of his mother, either. He was much too clean.

There was a little built-in bench in the corner where the phone hung on the wall, and I sank into that, my back to the pictures.

Eleanor said, "Avra? Is that you?"

Eleanor didn't know which way to be: annoyed that I was checking up on her, treating her like a child; or proud of herself for having got so much done. Her Princess Di voice bubbled through the wires to me, half-exasperated and half-ecstatic.

"I got a girl from a temp service," she said. "Nice girl named Deirdre Alcott. I've got her convinced I'm a nob, I think, at least an earl's daughter. Isn't that a hoot?"

"It sounds like about par for your course," I said. "Are you staying in the room?"

"I had to run into the office to show Deirdre where everything is."

"Eleanor."

"Don't *fuss*. I really did have to do it. It would have looked queer otherwise. And Belle changed all the filing to some American system. It's not that easy to explain. Nobody saw me."

"Or you didn't see anyone," I said. "What if that Mrs. Derme was hanging around and following you?"

"Nobody followed me. I took cabs. And Mrs. Derme wouldn't have recognized me if she'd walked right into me."

"Yes, she would have," I said.

"I can't spend six entire weeks locked away in a hotel suite, you know."

"I'm just trying—"

"Would you like to know what was in the mail?"

Actually, the answer to that was no. Mail isn't the best part of my day. I let Eleanor rattle on anyway, about bills we could pay now that Caroline Matthews's money was in the bank, about circulars, about a meeting of the Association of British Tour Guides. It was the usual stuff, without surprises, and when Eleanor was done I found myself feeling better. I think I'd half-suspected another note from whoever had sent the flowers, or maybe more flowers. It was odd how my grip on that particular subject came and went. I didn't like thinking about it, so I would blank it out. There were days when I kept it so well suppressed that it might never have happened at all.

The man from Foyle's, I thought. *That's who that reminds me of. The man from Foyle's.*

I turned around and stared at the pictures on the far wall. The room was narrow enough so I could make out the features in the studio portrait, but the particulars in the snapshots would always be unclear unless I stood right next to them. The studio portrait looked nothing like the man from Foyle's. In fact, it looked like nobody. All personality had been wiped away in the photographer's zeal to be professional.

I turned back to the phone. There was no reason for what I was thinking, no reason at all, and yet I was chilled. The house seemed to shudder and hulk around me, changing shape and attitude. Nonsense, I thought. Sheer nonsense. I had to be making myself paranoid. The man I'd seen in Foyle's had followed me, which had frightened me. I'd refused to do anything about my fear. Now it was coming back to haunt me. That was all.

I took my cigarettes out of my pocket and got one lit, wishing my hands would steady.

Eleanor said, "Avra? Are you listening to me? I just said you got a call from Mr. Benjamin Grade."

I shook my mind clear of fantasies. "You talked to Ben Grade?"

"I didn't talk to him," Eleanor said patiently. "Deirdre took a message after I was gone. I told you I didn't stay long."

"Yes," I said. "Yes, you did. What did he have to say?"

"He said he needed some peace and quiet, so he was taking a car instead of the train." Eleanor laughed.

I sighed. It figured. Benjamin Grade could have done us all a real favor and decided not to come at all, but the way my life was going, that was too much to ask for.

I tapped cigarette ashes into the wastebasket at my feet and decided that, paranoid delusion or not, I now had more than dirty sheets and dust balls against spending six weeks with Mrs. Henry Copplewhite.

——— FIFTEEN ———

By the time I got off the phone, the cocktail hour had broken up. I walked back to the foyer to find Belle and Caroline and Mariliee standing in a little knot around their still-dripping luggage, looking ill. I wondered what Mrs. Henry Copplewhite's sherry had been like. Vintageless rotgut from the local licenser's, I expected. She'd have laced her own with gin. I wondered where Mrs. Henry Copplewhite was and where her other guests were. The house was as quiet as the British Museum after hours.

I picked up the largest suitcase and said, "I take it there isn't anybody to help with the bags?"

"Mrs. Copplewhite didn't say there was." Caroline sighed. "Of course, she didn't say there wasn't, either. She just said our rooms were the first two doors at the top of the third-floor landing."

"Third floor," I said.

"I know," Caroline said. "I do understand. And I'm afraid you might be right about Mr. Grade, too. At least, he wasn't with the rest of them at, uh, at—drinks."

"I take it the sherry left something to be desired," I said.

"Cleaning fluid," Mariliee said.

"Don't be ridiculous," Belle said. "If it was cleaning fluid, we'd already be dead."

"Maybe I *am* dead," Mariliee said. "I certainly *feel* dead."

I picked up a light suitcase in my free hand. "Come on," I

told them. "Let's get upstairs. Much as I'd like Mr. Grade to just disappear into the London mist, I'm afraid he's probably coming. At least, he left a message saying he was."

"He left a message for you?" Caroline asked.

I started for the stairs, flushing a little. I hadn't told them everything that had gone on in my apartment the night before. I hadn't told them, for instance, that I rather liked Benjamin Grade. Now I felt as if it were showing on my face.

"He left a message for all of us, I think," I said. "Just saying he wanted some peace and quiet, so he was going to drive instead of taking the train. He'll probably be in later tonight. The weather must be holding him up."

"Maybe he'll come and see this place and decide he doesn't want to stay here after all," Mariliee said hopefully. "Then we could all move on to—to Mrs. Jergens's."

"If we have to stay in St. Edmund Cavateur, it will have to be Mrs. Jergens's," I told her. "But just don't remind me there's a first-class pub inn in Ramsmoor. *First*-class."

"With scones?" Mariliee asked.

"With a full cream tea," I said.

Mariliee sighed a sigh worthy of a suffering soul in Purgatory.

I reached the first landing and turned around to look at them. "Come *on*," I said again. "We might as well get as settled as we can get before we all collapse."

Our rooms were as bad as we had feared; worse maybe, because Mrs. Copplewhite believed in using as much electricity as possible. The bulbs that hung from wire cords in the center of each of our rooms were one-hundred-twenty-watt. They cast a harsh glare into every corner of the room, showing up the dirt on the floors and the stains on the walls and the balls of dust under the beds. There was dust on the furniture, too, *old* dust. It had first accumulated and then been invaded by some kind of oily grime. It was crusted in ridges on the tops of the Deal tables and the Sheraton chairs. Mariliee looked ready to cry. All those rare, prohibitively-expensive antiques—all those lovely things she couldn't afford for herself—all going to ruin.

Belle, who noticed things like that but didn't get sentimental about them, took a white lace handkerchief out of her purse, dusted off the seat of the nearest chair, and sat down.

"I'd clean up myself," she said, "but I don't want to provide that woman with the service."

"I may clean up anyway," Mariliee said. "I'm not too sure I can—I mean, everything is so—"

"Dirty," I suggested.

"Well, everything isn't awful," Caroline said briskly. "It's too bad you weren't at sherry, Avra—I don't mean for the sherry, for the good Lord's sake, I mean for the company. There are a great many very nice people staying in this house."

"Girls," Mariliee said helpfully.

"Too much makeup," Belle said.

I was confused. "She's got girls staying in the house?" I asked. "What kind of girls?"

"Just girls," Caroline said. "Very nice ones really, although Belle's right. Much too much makeup. But a lot of girls use makeup like that these days. It doesn't mean anything."

"I'm just surprised there were any girls at all," I said. "That's not the kind of clientele places like this usually have."

"What kind of clientele do they have?" Belle asked.

I thought for a moment. "Old-age pensioners," I said finally. "What are called 'OAPs' on the underground. Older people on fixed incomes looking for a holiday. There are usually a couple of younger men, too, university students or bureaucrats on hiking tours. They camp out for most of their stay and take rooms for a couple of nights to use the showers. Sometimes you get people who live semipermanently in places like this, because they can't afford a regular flat. Widows without families. Women who never married and spent their time typing for somebody or serving as salesladies and now don't have much to live on or anywhere to go. That sort of thing."

"Older people around here must have better sense," Belle said. "There was nobody like that here. Just the girls."

"Very *young* girls," Mariliee said. "Not more than eighteen, most of them, although with all that stuff on their faces it was hard to tell."

"And very nice," Caroline repeated. "All 'please' and 'thank you' and 'can I get you something else?' I don't think American girls have behaved like that for the past twenty years."

"American girls get better educations," Belle said. "I'll bet not one of the ones downstairs ever finished high school or whatever they call it here."

"It's not the same," I said, my mind wandering. "This is a country where fewer than ten percent of the population ever sees the inside of a university. Even a technical university. You have to have a college degree in America for a lot of jobs you wouldn't have to have one for here."

"I wasn't talking about college," Belle said. "I was talking about high school."

"Point taken," I said.

Mariliee stared at me curiously. "Are you all right, Avra? You look distant."

I brought myself back to the present. "Sorry. I guess I just—so much is strange about this place, I'm having a hard time handling a strange clientele."

"The clientele is all that strange?" Caroline asked.

"I don't know," I said. "Let's just say that in my personal experience, the kind of girls you're describing don't usually go on holiday. They don't often have the ready cash. Of course, I haven't seen them—"

"The descriptions were perfectly accurate," Belle said.

"I'm sure they were, but there could be some kind of cultural confusion going on. They could be an English type you're unfamiliar with, so you're misreading the cues. But if they are what you've made them sound like, it's very unusual to find them in a B-and-B. It's very unusual to find them in St. Edmund Cavateur. How many were there?"

"About a dozen," Caroline said.

"A *dozen?*" I'd expected to hear something like "three." "Good Lord, what are a dozen school-leaving-aged girls who wear too much makeup doing in St. Edmund Cavateur?"

"Maybe they're working," Caroline said. "Didn't you say there was an Arab who owned the manor house? Don't those people keep a lot of servants?"

"Servants live in," I said. "Especially minor servants like

165

housemaids. The pay for that kind of work is bad, but room and board at least make it feasible."

"Maybe they're barmaids," Belle said. "I saw a pub on our way in."

Mariliee shook her head, suddenly coming in on our side. "There are only two pubs in all of St. Edmund Cavateur. That was in that guidebook I sent you. Two pubs couldn't take on a dozen barmaids. Pubs in the country are mostly run by the people who own them. And if they did hire somebody who wasn't from the area, they'd just give her a room. That's the usual thing."

Caroline looked from Mariliee to me and back again, incredulous. "But this is absurd," she said. "You sound as if you thought something criminal was going on. What could those girls possibly be involved in?"

"Prostitution?" Mariliee suggested.

I shook my head. "I don't think so. Mrs. Copplewhite could never support a twelve-girl house in St. Edmund Cavateur. The local men just don't have enough money. The people with the holiday houses wouldn't want to get a reputation in the area for that sort of thing. They're too involved in politics. And the Arabs would go to London, wouldn't they? Not to this filthy house."

"Well, they weren't on drugs," Caroline said. "I know enough about drugs to be able to tell. If it isn't prostitution and it isn't drugs, what could it be?"

"I don't know," I said. Then I sighed. "I don't know it's anything," I admitted. "It's just out of whack, and I don't like it."

"I know what I'm ready for," Belle said. "Food. It's a wretched night and I refuse to go out—and I wouldn't let that woman feed me for anything—but I do believe Mariliee brought—"

"Oh, I did," Mariliee said. She reached for her oversize tote and started hauling out cheese and bread and tinned paté. Then she looked at the small round table she was about to put them down on and put them back in the tote instead. "Just a minute," she said. "I'm going to have to at least clean the table. I refuse to eat off that—that *dirt*."

"I refuse to sit through my first night in this hellhole

sober," Belle March said. She reached for *her* oversize tote and came up with a bottle of first-rate claret and a little box of those screw-together plastic wineglasses. "I've got three more bottles in the bag," she said. "I suggest we all get drunk."

Mariliee gave her a long-suffering look and marched out the door, holding a wad of linen handkerchiefs in one hand, to find the bathroom.

I sat back and decided Belle might have a point. We were tired, we were hungry, and there was going to be no way to get comfortable in this place without a little alcohol.

I didn't get drunk, maybe because I never do, but by the time I left the godmothers' room to find my own I had definitely mellowed. It was after nine o'clock, and the house was maintaining an unnatural quiet. The lights in the hall, unlike the ones in the bedrooms, were dim. They gave the high-ceilinged passageway a spectral look. I wondered if Benjamin Grade had arrived and, if so, where he was. I didn't think I'd have heard him come in. Old houses like this one were built for privacy and quiet: six-inch walls made of solid plaster, six-inch recesses between floors and ceilings. I thought about going downstairs and asking Mrs. Copplewhite about him, and then I decided against it. I would have liked to talk over the business of the girls with him, but it wasn't something I *needed* to do. The only thing I *needed* to do was get some rest. Besides, I had no stomach for wandering around that house alone or for another run-in with Mrs. C.

I let myself into my room, locked the door behind me, and decided to forgo the glare of the overhead bulb for my little portable battery-powered book light. In the interests of comfort, I stripped the bed, turned the mattress, and made the mess up again with three oversize scarves. I'd brought the scarves just in case the weather turned really nasty, which it often does in Yorkshire in the fall. Now I was grateful for their protection and doubly grateful for Mrs. Copplewhite's knee-jerk miserliness. She had apparently decided to spend not a single penny more than she had to on her guests. The bed was no more than a cot, as narrow as a nun's board. If it had been any wider, I wouldn't have been able to tuck in the scarves around the edges.

It was becoming increasingly obvious that if I was going to spend a significant amount of time here, I was going to have to do some of Mrs. Copplewhite's work for her, no matter how Belle felt about that. If Benjamin Grade didn't decide to decamp as soon as he put a foot in the door—and I had a depressing premonition he wouldn't—I was going to take the sheets to the washateria the first chance I got. I was also going to buy a plastic mattress cover. Mattress covers aren't a hundred percent effective against bedbugs, but they help.

I was also going to buy a pillow. The two Mrs. Copplewhite had provided looked suspiciously as if they were inhabited by fleas. I dumped them on the floor in a dusty corner and wound my down jacket—also brought in case of nasty weather—into a ball to use as a head support. Then I got the plastic glass and the nearly empty wine bottle Belle had sent me off with, poured myself a nightcap, and stretched out to read myself to sleep.

The nearly-empty wine bottle turned out to contain a full-to-the-brim glass. I took a long drink of wine to forestall spillage—that room didn't need any more spillage—and settled down to Mariliee Bonnard and *Death on the Water*.

I must have been exhausted. Just as I got to the part where the cruise-boat social director is found dead of a gunshot wound to the head in her dead-bolted-from-the-inside, impossible-to-unbolt-from-the-outside cabin, I fell asleep.

I awoke, I didn't know how long later, feeling itchy and disoriented and in desperate need of a trip to the loo. My sleep had been of that drifting, twilight kind that makes you think you aren't asleep at all, and for a while after waking I couldn't remember where I was. In my dreams, I had been back in my Putney flat, arguing with Eleanor about the cat. I stared at the vast, high-ceilinged room in confusion, wondering where on earth the Buddha with the clock in its stomach had come from.

"Bugger," I heard someone say. "There's not a thing you can do about it and you know it."

I pulled up on my elbows, shocked awake by the similarity of that voice to Eleanor's. *Death on the Water,* which I had left lying open on my stomach, dropped to the mattress beside me, losing my place. I swiped at it without much effect. Of course, I knew the voice did not belong to Eleanor. Eleanor wouldn't have come to Yorkshire.

I sat all the way up and drew my legs underneath me. The pressure on my kidneys was enormous, but I didn't want to move just yet. The house was quiet again, as quiet as if I were the only one in it, but I knew that what I'd heard had to be just one small piece of a conversation. Somewhere out there, two people were talking. One of them was very angry.

I went through the possibilities, just to make sure I wasn't still half-asleep and fooling myself. The voice had had a thick Yorkshire accent. It couldn't have been one of the godmothers. Not one of them had even the smallest talent for mimicry. Neither did Benjamin Grade, and besides, the voice I'd heard had been unmistakably female. That left Mrs. Henry Copplewhite to round off the usual suspects. Mrs. Henry Copplewhite had the gravelly croak of someone who's spent too many decades with whiskey and cigarettes. The voice had been soprano and clear.

I closed my eyes, lowered my head, and listened intently. A moment later, the soprano came back, angry and bitter.

"You're going to get all of us into a lot of trouble," it said. "You're going to ruin everything."

"Shh," someone else said. "She'll hear."

The someone else, I decided, wasn't one of the usual suspects, either. Her voice was much too young and nervous and uncertain to belong to any of the people I'd met so far.

"I don't care bloody hell who hears," the first one said, "as long as you do. I can't make you understand a thing."

"I've changed my mind," the second one said. "Isn't that all right, then? Can't I change my mind!"

"Bugger," the first one said again.

They had to be out in the hall. If they'd been closed up in one of the rooms, I wouldn't have been able to hear a thing. I opened my eyes and climbed off the bed, as carefully and quietly as I could. These had to be two of "the girls," as the godmothers had called them. If they were what the godmothers had described, or what their voices made them sound like, I'd do better not to make any sudden moves. There is no vocal equivalent to The Look. There is no way to tell if a girl is a runaway from the sound of her voice. I was convinced by other things. The descriptions I'd heard of them fit. Their presence in this house and in my life, after everything else that had happened to me over the last few weeks, also fit. Most terribly, their conversation fit.

I walked to the door on stockinged feet, prodding carefully for loose or creaking boards. Outside, there was a rustling and the sound of agitated whispering. The two I'd been listening to had been joined by others. All of a sudden, the hall seemed stuffed and fluttering with girls, like a bevy of wild birds trapped and struggling in a barn.

"Let's get out of the hall," the first voice said. "We'll wake the old ladies up."

I got into the hall just in time to see what door they disappeared behind.

I really did need to go to the loo, but I might have gone even if I hadn't had to, just to give them a little time. I didn't want to barge in on them so quickly they'd know I'd overheard their conversation. Whatever was going on was supposed to be a secret, and girls like that share their secrets with nobody. I wondered what they had promised and what had been promised to them. Nobody has the sense of a gnat at the age of fifteen, or eighteen, for that matter. They might have become involved in anything. A dozen nasty ideas ran through my mind, each worse than the one before it: dope, prostitution, petty crime, grand larceny, weapons. I believed what I'd said to the godmothers about a bawdy house's chances of success in a place like St. Edmund Cavateur, but there were other things not-very-nice people might want of very young women besides a lay. Girls are good camouflage. They can carry weapons, or bomb parts, or a hundred other kinds of contraband with a fair chance of going unsuspected. The Arabs at the manor might have all the whores they could use stashed away in London, but they might also be in the business of running guns for the PLO or providing random terrorists with passports and working papers. Or hiding fugitives who needed food, clothing, books, and a few more-esoteric items their hosts didn't want to be caught buying.

I threw cold water on my face—the only kind of water Mrs. Copplewhite provided free of charge—and told myself to calm down. The chances were, whatever these girls were involved in was much less bizarre than the kinds of things I'd been thinking up. Illegal gambling would fit. That needs runners. Bootlegging would fit, too. Alcohol is heavily taxed in Britain. Alcoholism is high and salaries are low. There are always people looking for bargains on their little medicinal nips.

I straightened my hair, bit off the rest of the lipstick I'd put on just before we got off the train—I didn't want to look too respectable—and went back into the hall. As it turned out, I'd have been able to find them even if I hadn't seen which door they went through. They had the damn thing open. It was just a crack, but it was visible even in the dim light. So was the smoke that was poring out of it. They must have had a window open in there, too.

I went straight to the door and pushed it open all the way, without bothering to knock. I looked in on a sight I hadn't seen since leaving Santa Clara ten years before: fourteen faces stamped and branded with The Look, like a dormitory room at some benighted juvenile center.

Caroline Matthews had been accurate about one thing. They were very polite—too polite. As soon as I walked in, they went on automatic pilot, suddenly proper little children for a scrutinizing adult. They had the overhead light on and I looked at each one of them in the glare. Their clothes were an orgy of excess and ostentation: feathers, beads, spangles, shiny synthetic satin, glitter-paste appliqués, glow-in-the-dark decals, fringe. Their eyes were shuttered. Not one of them was more than sixteen years old.

I shut the door behind me with a sharp click, not caring how smoky the room got. I needed privacy and I needed to make an impression. I managed both. I knew I'd surprised them. I could see it in their faces. I'd even made one or two of the oldest ones very nervous. I wasn't the bumbling, ignorant grown-up they'd expected me to be.

There was a rickety desk shoved against one wall, covered

171

with dust and a film of something that might have been growing. I sat down on it anyway. Most of them were on the floor. Two were sprawled out over the edges of the bed. I needed the authority a little height would give me.

"Okay," I said, "my name is Avra Mahon. Ten years ago, I ran away from a foster home in Santa Clara, California. I was on the run for nearly three years. None of you is fooling me in the least. We're going to *talk*."

The reaction was a mixture of awe, surprise, and tentative curiosity. Only the oldest girls, the ones on the bed, closed in hostility against me. The ones on the floor, all as young as they could be and still have a chance of running successfully, looked distinctly interested. One or two even looked hopeful.

A small girl with pale brown hair and a green-and-yellow scarf around her throat said, "Is that really your name? Avra Mahon?"

I smiled. "No," I said. "I made it up when I was on the run."

"No one ever knew mine," a fat girl said.

"I know what that's like," said a redheaded girl. "I knew somebody like that at the Margaret MacCauley Home. She was just left off on the street one day, with no note or anything, and no one knew what to call her—"

"Shut *up*," a larger girl on the bed said. "Don't you know what she is? She's from DS, that's what she is. You can tell—"

"No, she's not," the redhead said. "She's American. She's got an accent."

"She could be informing for them," the big girl said. "She could have come up here just to find us and turn us in."

"No," said the redhead softly. Then she looked up at me and blushed a little. "I'm sorry," she said. "Gemma gets a little . . . it's because it's been so hard, you see. You must know about that."

"Oh, good Lord Jesus *Christ*," Gemma said. "She's never been in a home. Just *look* at her."

They all looked at me. Twelve pairs of eyes were trained on my face. The other two did a quick, longing survey of my clothes. I don't own what I think of as a fancy, expensive wardrobe, but to these girls a skirt and a twin-set of good but not particularly fine wool probably looked like a luxury beyond dreaming about.

The redheaded girl got up, crossed the room to me, and held out her hand. "I'm Molly Larkin," she said. "And it's my real name. I tried to make one up, but I could never remember what it was." She paused and looked me over one more time. Then she said, "I'm very glad you're here."

"Why don't you ask her why she *is* here," Gemma said. "That ought to be good."

All those eyes, trained on Gemma for the length of her remark, turned back to me. I felt like the backboard to a basketball hoop. I also felt nervous. I had just lost a little ground. Gemma had had the experience to see what the others had not: that my arrival, and my methods, were unlikely to be part of something as innocuous as a social chat.

I did the best thing I knew how to do. I went on the offensive. It had worked up to that point. I was hoping against hope it would go on working.

"I was in a home," I said. "Actually, I was in several. I got kicked out of a few and I ran away from a few others. I had foster parents, too. Those never worked out either. Then, when I was fifteen, I just ran."

"Fifteen?" someone squeaked.

I turned my attention to the center of the room, where the squeak had come from, although I didn't know who'd spoken. "Fifteen," I repeated. "I spent three months living under bushes and on benches in Central Park in New York City. Then I headed north, and I got a job. It wasn't a wonderful job, but it brought in money. And when I started to get some money together, I started studying. I got my high-school diploma when I was nineteen—"

"Bloody, fucking *marvelous*," Gemma said savagely.

I swung around. "You bet your ass it's marvelous," I told her. "There are eight million people out there who'll tell you that what's happened to you so far has ruined you. You haven't had the advantages, so you'll never have anything.

Well, bull*shit*. The systems suck—in Britain and America—but you're all growing up. You ought to know right from wrong by now and you ought to know what kinds of stupid behavior are going to really mess you up. If you don't, you damn well deserve to be caged."

"Cor," the little girl at my feet said. "I didn't know people who dressed like her could swear like that."

"I haven't started swearing yet," I told her. "Get me mad enough and I'll *show* you swearing."

"Why don't you just *show* us what *intelligent* behavior is," Gemma said. "Going back to the wonderful world of St. George's Children's Home? Seeing a therapist? Signing up for the dole?"

I turned back to her. "I think intelligent behavior would be getting the hell out of St. Edmund Cavateur. Getting out and not telling anyone where you're going. Because I don't know exactly what's happening here, but I can smell it. And it's bad."

"Bloody ass," Gemma said.

I looked down at the younger girls again, expecting to see nods of agreement or at least the dawn of understanding. I was flying. I didn't think I'd ever been so persuasive in my life. And I was right. If you survive running, you develop an instinct you never lose for bad places and bad people. This whole situation vibrated with nastiness.

The first face I caught was Molly Larkin's. It gave me the shock of my life. She had completely closed up. I might never have spoken a word to her. I jerked my head around and looked at the rest of them, one after the other. It was the same with every one of them. I had lost them in a snap.

Closed, hostile, stubborn, secretive: They had put up the walls against me and gone into hiding. I almost couldn't make myself believe it. What the hell were they involved in, that the mere suggestion of giving it up could turn them around this quickly? The only thing I could think of was drugs—addictions are like that—but I knew it wasn't that. I would have spotted the telltale signs of abuse in a second. These girls were cold sober and stone straight, and they no longer wanted any part of me.

I raised my head, slowly. Gemma was sitting up on the bed now, squaring her shoulders and pulling her spine straight, grinning at me.

"Get the hell out of here." She hissed. "You never saw us before. You never heard about us. You don't know anything. Get the hell *out* of here."

─── SIXTEEN ───

I got out of there. I got out of there fast, although I think I kept my head enough not to look as if I were running. My mind was playing a tape that said: *You did the right thing with Eleanor, you did the right thing with Eleanor*. It was as if doing the right thing with one person made it unimportant that you did the wrong one with others. Maybe I was just trying to reassure myself that I had not become totally alien to my childhood self. In the end, they had looked at me as an enemy. I didn't want to think that that's what I was.

Of course, they might have had a point. Even when I'd been in the position they were in, I'd never had the all-consuming hatred of the settled, middle-class world that was the defining principle of Gemma's soul. I'd had Sister Tom, and later I'd had other people. I'd had luck.

I paused at the door to my room and looked back across the dim hallway to the room I'd just left. The muted sounds of angry whispering poured out at me, like a hiss. I knew they were talking about me. I couldn't help wondering what they were saying. In the conversation I'd overheard coming from the hall, one of them had said she'd "changed her mind." I hoped they were talking about that.

I turned away and looked back at my bedroom door. I knew I should march in there and get some sleep. The day was catching up with me. My body was trembling with the surface shakes that are the start of true, bone-deep exhaustion. The air in front of my eyes was full of tiny sparkling dots, my mind's revenge for sleep deprivation and overexertion. If I'd thought I could get to sleep, I would have gone right to it.

I wasn't going to be able to. I was feeling too guilty and too frustrated. This made me restless. Dog-tired as I was, I couldn't stop moving. My feet were shuffling fretfully. My hands kept picking at lint on my skirt and strands of hair on my neck. If I tried to lie down, I'd just get up again seconds later, feeling like a fool for the effort.

In most bed-and-breakfasts, guests have the run of the guest floors and the common rooms of the house. I had no reason to suspect the rules at Mrs. Henry Copplewhite's were any different. I didn't think she had a lot of people wandering about—who would want to risk disturbing a nest of spiders in the dark of that living room?—but she hadn't said anything about the first floor being off limits, so I supposed I could go there. I stopped at the door to the godmothers' room on my way to the stairs, half-hoping to see a light and an offer of another glass of wine. I was out of luck. The only sound that came from it was Mariliee Bonnard's faint, whistling, ladylike snoring.

The stairs were lit by a single, underwatted bulb in the ceiling over each landing. There were small octagonal windows at each landing, too, but they weren't much help. Dark comes early to the north countryside, and in an autumn storm that dark is black as tar. At the second floor, I pressed myself against the wall, stood on tiptoe, and tried to look out. All I saw were the staccato splatterings of raindrops on the pane in front of my face. I wondered what time it was, and what direction I was looking in. There were churches in St. Edmund Cavateur, one in the very center of town. If midnight had come and gone, I would have heard the bells. Even after midnight, there should be lights coming from the village. There had been two streetlamps on the high street. I'd seen them.

I was stalling. Below me, the foyer was a black pool. Outside, the wind was rattling the gingerbread trim and making it creak.

I told myself not to be a fool and forced myself down the last half-flight into the dark. When I reached the first floor, I searched around on the wall for a light switch. I couldn't find one. Maybe Mrs. Copplewhite had installed remote switches somewhere where the guests couldn't get to them. I turned in what I thought was the direction of the living-room doors and groped my way toward the back.

It was darker in that foyer than in any place I've ever been. There was a tall, thin, ornamental window next to the front door, but it was stained glass and let in little light. My eyes adjusted to the dark and then adjusted again. I lost that blind feeling without ever being able to see anything. After a while, I began to get spooked by wandering around in the open, and so I edged sideways until I bumped into a wall. Hanging on to it gave me a sense of direction. I searched for a wall switch and searched again. I never found one.

When I got to the doors, I was sure I had found the living room, although its placement confused me. I'd thought I'd been traveling from the front of the house toward the back, that when I'd edged over to the wall I'd have to move along it and then turn a corner before I came to the living-room doors. The wall I'd bumped into, I decided, had to be the one *facing* the front door. I had my hands on a pair of twin knobs, and from what I remembered there was only one set of those leading off the foyer. The door to the back hall where the telephone room was had a single.

I turned the knobs all the way and pulled them toward me. Nothing happened. I turned them in the other direction and pulled again. This time, something did happen, but it wasn't what I had expected. I felt the sliding catches give and a sudden looseness under my hands, but instead of sagging outward, *toward* me, the doors seemed to be sagging inward. I let the knobs go and stood back. Somewhere in the dark in front of me, the doors creaked open.

Nonsense, I told myself. I just wasn't remembering right. I rubbed the palm of my hand against the side of my face, nervous beyond all reasoning. I'd been left standing in that foyer long enough to examine it minutely. There were *three* doors. I would bet my life on it. The double set went to the living room. The single went to the back hall. I didn't believe in secret passageways and I certainly didn't believe in corridors leading in to other dimensions opening up in blank walls.

By then I was completely disoriented. At gut level, I no

longer *knew* I was in the foyer. Part of my mind was going over and over my route from the third floor: I'd turned here, walked across there, moved sideways then. The dark and the silence were all I had for landmarks. The harder I tried to remember, the more confused I got.

This is *nonsense,* I told myself again, spelling it out to make myself believe it. I reached for the doors again and pushed, thoroughly angry at myself for my cowardice. The doors shuddered and creaked and moved back, sending up a small breeze.

I took a deep breath and stepped between them. There was a stiff draft coming from somewhere, a ragged stream of cold that made its way up my legs until the muscles in my thighs and calves felt frozen solid. I forced myself to walk toward it. A draft meant a window. A window might mean light. I'd never made it to the living room with the others, but my impression of Victorian houses was that they always had large banks of "view" windows covered in heavy curtains.

I kept brushing against furniture I couldn't identify and telling myself not to worry. I didn't know much about antiques. At one point, I stumbled over a low piece that might have been an ottoman and, reaching out to steady myself, grabbed a tall stack of paper that shifted and toppled under my hand. I kept my balance only by determination and the force of panic. I should have fallen on my face.

Upright again and even more shaky than I had been, I made myself move again toward that draft. The air around me was much colder than it had been, and I thought I might be near its source. I reached out and touched cloth: curtains. I took a deep breath and went at them.

There was something—a bench? a sewing box?—lying on the floor at my feet. This time, I didn't have the luck I'd had with the ottoman. I pitched forward, stumbling uncontrollably. The palms of my hands hit the cloth of the curtains and then a flat surface that felt thin and fragile and had to be glass. The flat surface gave way. For a second, I thought I'd broken a window.

I was already out in the rain and cold before I realized what had happened. It hadn't been a window I'd found, after all. It had been a set of French doors, insecurely latched. My weight had been too much for them. They'd popped open and dumped me into the back garden.

I jerked upright and whirled around, meaning to get back inside as quickly as possible. The rain was coming down in heavy sheets, and it was freezing. As I turned, my arm caught against a bush and I heard the sound of cloth ripping. I jerked away and slammed my hand into the bushes on the other side. My hand sank wrist-deep into a tangle of thorns.

Above me, something flashed, flashed again, and then started to glow: Someone had turned the garden lights on. I blinked twice, hard, trying to focus—and then I wished I hadn't.

I was standing in a garden, a rose garden. I was surrounded by hundreds and hundreds and hundreds of white roses.

Then I turned back toward the door and saw him standing there.

Benjamin Grade.

"They're fake," Benjamin told me, when he finally had me installed in Mrs. Henry Copplewhite's kitchen. "They had me confused, too, when I first saw them. I kept telling myself roses couldn't possibly survive in this weather. Well, they don't. I went out and checked, must have been just before you came down. They're silk."

I looked around the kitchen, my head aching in confusion. It was a large room, large enough to have been the working kitchen in a good-sized inn, and it was the antithesis of everything Mrs. Henry Copplewhite stood for. Every surface shined. Even the floor looked as if someone had scrubbed it down with a toothbrush. The idea of Mrs. Henry Copplewhite with a kitchen-cleaning fetish blew my circuits completely.

The kettle went off and Ben went to get it; that was what we were doing in the kitchen. It felt much longer than the few minutes it must have been since I'd first seen him in the garden. Standing in the door like that, he had been frightening. Now he was comforting, a large, gentle man fussing over housewifely matters. The fuss was not the bumble of inexpertness. He put tea and coffee and sugar and milk together as if he did it often and well.

I shifted slightly in my hard kitchen chair in a vain attempt to get more comfortable and thought that Benjamin Grade and I spent a lot of our time in kitchens—especially for two people who had got themselves involved in so much craziness. I tried to figure out if that meant something, but couldn't. I was just too tired.

He brought over a mug of tea and set it down in front of me. "My sense of justice says our Mrs. Copplewhite deserves to be ripped off for a midnight tea, but my sense of everything else won't let me do it. I brought this stuff down in my grip. You may drink in blissful moral peace."

"I'd have drunk in blissful moral peace in any case," I said. "I'm ready to burn the place down. I wouldn't have stuck at a little tea."

"Yeah, well. I buy better tea than she does. Have a good time. That's expensive stuff."

I took a sip and nodded. "Nice," I said. "Now will you please, *please* tell me what's going on here? Why would she do something like that: fill her back garden with fake white roses? Why—"

Ben held up a hand. "Slow down. It may be nothing. This is Yorkshire, for God's sake. They've got white roses all over the place. The official name of this magnificent establishment we find ourselves in is The White Rose Bower."

"Marvelous," I said. I got a cigarette out, lit it with a match from a book left lying in a wicker basket on the table, and dropped the spent match in a clean and polished ashtray. It bothered me. All the ashtrays I had seen before this had been overflowing and filthy, as if they were emptied twice a year and never cleaned. "You know," I told him, "I don't like this. I really don't. Somehow, I just can't believe Mrs. Copplewhite keeps this room like this and the rest of her house like . . . like that. It just doesn't fit. And the roses just don't fit, either. Someone spent a lot of time on that garden, a lot of *careful* time. It looked real in the dark and I'll bet it looks real in the daytime, too. I don't think Mrs. Henry Copplewhite is careful about anything."

"It doesn't seem like the same person, does it?" Benjamin said carefully.

I gave him a long look, making it as heavy with significance as I could manage. In books, when people do that, their target always gets nervous and flustered. Benjamin didn't. He got up and got his coffee, moving as slowly and casually as if we'd been talking about the weather. I wondered crazily if anything but the godmothers ever really got to him. Murder charges, official and unofficial harassment, even serial slayings on both sides of the Atlantic; he seemed to take it all in stride.

I commanded myself to make sense. Of course he didn't take it all in stride. He had been deeply affected by Julie's murder. I was sure of that, even though he didn't express it the way most people would. Sometimes I even thought he'd been affected by me, that he *worried* about me. That, of course, might have been wishful thinking.

He came back and sat down across from me at the table, and I gave him a little smile. "I'm really not trying to annoy you," I said, "but things are strange and getting stranger. You don't know how strange. You weren't here earlier in the evening."

"Did our Mrs. Copplewhite hold a séance?"

"No," I said. "She's just got a very weird clientele. With the exception of the two of us and the godmothers, everybody staying in this place is a runaway from a children's home. A female runaway."

"What?"

Finally, I'd managed to shock him. I'd managed to shock him big. He looked as if he'd been run over by a truck.

"Did you talk to them?" he asked. "Are you sure?"

"I talked to them," I said, "but I wouldn't have needed to to be sure. I was one, myself, ten years ago. I can spot them on the street, and often do. But you haven't heard the half of it. I don't know who Mrs. Henry Copplewhite is, or what she's doing, but she's definitely doing something."

I gave him a quick sketch of what had gone on upstairs, watching his eyes grow wider and his body grow stiller with every word.

"I couldn't begin to guess what the story is," I said, finishing up, "because none of the usual things fit. If they were involved in prostitution or something self-evidently criminal, they wouldn't have turned on me like that. Not all of them, and not all at once. Whatever it is, it's something they've been convinced is good for them."

Ben grabbed a cigarette out of my pack and lit up himself. "Dear Lord Jesus Christ, why do they *do* things like that? An entire social-services network set up just to protect these kids from what happens on the street, and they haven't got the Goddamned common sense to stay in out of the—what the hell's the matter with you?"

I told him. I gave him the whole thing, from Mrs. Catherine Hobart and Miss Anne Durbin to Sister Tom and the time I'd spent sleeping in Central Park. When I was done, he looked uncomfortable but also unconvinced.

"If you think I'm going to say you were right to do what you did," he said, "I'm not. You make it sound as if all the people involved in children's services are monsters, vampires. It just can't be true. There had to have been other solutions. There had to be someone in authority you could have gone to."

I sighed. "It's the people in authority who are the problem," I said. "I'm not saying they're all vampires. I'm saying that the way the structure is set up, it not only attracts vampires, it shields them. In England, you've got these damned children's homes stuck out in the middle of nowhere, because somebody in Parliament once decided the countryside was good for children. Well, it's impossible to monitor what goes on in these places. They're too far from the centers of power. If you've made a mistake in your choice of director, you've got real trouble. And as long as she doesn't actually kill off her charges, nobody's ever going to know. In the American system—"

"Foster homes are a good idea, Avra. You might have had trouble with the ones you were placed in—"

I shook my head vigorously. "Foster homes are a lousy idea," I said. "You take a child who's just been through a tremendous upheaval. You put her with a family. The problem is, most times, they ask these families, before the child ever gets there, if they're thinking of adopting. If they say no, everything possible is done to ensure that the child and her foster parents don't form what's called an 'inappropriate bond.' They do that if the child's natural mother is still alive, too, even if the reason the child's in foster care is that the natural mother put her in the hospital—with two broken legs. Good Lord, a good foster situation is almost worse than a bad one. As soon as your friendly neighborhood social worker finds out you actually love those people and they actually love you back, they drag you out of there. Your whole life becomes a series of displacements. After a while, you don't dare care about anything."

"But with the abusers—"

"No, Ben. They just don't believe you. All foster children complain about their foster parents. It's their way of keeping their distance. If you don't have any broken bones to show, the judges just think you're exaggerating."

"And sometimes you are?"

"And sometimes you are," I agreed.

Ben sighed. "You ought to go into politics," he said. "You almost have me convinced. And that's when I know there's a Ripper running around London killing these children off."

"Actually," I said, "I think about going into politics a lot. Going back to the States and starting one of those advocacy groups. Getting a lot of ex-foster children together and starting to put some pressure on the system. Somebody's got to do something."

"In the meantime—"

"In the meantime," I agreed, "we have fourteen girls upstairs and something weird going on. And you're not telling me everything you know."

He got up and went back to the counter near the stove, turning his back to me. From the movements of his shoulders, I knew he was packing up his tea-and-coffee things. He seemed to be operating on autopilot, thinking about something else. I didn't disturb him. I'd given him a lot to think about. I'd even delivered one of my lectures, something I usually do only to myself on long sleepless nights alone. Besides, I knew he'd start talking to me again when he knew what he wanted to say, and how much he wanted to tell me.

Somebody else—a detective, a cop, even Mrs. Henry Copplewhite—might have tried to bludgeon the story out of him. He was in a weakened emotional state. I couldn't do it. I didn't know how. I couldn't decide if I'd feel right about it.

He got his things straightened away, and the cups washed and set up in the rack, and then he came back to me. He looked troubled and uncertain—emotions I would have said, only a few moments before, he had no capacity for. He dropped back into the chair he'd been using and leaned over the table, getting as close to me as he could.

"Look," he said, "at the moment, I have no reason to think these two things are connected. I'll agree that there are disturbing concurrences—"

"Like the fact that all the dead girls are runaways or ex-runaways?" I said. "Like the fact that the killer is impaling white roses into his victims' chests and there are a million white roses all over this place? Like the fact that anyone who looked through this house would know Mrs. Copplewhite couldn't be living alone? There has to be someone here who's a nut about neatness and precision."

"I know, I know. But Avra, I've spent the past year of my life working on this. I've missed two deadlines and canceled an author tour, just because I didn't want to take time away from the investigation. I know a lot, even if I don't know enough. And I know at least one thing that just doesn't fit with what you're trying to tell me."

"Meaning one thing that doesn't fit with the girls being gathered in this house for something strange?"

"The attitude, not the circumstance," Benjamin said impatiently. "Avra, this guy isn't killing girls in a house full of people. He'd get caught—by Mrs. Copplewhite if no one else. He's not killing them in Green Park or the Cape Cod beaches, either. Julie's body had been moved. The police never said so right out loud, but I've got contacts and I know the police believed it. If I had contacts at Scotland Yard, I'd bet I'd find out the same thing about what's been happening here. These are slow deaths. He can't be doing them in crowded places. He's got to be getting these girls out to some remote place. He could be kidnapping them, but if he has been, he's been very lucky. Nobody's ever seen him do it. I'd say he has to be convincing them to go with him. They have to be going willingly."

"There are plenty of places to go around here," I said. "We're on the edge of the North York Moors National Park. That's a wasteland out there."

"Okay," he said. "But you just told me that when you tried to convince them to leave this place, they turned on you. Obviously, whatever they're involved in—and I'll give you that they're probably involved in something—depends on their staying here."

"They might go with someone they knew," I said. "Someone they trusted. For a walk on the moors, say."

"How could they know him? As far as *I* know, he'd been in America for a year and a half until a month and a half ago. At best, they might just have met him. And they're street-smart, Avra, just like Julie was. They wouldn't go wandering off to a dark place with someone they'd just met."

"Girls like these have done less intelligent things before," I said.

"Maybe. But don't forget, I've seen the guy I think is doing this. He's not young. He's not handsome. He's not wealthy. Why would they bother? And now that I think of it, he couldn't be killing them in the moors."

"Why not?"

"Because he's dumping the bodies in London. It's too long a trip. Which brings me back to where I started. If whatever's going on in this house has something to do with my man, then there'd have to be some way for him to convince your girls to leave with him. And even if he managed that once, what then? What happens when they see one of their former friends on the BBC evening report?"

"I see what you mean," I said.

"I thought you would. I came up to this place because Julie had it in her address book, don't ask me why. Maybe he'd stayed here once and gave her this address just to get her off his back. I've got no reason to believe he actually knows Mrs. Copplewhite, or that she knows him. And I can't, for the life of me, think of how your girls and their trouble could be connected to him."

I sighed. "I don't know. It just seems impossible to me, the Ripper and you finding this address in Julie's address book and then a lot of runaway girls involved in something nasty and none of it having anything to do with anything else."

"Well, I think the Ripper and Julie's murder are probably connected," Benjamin said. "You have to give me that."

"I will give you that. But the rest of it just seems to be too damn much coincidence."

"So give me a connection," Ben said. "I'd be more than happy to hear it. From what I know about this guy, I'd believe anything."

He had his tea-and-coffee things all packed away in a little leather bag. He picked them up and put them under his arm. "Come on," he said. "I'll walk you to your door. I don't think the Ripper's here, but this place gives me the creeps anyway."

"Do you really think I need an escort?" I asked him.

"Probably not," he said, "but it's a hell of a lot more subtle finding out where your room is this way than trailing behind you after dinner some night."

That made me laugh, the first time I'd done that in what seemed like forever.

It felt wonderful.

─── SEVENTEEN ───

I slept better than I had since I'd first learned that Sheila Ann Holme had been murdered. I got up to find the sun forcing its way through the grime on my window. I got out of bed without bothering with my morning cigarette. I was in too good a mood.

It was after nine. The godmothers were already gone by the time I got to their room. I headed down the stairs and made my way along the second-floor corridor until I found the corner door Benjamin had told me was his the night before. The godmothers were probably having their morning tea in Mrs. Henry Copplewhite's dining room, but I couldn't be sure. They might have decamped for the nearest restaurant in the hope of getting a decent meal. I didn't want to spend the morning by myself or alone in a corner table while the girls pointedly ignored me. I didn't want to put myself in any circumstance that might destroy my morning good cheer.

I knocked on Benjamin's door, got no answer, and knocked again, harder. I must have been really pounding. The door rattled and then jumped open, creaking on its hinges the way all the doors in that house did. I knew that if Benjamin had been inside, he would have heard me, but I was reluctant to give up. I couldn't see that it would hurt anything if I just stuck my head in and made sure.

I stuck my head in. I'd expected an empty room and a made-up bed. I saw a cavern of darkness and a huddled shape under the quilt. God, the man must have been exhausted, I thought. I'd been knocking loud enough to wake the dead.

I propped the door open and went in, wishing I knew Benjamin well enough to do something really outrageous, like waking him by kissing his feet. I did the ordinary thing instead. I reached out and shook him by the shoulder.

The shape under the quilt slid, and shifted, and then came tottering toward me. Its head twisted in the fall so that its eyes were clearly visible to me in the light coming in through the doorway. The eyes were glazed and empty.

Then the shape hit the floor and the quilt fell off, and I saw it all: the slash in the throat, the slashes in the face, the knife sticking out of the chest with the shredding petals of a white rose under its haft.

It was not Benjamin Grade.

It was Gemma.

PART FIVE

—— EIGHTEEN ——

The aftermath of a murder is much like the aftermath of a battle: much confusion, much fear. In this case, it was made worse by side issues I knew something about, but which the police did not. They didn't hear about them from me. At first, that was because I didn't think of them. Walking in on that body set off a series of eruptions in me that made me feel as if I were trying to cross the street in an earthquake. There was a split second in there when I must have been absolutely frozen. If I hadn't been, I'd have jumped back before the corpse fell on me. As it was, I didn't move until Gemma's dead hand brushed against my slacks, and then I was slow, mentally as well as physically. I stumbled backward, toward the hall, and all the time I was thinking: *These slacks cost thirty pounds and the blood is going to ruin them.*

I'd never before in my life given a damn about that kind of thing.

I was all the way out in the hall, standing under the swinging ceiling light, when the full significance of it hit me. I doubt if I was thinking clearly, even then. I could only think of one thing to do, and although it was in many ways the least sensible, I did it. I ran to the stairwell, leaned over the rail, and started screaming.

To this day, I have no idea what I was saying. Nobody else does, either. The others came at the sound, because a sound like that is at once a plea for help and a call to action. Fortunately, they came quickly.

Mrs. Copplewhite came first. I'd had no idea she could

move that fast. I heard the heavy pounding steps, that could be no one else, in the foyer, and then the stairwell was filled with rumbling and shaking and the slap of plastic soles on hardwood. All that bass clatter was followed by lighter notes, like a soprano counterpoint. The godmothers were on the chase.

The girls didn't need to be on the chase. Most of them were in their rooms, and when Mrs. Copplewhite and the godmothers reached the landing, they came out. I saw Molly Larkin in the background, looking curious and a bit bemused, as if I'd gone off my head but was probably harmless. None of them looked frightened.

Mrs. Copplewhite came running up to the floor without pausing for breath. It was a long, steep flight. She saw the door open behind me, brushed past me. Actually, what she did was push me out of the way, hard enough so that I almost fell. I got myself turned around just in time to see her charge through Benjamin's door and come to a stop a foot inside the room.

"Bloody hell," she said. "Bloody buggering idiot."

Caroline, Belle, and Mariliee reached the stairs just then. Caroline and Mariliee stood on the landing, out of breath, but Belle had more energy. She went right up to Benjamin's door and tried to push Mrs. Copplewhite out of the way.

Mrs. Copplewhite wasn't having any of that. Belle had to duck under the fat woman's arm to get a look at what I'd already seen.

"Oh, my God," she said. *"Oh, my God."*

"Belle?" Mariliee said.

Belle came back into the hall, shaken and sick. She looked Caroline and Mariliee over and made her decision.

"Caroline," she said, "go downstairs and call the police. Tell them someone's dead. Tell them they have to come now."

"Someone's dead?" Caroline said. "But—who's dead? Who . . ."

She started to walk toward the door, but Belle held her back. "Don't go in there, for God's sake. You don't want to go in there."

"But . . ." Caroline said.

Mrs. Copplewhite marched into the hall, slamming the door behind her. "No one's going in there," she said. "And nobody's calling the police, either. I'm not having police in my house."

"Don't be an ass," Belle said. "Of course you're going to have police. There's been a murder."

"Murder?" Mariliee said.

"There's been no murder," Mrs. Copplewhite said. "That fool girl went and killed herself, that's all. They're like that, these girls. I won't have police—"

I tried to shake the cobwebs out of my head. I didn't quite succeed. "Mrs. Copplewhite," I said, "didn't you see what was in there? She bled to death. People don't kill themselves by making themselves bleed to death."

"No?" Mrs. Copplewhite said. "And what do you know about it?"

"People do kill themselves by bleeding themselves to death," Mariliee Bonnard said. "That's what happens when they cut their wrists in the bathtub."

"She doesn't have her wrists cut," I said frantically. "She has her neck cut. And she's got, she's got—"

"Just like the murders in London," Caroline said quietly.

"Yes," I told her. "Just like. Right down to the rose."

Mrs. Copplewhite looked from one to the other of us. "I don't know about any murders in London," she said. "And I don't think that girl bled to death, either. There isn't enough blood. You know what? That's a man's room. I think she killed herself and she killed herself for *spite.*"

"A man's room," Caroline said slowly.

I turned to her. "It's Benjamin Grade's room," I told her reluctantly. "That's what I was doing here. I went wandering around last night and met him downstairs. I came down this morning to see if he was awake."

Caroline didn't bother to ask me about the hole in that explanation: why I'd go get Benjamin Grade at all. She just turned around and started walking stonily down the stairs, toward the foyer and the telephone room.

"Hey!" Mrs. Copplewhite called after her. "Where are you going? I told you no police—"

Belle March stepped in front of her and hooked ankles,

195

making Mrs. Copplewhite trip. "You just shut up," she said. "There's been a murder done and we're going to get the police. Get used to it."

From the back of the clutch of girls that now seemed to surround us like a wall, someone started wailing.

The first thing I noticed about the man from the village police station was that he didn't want to be there. He was a small, round man with the kind of bulbous face that looks good only when it also looks happy, and the murder made him very unhappy indeed. Caroline had to run interference for him with Mrs. Copplewhite. He would have been relieved to let her keep him out. He didn't stay in very long. He just looked around the room, prodded a toe against Gemma's rigidifying arm, then walked into the hall again. The sight of the body hit him worse than it had any of the rest of us, even me. I thought he was going to be physically ill.

He took a handkerchief out of his mouth, wiped his face, and said, "Awful thing. Awful thing."

"Yes," I agreed, not knowing what else to say, "it is."

"We had our Peter, of course," he said. "But he didn't get up here. Did most of his work south of us. We don't get this kind of thing up here."

"You're lucky," I said.

"It's a city crime," he said. "I'll have to call in Scotland Yard. I've never had to call in Scotland Yard about anything." The thought of Scotland Yard seemed to cheer him. "Scotland Yard will know what to do," he said.

He trotted off, presumably to find a phone and call the Yard.

Until then, I hadn't thought much beyond the need to find someone in authority and put the whole mess in his hands. I hadn't thought about the girls, or the godmothers, or even Benjamin. When I'd been looking at the body, the how and why of it had seemed perfectly obvious. Now it began to occur to me that nothing was obvious. Some things were the same: the mutilation, the multiple stab wounds, the rose, the fact that the body had been killed elsewhere and then moved. Some things were not the same. The body had been moved, not to a nice leafy park somewhere, but to

Benjamin's bedroom. Why? The body had been covered, too, which none of the others had been. What had been the point of that?

I looked up to see Belle March standing beside me, looking grim. "We're going up to the room for a talk," she said. "We think you ought to come with us."

I gestured to Benjamin's room. "Somebody ought to stay here," I told her. "The way Mrs. Copplewhite is, I wouldn't put it past her to just walk in there and pitch the body out the window."

"Police seals," Belle muttered cryptically.

I supposed she meant there weren't any, but should have been. She went to Caroline and Mariliee and held a whispered consultation. Then she came back to me.

"It's going to be hours before Scotland Yard can get here," she said. "We can't wait that long. We'll just have to risk it."

"I thought the point was to make sure the killer was caught," I said.

"Come on," Belle said.

I got up and went. In some strange way I felt I was obligated to, as if taking part in murder discussions was one of my duties as a tour guide.

They had cleaned their room—scrubbed it down, as a matter of fact. They must have been at it all morning. Surfaces were not only dusted, but washed and polished. The bedsteads and bureaus showed a deep brown gleam that can be coaxed only from very old wood. The floor had been swept and the carpet either vacuumed or beaten—beaten, probably, because I didn't know where they would have found a vacuum cleaner. They must have held the carpets out the window and shaken them hard. They'd done it to the mattresses, too, because the mattresses were standing upright against a wall. The linens were in a folded pile on the floor. They must have meant to take them to the washateria.

I took a seat on one of the bed's bare springs that the mattresses had covered. My godmothers were not in their usual form. They looked devastated, and once or twice I picked up from them a twinge of guilt. Caroline kept rubbing the palms of her hands against the sleeves of her dress, a fitful, obsessive gesture that made her look one step away from a breakdown. Belle March paced. Mariliee Bonnard just sat.

After a while, it became obvious that although *they* had asked *me* up to the room, nothing was going to get started unless I started it. They were just too upset. I'd never seen the godmothers speechless before. It didn't seem natural.

I said, "You know, even if you can think of something to do, you probably shouldn't do it. Scotland Yard is supposed to be very good at this kind of thing."

"The Boston police are supposed to be very good at this kind of thing, too," Belle March said sharply. "They were useless."

"I don't understand how he could have done this," Caroline said. "I just don't understand it."

I stared at them, light dawning in my brain. "Wait a minute," I said. "You think Benjamin Grade murdered that girl?"

"Of course he did," Belle said. "Who else could it have been?"

"Any one of eight million people," I said. "Don't you realize you're not making sense?"

"Of course we're making sense," Caroline said. "He's in Boston and Julie gets killed—like that. He's in London and three other girls get killed—like that. He's in Yorkshire and another girl gets killed. *Like that!"*

"Right," I said. "He gets her off someplace, slits her throat"—Caroline winced, but I went on, inexorable— "and then he wraps her up and puts her down in his own bed."

"Why not?" Caroline asked defensively.

I got out a cigarette and lit it. I hadn't had a cigarette in hours. In all the confusion, I'd forgotten about them. Now I needed one badly, and something told me I might need something stronger by the time the conversation was over. The cobwebs in my head were clearing. The situation we were in was before me, clear and undiluted by emotion. I knew they thought Benjamin killed Julie Matthews. They needed to have solid proof against that before they changed their minds. But this—

"Make sense," I told them. "You're saying Ben got this girl somewhere safe and private, in the basement or on the moors or somewhere, killed her, waited until she was nearly drained of blood, and then carted her upstairs to *his own room?*"

"Maybe it was the only place he could cart her," Belle said. "He wouldn't have expected you to go barging in there in the middle of the morning. Maybe he needed someplace to keep her while he was—well, looking for a park. The kind of place he usually uses. So—"

"Why cart her anywhere at all?" I asked. "If he killed her here—and he would have had to kill her someplace close; I talked to her last night—the only place that would incriminate him is where we found her. He could have done her in, in the basement or the back garden or the high street, and have been no more under suspicion than he ever was."

"Maybe he didn't want to come under suspicion at all," Mariliee said. "Eventually, there'd be too many coincidences for anybody. In three places he's been and in three places these murders have happened. Maybe he wanted to hide her so no one would find her, but he couldn't do it right away, so he put her in his bed until he had a chance to move her. Get her out of sight."

"Why not get her out of sight last night?" I said. "It was dark. He'd have had a better chance than in daylight."

"Maybe not," Caroline said. "This is a small village. Somebody might have noticed a stranger moving around in the dark."

I got off the mattress springs and started pacing. "You're all crazy," I said. "Do you realize that? I know you think Ben Grade killed Julie Matthews. I know that. I'm not even arguing with you about it. But this is nuts. Nobody who isn't a raving, hallucinating schizophrenic would do what you're talking about."

"Maybe he is a raving, hallucinating schizophrenic," Mariliee said.

"Have you ever seen one of those?" I asked her. "I've seen several. They're very hard to miss. All that psychotic-but-nobody-knows-it business that goes on in mystery novels makes for very entertaining reading, but it doesn't exactly correspond with reality. Those people talk to themselves, ladies. They jerk around. They act weird. The fact that they're a little off is usually perfectly obvious."

"Usually," Belle March said, "but not always. You know as well as I do what I'm talking about exists. That's how these serial killers get away with as much as they do for as long as they do. Some of them can look quite sane—"

"The ones who look sane behave more sanely than what you're trying to hand me here," I said.

"In the beginning," Belle said. "But when they start to fall apart—"

"Belle, I talked to Benjamin Grade at midnight. He showed no signs whatsoever of being about to fall apart."

"Maybe you wouldn't know what to look for," Belle said. "You've told us yourself that you haven't looked in to this sort of thing. You don't like thinking about it. You haven't read mystery books except for ours. These men are very clever, you know. He could be fooling you."

"He could be," I said, "but he isn't."

"He took in Julie the same way," Caroline said gently. "She thought he was the most wonderful man on earth."

I stopped my pacing and took them all in at once. All three of them pitied me. I wanted to shake them. I hadn't known Julie Matthews, but I was sure a dangerous man couldn't have taken both of us in—and Gemma, besides. Gemma I *had* met. She had been naive, unsophisticated in spite of her veneer of hostility and worldliness, but she had been a survivor. If Ben were a killer, one of us would have picked up on something seriously wrong in his personality, if it had been there.

If he were killing these girls, he had to be doing it cold-bloodedly. That way, he might be both guilty and not giving off anything I could pick up. The way these girls had been killed argued against it. The mutilations, the multiple stab wounds, even the rose, spoke of a savagery beyond hiding.

I sat down again, determined to get this across. One of two things was happening. Either the Ripper had followed us to Yorkshire, or the man who killed Julie Matthews was not the Ripper but trying to make it look as if Benjamin Grade was. I thought I understood how that would work. Ben was investigating the man he thought was Julie Matthews' murderer. Julie Matthews' murderer was tired of being investigated. He therefore—what?

My head was swimming.

Belle March's head was not. She came over and patted me maternally on the shoulder. "I know it's hard to accept," she said. "We've all known him, on and off, for years. But there really isn't any other explanation. Coincidences may happen, but this many of them just don't."

"And besides," Caroline Matthews said, "there's a dead girl upstairs in that man's bed—and where is he?"

It was, I decided later, when I'd finally convinced them I didn't want coffee or tea or breakfast or anything else they could make on the shiny new equipment they'd bought in the village that morning, a very good question. If I was right and Benjamin Grade had not killed Gemma, then either she had been put in his bed this morning, after he was dressed and gone, or she'd been put there the night before, which would mean he'd never gone up to his room. But I was sure he had. He'd been tired when he left me. Whatever he'd thought he was going to find at Mrs. Henry Copplewhite's, it wasn't the Ripper in person. Could he have gone skulking around the house after he'd seen me to my door? Could he have gone somewhere so far away he'd not been able to return in time for breakfast? Where? The whole point of our ridiculous sojourn among Mrs. Henry Copplewhite's legions of dust was that there was something besides dust worth finding.

I walked down to the second floor, found the corridor cordoned off—our village constable had probably been given some very specific suggestions by the good men of the CID—and proceeded down to the foyer. In the sunlight it looked dirty and sad, but not sinister. I passed through it, looked into the empty, darkened, and close-smelling living room, and then kept going until I got to the kitchen. I think I was half-hoping I'd run into Benjamin. It was silly. If he'd been in the house, I would have seen him by then. He'd at least have emerged from whatever he was doing to find out what all the noise was about.

I stuck my head through the kitchen door and found, not Benjamin, but Mrs. Copplewhite. I started to withdraw, expecting another discourse on how she didn't want police in the house or a lot of screaming invective about how I wasn't allowed in the kitchen. Instead, she raised her head and beckoned to me. I stopped backing up, astounded. It was almost a friendly gesture.

"Well, you don't have to stare at me," she said. "I was just letting you know you could come on through."

"Right," I said. I went into the kitchen, noticing as I did that Mrs. Copplewhite looked as deflated as the godmothers had. She looked scared, too, and although that surprised me at first, I soon found what I thought was the answer. If Mrs. Copplewhite really was using those girls for something unsavory, she was about to lose her hold on them. The night before, they'd told me nothing would ever make them leave. This, I was sure, was going to be the exception. A murder in the house wouldn't necessarily scare them off, but the police that came with it would. Police meant investigations and investigations meant exposure and exposure meant being sent back. I didn't think those girls would risk being sent back for anything.

Mrs. Copplewhite stabbed her spoon into a cup of muddy-looking coffee. "American, aren't you?" she said. "You and them women."

"And Mr. Grade," I said. "We're all American."

"Thought so. It's the accent, you know. Hear it at the pictures. My son Charlie went to America once."

"On holiday?" I asked.

"What? Oh, yeah. I guess you could say that. Went to see about emigrating, he did. Thought we'd do better there. Turned out, you can't emigrate for money. It takes years and they don't want to let you in."

"I wouldn't know," I said. "United States immigration laws aren't something I'm really up on."

"Well, I didn't want to go, anyway. I like it here. Been here all my life. Have the house. Or at least I used to have the house. Don't know what will happen with all this."

"They'll clear the murder up and then they'll go away," I said. "What would it have to do with the house?"

"Well, it's going to give us a bad reputation, isn't it? Place where murders are done and police have been. I'll lose my clientele."

I almost told her she didn't have a clientele, but there didn't seem to be any point in it. There didn't seem to be any point in the conversation, either. I started to edge back toward the door, making noises about how I had a few things to do in the village. Mrs. Copplewhite wasn't fooled.

"You're all a nice bunch," she said. "Think you're too good by half. Those old ladies, cleaning up after me as if I didn't know how. Making tea in their rooms when it's not allowed. What are you doing here, anyway? People like you don't come to villages like this. It isn't natural."

"The ladies write murder mysteries," I said. "I think they want to set one here."

"Murder mysteries? Here? In my house?"

"Not in your house," I said, "in St. Edmund Cavateur. You know, a nice out-of-the-way English village? It's traditional."

Fortunately, Mrs. Copplewhite knew even less about murder mysteries than I did. She took me at my word and got indignant.

"They put this house in a murder mystery, I'll take them to court," she said righteously. "They aren't allowed to ruin my reputation when I haven't done anything. I know that. I've got half a mind to throw you all out. It's all your fault, the police being here and murders going on. You've made a mess of everything, and now that bloody fool—"

She came to a cold stop. It was so abrupt, I immediately came to attention. I always managed to think of something else when I had to be around Mrs. Copplewhite. If I didn't, I wanted to strangle her.

Now I looked at her more closely than I had before. "What bloody fool?"

Mrs. Copplewhite rubbed her lips. Purple lipstick smeared across her cheek, shading to violet as it thinned out. "That bloody fool girl," she said halfheartedly. "I told you what I thought went on, and you'll see I'm right. Killed herself over some man who wouldn't have her. Thought she was going to get herself a rich American, and when he wouldn't have her she decided to cause him trouble. They're all like that. No morals, these girls."

"She couldn't have killed herself," I said, feeling as if I'd repeated that statement more times than should have been necessary for anybody. "She didn't die in that room. She didn't bleed there."

"Just like a murder mystery," Mrs. Copplewhite said

maliciously. She got to her feet. "You know what the trouble with Americans is? Americans always want to blame their troubles on somebody else, that's it. No sense of responsibility. I'm going to get some work done. There's a lot, keeping up a place like this."

I stood still and let her pass, impressed with myself for not shouting at her or braining her or doing something drastic. She'd left her half-filled coffee cup on the table, and the spoon and the sugar bowl with it. There was a fine coating of sugar on the tabletop. I had to be right. Mrs. Copplewhite spread dirt and mess wherever she went. Somebody else had to have cleaned that kitchen.

Some other time, I might have been interested in finding out who. That time, I was too tired. It had been a long morning and promised to be an even longer afternoon. Once the Scotland Yard men got there, we were going to be in for a long, grueling round of questioning. I thought of the godmothers' newly cleaned room and wondered if they'd let me sack out there while they went to the washateria. It was only eleven o'clock in the morning, and I already wanted a nap.

I wandered into the foyer, aimless and exhausted, my mind pulling back and forth and sideways among all the theories I had heard in the last twenty-four hours.

I was just coming back to the Problem of Benjamin— where was he?—when the doorbell rang. I should have let Mrs. Copplewhite answer it, but I was distracted. I went right to the door and pulled it open.

Standing on the porch outside, looking bedraggled and on the edge of panic, was Eleanor.

——— NINETEEN ———

She had made an effort to disguise herself. She hadn't been able to ditch all the lovely expensive clothes, or do anything that might ruin them, but she had rearranged the accessories and added a few bright-colored scarves and changed her makeup. She now looked less like Caroline Matthews's well-heeled British relative and more like my well-heeled American one. Unfortunately, she couldn't do American accents. The voice that floated up at me from the door was still pure Princess Di. It was the only upper-class accent Eleanor knew.

I grabbed her wrist and pulled her inside, slamming the door behind her. Eleanor in Yorkshire, even disguised, was in danger of being spotted by the authorities from her children's home. Then I remembered where I was and what I was in the middle of, and I winced. In no time at all, Mrs. Copplewhite's tattered excuse for a bed-and-breakfast was going to be crawling with representatives of Scotland Yard, probing, asking questions, looking into everyone's background. It was the worst possible circumstance for a girl like Eleanor to find herself in.

Which, of course, was why I hadn't seen any of Mrs. Copplewhite's girls since the village constable showed up this morning. Whatever they had been promised, it would count for nothing against the possibility of being caught. They were probably long gone.

I pulled Eleanor through the foyer and shoved her through the single door leading to the back hall and the telephone room. It was a shorter route to privacy than taking her all the way upstairs, and besides, going upstairs meant passing the temporary constable on the second-floor landing. Get one thing out of the way and another comes up and hits you on the head: That was how Jasmyn Cole had once described being in business. It was beginning to look like a good rule of thumb for living with Eleanor.

I got us both into the telephone room and I closed the door behind us. I was panting, although dragging Eleanor around does not require all that much physical exertion. I couldn't decide if I was furious or scared to death.

"What are you doing here?" I exploded. "You know damn well you shouldn't be within a hundred miles of this place. What were you thinking of? I—"

"I got caught," Eleanor said quietly.

I stopped. I'd heard the words, but they wouldn't register. "What do you mean, you got caught?" I asked her. "How could you get caught in the Connaught? The Connaught wouldn't seat your Mrs. Derme for tea."

Eleanor sighed. "It wasn't Mrs. Derme," she said. "I don't know who it was, but I know the type. *You* know the type."

"I know the type," I said, "but I still don't understand how the Connaught—wait a minute. How did you get up here? If you took the train, you had to have left—"

"Right after I talked to you last night," Eleanor finished miserably.

"You mean you were lying to me?"

"Not exactly," Eleanor said. She stared at the shadowed walls of the telephone room. "Creepy place, isn't it?"

"Get to the point," I said.

"Yes, well. I went to show the girl the office, like I said. And when I came out, there was this woman in the street, only—" Eleanor laughed. "She was a terribly ugly woman. Looked like a man. If I'd been in Camden Town I'd have thought she was a man, dressed up like a woman; what do you call it in America?"

"Drag," I said.

"Right, drag. Except most of them who dress up in drag look prettier than we do. She was standing on the corner where you turn for the tube stop, and when I passed her she came along behind me. Then I got on the tube and she was on the same car. Then I got off the tube, and went up to the street, and when I turned around to look back, she was gone."

"That's it?" I asked incredulously. "You came running up to Yorkshire because of that?"

Eleanor shook her head. "There was another thing. Just before you called, I went down to the dining room for tea." She saw my look and exploded. "Well, I couldn't just stay behind doors for six weeks, could I? And it wasn't like leaving the hotel. I just went down to the dining room and ordered myself a cream tea and felt like a lady. It was nice. Only—she was there."

"Having tea at the Connaught," I said doubtfully.

"I had a table in the corner and she had one in the middle of the room. There weren't a lot of people there. And then she turned around and smiled at me." Eleanor shuddered. "That one's got a nasty smile. Let me tell you."

I ran my hands through my hair. "It could have been paranoia," I said. "You could have—"

"No," Eleanor said. "I thought of that, too. When I got to Euston Station I felt like a fool. I was ready to turn around and go back when I saw her again. She was two people behind me on the ticket line *and* she was on my train."

"When was this?"

"I don't know. The train was at quarter after seven."

"'Quarter after seven,'" I repeated, counting in my head. "You should have been here around eleven, last night. Even if you had to wait for a car hire, you shouldn't have been later than eleven-thirty."

"Yeah, well. That was a funny thing. When I got to the ticket window at Euston Station, I asked for two express tickets, but I could only get one. From Euston to York. The express train from York to Ramsmoor was all full up. But the man behind me must have canceled on that, because when we got to York the woman who was following me transferred to the express. I had to wait around in York until this morning. But she was following me, Avra, she really was. She was sitting in Ramsmoor Station when I got off. Just sitting in the waiting room. And she *smiled* at me again."

"Eleanor, if she was sitting in Ramsmoor Station when

you got off and she smiled at you and she was following you, then she knows you're here."

Eleanor shook her head. "I got a really nice man for the car hire. He ditched her. That's why I'm so late. It took a lot of driving around."

"It still doesn't wash. If she was one of those people and she was trying to find you, why didn't she come up to you? She's got a perfect legal right. In fact, she's got a legal obligation."

"You know how those people are," Eleanor said. "Maybe she was just playing with me."

"I suppose it's not outside the realm of possibility," I said, "but why bother? She'd have more fun playing with you if she picked you up."

"She was following me," Eleanor said stubbornly. "I wasn't just being a twit. She was *following* me."

"I never said you were being a twit." I took my cigarettes out of my pocket and then put them back again. I seemed to be quitting smoking without thinking about it. I kept lighting the things and never getting a chance to inhale them. "All right," I said. "Let me think for a while. There has to be some way to keep you out of trouble."

Eleanor was standing near the far wall, looking at the framed pictures I'd noticed the night before.

"This is creepy," she said. "Wouldn't think a child could be so creepy, would you? Reminds me of someone."

I looked up sharply. "Who?"

"Don't know," Eleanor said. "Can't place it. Gives me the awfullest feeling, though."

The best thing would have been for Eleanor not to have been there. The second best thing would have been to get her away as quickly as possible. Neither of those things was in the cards. Not only was Eleanor already in Yorkshire, but her coming would have been marked. St. Edmund Cavateur is a small town and Ramsmoor is not much larger. The arrivals and departures of strangers in places like that are topics of conversation even on ordinary days. On a day when a bloody murder had been discovered, the populace would give them all the significance of clues in an Agatha Christie novel. It would be a good idea if Eleanor, who had already been seen arriving, was not also seen leaving. Two trips through Ramsmoor station in one day would cause too much comment.

I filled Eleanor in, as well as I could, on what had happened so far. She went a little gray around the edges, but she kept her head. I was relieved. I'd expected her to panic. The chances of her ending up back in her children's home before this was over were incalculable.

"I'd just run away again," she said. "They wouldn't be able to keep me there."

"Why don't we just try not getting you caught to begin with?" I said. "We'll have to hide you somewhere. I wish I wasn't so angry at the godmothers. They'd probably know a place."

"What are you angry at the godmothers for?"

I gave Eleanor a quick rundown on the godmothers and Benjamin Grade. "What they want to believe just doesn't make sense," I said. "And now we've got that poor girl dead, and either we've got the Ripper following us around or a copycat killer. I don't know which is worse."

"I think when this is over, I'll fake an identity and go back to the States with the godmothers," Eleanor said. "You come, too. I'd much rather trust our lives to nice sane muggers."

"Maybe we'd better go find the godmothers," I said. "I haven't read enough thrillers to begin to know how to go about this."

Eleanor hoisted her tote bag onto her shoulder. "From what you say, there'll at least be plenty of rooms in the house," she said. "I won't be put out on the road."

I let that comment pass—Eleanor regressing to her pre–Avra Mahon state—and led her out the back in search of secondary stairs.

The secondary stairs were there, at the very end of the back hall, as I'd known they would be. Houses of the era of Mrs. Copplewhite's always had servants' passages and servants' staircases, because servants were supposed to be seen as little as possible. These servants' stairs were solid but very narrow, so narrow I couldn't help thinking what a trial it must have been getting trays and laundry up them. They were also very badly lit. There was a dim bulb glowing above the second-floor landing, but none above the third. There was a single opaque window near the bottom and another near the ceiling line at the very top, neither admitting much sunlight.

Eleanor's tote bag weighed a ton. We took turns carrying it. She would haul it up four or five steps, then I would. If I'd heard the smallest sound or sensed the least movement, I would have thought she'd brought the cat. The bag, however, was inert. She'd left the cat to the luxurious administration of the hotel's pet-sitters. She'd just brought the rest of her life with her.

At the second-floor landing I stopped, put the tote down, and said, "This stuff could have stayed at the Connaught. They have very good security."

"I know," Eleanor said. "I wasn't thinking. I was just trying to get out of there as fast as I could." She looked around the landing. "What about that door? Can we go through there?"

"Wrong floor," I said. "On the other side of that, you've probably got a hundred police officers. Ben's room is way down at this end. I think the CID gave our village bobby a good talking to. He had a barrier up last time I came down, and I heard— That's funny."

"What's funny?"

"Listen," I told her. "What do you hear?"

Eleanor gave me a measured look. "I don't hear anything, Avra. There isn't anything to hear."

"I agree. Don't you think that's strange?"

"No."

"I do. There's been a murder committed here. There were supposed to be people coming, technical people: coroners, fingerprint men, that kind of thing. We should be hearing all sorts of things."

"Maybe they haven't arrived yet," Eleanor said patiently. "Maybe they've been and gone. Maybe the door's too thick. Avra, if we have to climb another flight of stairs, I want to *do* it."

"Right," I said.

Eleanor grabbed the tote and pulled it up another half-flight. "Come *on* then. I'm going to break my back carrying this."

I turned away from the door and followed her reluctantly.

Somewhere at the back of my mind, a light had gone on. It wasn't a very strong light, but it had a magnetic quality. Back stairs, back rooms, that smell of perfume—

There, that was it. I stopped. I was halfway up to the third-floor landing by then, and I couldn't smell anything, but I *had,* down below. I hadn't caught on to it at first because the scent wasn't very strong. Perfume, yes, but not Mrs. Henry Copplewhite's. Hers would have permeated the woodwork. This was something delicate, ethereal, but persistent. It had come to me through the smell of must and filth that hung over those back stairs like a poisonous cloud.

I turned around and started down again. Eleanor stopped and stared after me.

"What are you doing? You said we had to go up."

"Just a minute," I said.

"If you'd said we could go through that door, I wouldn't have hauled this thing all the way up *here."*

I stopped in front of the door and tried the knob. It was locked, but standing this close the smell was unmistakable. Roses. Behind that door there were roses, real, fresh flowers—a greenhouse? I couldn't see how, this deep in the house. I'd been in the back garden last night and I hadn't noticed the necessary windows. Cut flowers, I decided. Cut flowers, fresh ones, smell much more strongly than live buds still on the bush. Even with that, though, there had to be a lot of them in there.

I tried the knob again. Still locked, of course. All of a sudden I was both desperately frightened and desperately in need of getting past that door. I kept remembering Benjamin saying how easy it was to open skeleton-key locks. All you needed were a couple of hairpins. I didn't have any hairpins and I wouldn't have known what to do with them even if I'd had.

"What's the matter with you?" Eleanor said. "Have you gone off your head?"

"No," I said. I could feel the sweat coming off me, and none of the sensible things I told myself had any effect on it. This was Yorkshire. There were roses everywhere. A lot of people liked cut flowers. The mere existence of roses, even large numbers of them, did not a Ripper make.

What wiped all this out was the simplest thing: There is

such a thing as one coincidence too many, and for me, this was the one.

Up until then, part of me had always been skeptical. Serial murders, old ladies following private-eye writers, mysterious Victorian houses in the Yorkshire moors: It had been too much like one of Belle March's plots. I'd taken it as seriously as I could, because I had to, but at bottom I'd always thought it would turn out to be nothing. The Ripper was real, he might even have been in America once and killed Julie Matthews, but he wouldn't be Benjamin Grade or anyone else the godmothers knew.

I backed away from the door. Murder could happen to anyone. It happened to all the girls murdered by Ted Bundy and all the girls murdered by the Son of Sam and all the girls murdered by this Ripper, the girls whose pictures appeared in the paper in black-bordered boxes week after week as the killing went on. I didn't know how to fit it together yet, but I knew it was here. The answer was behind that door, with the roses.

There had to be a connection between whatever else was going on in this house and the Ripper. There had to be.

"Leave the tote bag," I told Eleanor. "I want to get upstairs fast."

"We'll just have to come back and get it," Eleanor said.

"We'll come back and get it. I've got to find the godmothers. *Now.*"

But I didn't have to find the godmothers. They were standing out in the hall, looking for us, when we got to the third floor. They were triumphant, ecstatic, vindicated. They thought they had every right to be.

"We got him," Belle March announced. "We followed him and he went back in the brush out there and he started digging. There are four more bodies out there *and he knew where they were.*"

——— TWENTY ———

They were in the back, in a tangle of bushes and weeds just beyond the clipped edge of the garden. They might have been on Mrs. Copplewhite's property or off it. There was no way to tell. The garden had a schizophrenic quality. The fake roses were definitely Mrs. Copplewhite's style. She tended to fake everything: fabrics, furniture, gin. The precision belonged to whoever it was who had cleaned the kitchen. There was an obsessiveness to it, a mania for neatness and order that bordered on the abnormal.

The godmothers' bedroom windows faced the garden. Standing against them I could see what was going on out there. The fake roses and very real weeds had been invaded by a platoon of tan-raincoated men. I assumed they were the gentlemen from Scotland Yard. They stood surrounded by loose dark earth and equipment, looking down at two other men in denim and plaid flannel who were digging. The two bodies they had already dug up were in black plastic bags, lying one on top of the other in what was almost the exact center of the tended square. As I watched, the denimed men jumped out of the hole and started making gestures at the ground. I moved away from the window as quickly as I could. They'd found another one. Any minute now, one of the men in raincoats was going to start the process that would land it in a body bag.

I turned around and looked at the godmothers sitting with their hands folded on their still-stripped beds. Their faces were terrible: sick and frightened on the one hand, alight with retributive triumph on the other. They'd done such a good job of presenting themselves as fluffy, benevolent little old ladies, I'd got into the habit of thinking that's all they were. Now I could see they were something more, or at least something else. They looked like three avenging goddesses from Norse mythology, both vindicated and vindictive.

I sat down in the room's one chair, took out a cigarette, took out my lighter, and lit up. I looked at Eleanor, who looked away quickly, as if she didn't want any part of what was happening here. I didn't blame her.

When I thought I had myself sufficiently under control, I said, "I want you to start from the beginning. I want you to tell me everything that happened here."

I must have hit the right note. Their triumphant looks wavered, broke, and crashed into something more human. Underneath their obsession to see Benjamin Grade punished for Julie Matthews' death, their sense of decency remained.

It was Mariliee who spoke first. "We were talking to Mrs. Copplewhite," she said, "and her friend, Mrs. Ewern. Mrs. Ewern had come over for tea. And——"

"And Mrs. Ewern was an awful woman," Belle said dryly. "Looked like a man in makeup." Eleanor looked up quickly. So did I. "And they were giving us a lot of bunk about Mrs. Copplewhite's son and his trip to America. About how he might have to go to Australia, because he'd been ruined."

"Ruined?" I said.

"By a woman," Mariliee said. "A girl, really. One of the girls who stay in the house. Apparently, she's been doing this for years. Taking in the girls. That's how she makes her money. Not from the rent they pay. They don't pay any. She gets them jobs in service in London and Liverpool and Edinburgh and she takes a commission. Anyway——"

"Anyway," Belle went on, "it was a lot of nonsense. According to Mrs. C., this girl took a liking to dear Charlie and got hysterical when he wouldn't have her and accused him of rape, and he was ruined. But you know what rape law is like, here and in the United States. Even when there's something to go on, they don't get them. They got Charlie, so there had to be a *lot* to go on."

"They sent him to Dartmoor," Mariliee said, "for three years."

"What does this have to do with Ben?" I said. "How did you—"

"I got *upset*," Belle said. "We all did. Listening to that terrible woman go on and on and thinking about that poor girl who'd probably been beaten half-dead. So I got up and began pacing around so I wouldn't throw anything."

"We all got up and started pacing around," Caroline said. "But it was Belle who went to the windows."

"I was thinking about breaking the glass," Belle said.

"And you saw Ben out there," I said. "Digging."

"I didn't know he was digging, not then," Belle said. "Those idiotic fake roses were in the way. He was kneeling on the ground, though. And he wasn't doing anything that looked regular."

"She called me over and I went and looked, too," Caroline said. "And then so did Mariliee. And then so did Mrs. Copplewhite and Mrs. Ewern. Mrs. Ewern smells even worse than Mrs. Copplewhite. She's so clean she puts me in mind of hospitals."

The ash had grown long on the end of my cigarette. I was failing to inhale again. I reached over to the table and took the ashtray that rested there and tapped into that. The connections were falling into place. A woman who looked like a man and was so clean she smelled of hospitals: I'd have to get Eleanor downstairs to make sure, but I had that worked out. A son ruined by a runaway teenaged girl. A lot of other runaway teenaged girls stuffed together in a house for—what? I didn't know that it mattered. For something that paid enough—white slavery, maybe, shipping them off to North Africa where Caucasian whores brought a high price. Whatever it was, it had probably become secondary since Charlie Copplewhite got back from Dartmoor.

I stubbed the butt of my cigarette out and got another one lit, thinking I might actually smoke this one. What I was thinking was so horrific, it was almost inconceivable. It made me numb. Unfortunately, it also made a grinning, leering, insane kind of sense.

"I wish I'd met your Mrs. Ewern," I said.

Belle looked surprised. "Whatever for? She's just an unpleasant old woman."

"Are you sure of that? Are you sure she's an old woman?"

"Well, of course I'm—" Belle stopped.

Mariliee looked distressed. "You know," she said, "now that you mention it—"

"Too spry," Caroline interrupted. "And too—"

"Masculine?" I suggested.

"Why don't you tell us what you're getting at?" Belle said.

"Not yet," I told her. "I want to hear the end of this, first. You all saw Ben Grade and then what?"

"Belle started to call to him," Caroline said. "He looked up and saw us and then he waved."

"Waved like he was calling to us," Mariliee said. "Calling us over. So we all went trooping out—"

"We didn't all go trooping out," Belle corrected. "Mrs. Copplewhite went running out. And Mrs. Ewern just sort of drifted in behind us, as if she weren't interested."

"She had this awful smile on her face," Mariliee said. "As if the whole thing were terribly funny."

"Anyway," Belle said, "he was standing there, at the edge of the garden. And there were these four mounds. Old, I think. One of them had sunk. But there wasn't any way of mistaking what they were. There really wasn't. And then Mariliee—"

"It was like I could see what was under the dirt," Mariliee said, embarrassed. "Bones and blood and skin. And I just ran—"

"And I went for the telephone," Caroline said, "and I called the police. And when the police got here, he was *still out there*. He was *digging.*" She looked sick.

I *felt* sick. Where had I been while all this was going on? Talking to Eleanor, of course. In the back hall. The walls were thick and had cushions of air built in between them, to eradicate noise. I took Caroline's wrist and turned it so I could see the face of her watch. That confirmed it: We'd been longer than I thought we had. It was almost one o'clock.

My cigarette had a long cylinder of ash on it again. I was failing to smoke it again. I grabbed the ashtray and put the cigarette out.

"Okay," I said, "now he was out there digging, and he made no effort to get away, right? In fact, he called you over to look."

"That's right," Caroline said.

"And was he—strange—when you got there?"

"He looked upset," Caroline said. "But he would, wouldn't he? After all—"

"After all *what,* Caroline? Why would he look upset if he'd put the bodies there to begin with? Why would he dig them up at all? You didn't know they were there. The police didn't know they were there. It was high noon on a sunny day. Why call attention to them?"

"I—" Caroline started. She subsided. Mariliee and Belle said nothing. I could see them working through the possibilities, and deciding none of them would wash in a tenth-rate mystery novel. As the minutes ticked by, they even had the grace to begin looking guilty.

"Oh, dear," Mariliee said. "You think we made a mistake. But we couldn't have. Everywhere he goes—"

"Not everywhere," I told her. "In Boston, there was Julie. Then there's nothing that anybody knows about until a few weeks ago, when he came to London, according to him, looking for the man he thinks killed Julie, following him."

"Benjamin Grade says he's following a man he thinks killed my niece?" Caroline sounded strangled.

"He says he found the address of this place in Julie's address book," I said. "He also says he doesn't think Julie was the only one in Boston. He thinks this guy usually covers himself pretty well. Until recently. He thinks the bodies strewn all over the landscape are an indication that this guy is losing control. I have decided, ladies, that I don't agree with him."

"We were being *manipulated,*" Mariliee said, horrified. "We were being—"

"We still are," I said. "I take it Ben got carted off to jail. The village jail?"

"Oh, yes," Mariliee said. "Things aren't organized yet. There are some men down from the York police, you know, and a man from the London CID who was in York for something else and is looking in on this. But that's all."

"And that's good," I said, "because I've got to talk to Ben

217

and getting to him in a regulation CID lockup would probably be impossible. Look, we left Eleanor's bag on the back stairs. Go get it for us, will you please? I need Eleanor for a minute. I'll send her back up when we're done. Oh, and ladies? Start thinking. Because we're not going to be able to straighten this out until we've had a talk with Ben, and if the police won't let me see him, we just might have to spring him. You're the mystery writers. Come up with a plan."

"Actually," Mariliee said thoughtfully, "it might not be that hard—"

I grabbed Eleanor by the arm and dragged her out of there.

We were nearly at the staircase when we heard the girls giggling and rustling, sputtering and whispering. I stared at the door to the room where I'd spoken to them the night before. They were definitely in there, a lot of them, making no effort at secrecy. I stopped Eleanor in her single-minded march to the stairs and said, "That's odd. Can you hear them? The girls are still here."

"Maybe it's somebody else," Eleanor said. "They wouldn't stay with all the police around, would they? I wouldn't."

"No," I said. "I wouldn't either."

I hesitated. Confirmation of my theory, or at least one part of it, was downstairs in the telephone room. Time was important. Once Scotland Yard had formally arrested Benjamin, it would be difficult to get them to switch theories. I wanted the evidence collected and the solution mapped out before the police had too much time and emotion invested in Benjamin's guilt. On the other hand—

"Come on," I told Eleanor. "I have to see what this is all about."

What all this was about, it seemed, was a convention, or a midday slumber party. I knocked on the door and opened it without waiting to be invited in, just as I had the night before. I counted and came up with thirteen pairs of eyes staring up at me. Not only had all the girls not left, but *none* of them had.

This was crazy, almost as crazy as what I thought was really going on in that house. I was speechless. They were sitting on the floor and on the chairs and on the bed, looking almost happy. Molly Larkin was positively glowing. The emotions they were giving off were so inappropriate, I didn't know what to do with them. I didn't think they'd liked Gemma very much, but they were behaving as if she'd never existed. They didn't look sorry and they didn't look afraid. I thought they ought to look both.

I heard the door close behind me and turned to see that Eleanor had swung it shut. She was more used to shocks than I was. The girls' odd behavior had not put her off. She went marching to the center of the room and glared at them.

"What are you all, daft?" She had her Yorkshire voice on again. "There's coppers all over this place. You're going to get sent back to the home, you are."

They stared at her solemnly, not in the least disturbed. They looked like people who have just found God, and whose new knowledge has wiped out the knowledge of everything else. They listened to Eleanor only because they recognized her as one of their own. Maybe they thought they could convert her.

A form stirred at the back of the room. When I focused on it, I saw it was Molly Larkin. I'd blocked her out after my first sight of her.

"It's all right," she said tentatively. "We won't get sent back. We've had police here before and—" She clamped her mouth shut. There was no Gemma here to tell her she was giving away too much, but she had *some* instinct for self-preservation. She looked around at the others and smiled nervously. "It's all right," she repeated. "It really is."

Eleanor sighed, with great and deliberate exaggeration. "Scotland Yard," she said, "is not the local bloody constable. This is a murder investigation. Don't you read books? They go into everybody's background. They find out everything."

"But the investigation is over," the little fat girl said in confusion. "They caught the man who killed Gemma. He was some American. They have him in jail, they do."

"They've just pulled him in to help the police with their inquiries," Eleanor said. She was lying, but she was lying convincingly. "They could let him go at any moment. Then they'll start in on all of you. Don't you at *least* watch the telly?"

The little fat girl looked morose. "Mrs. Copplewhite doesn't like the telly," she said. "She won't have one in the house. I went down to the pub once to watch it there, but they wouldn't let me stay. Said I was underaged."

"You weren't supposed to go down to the pub, either," another girl said. "We're not supposed to get around the village much, you know, in case—"

"In case somebody begins to think something's funny, with all of you here like this?" I had found my voice.

Molly Larkin flushed. "It's all *right,*" she insisted for the third time. "It really is. I know you're very concerned. It's very nice of you. But we'll be fine. We really will be."

"Bullfeathers," Eleanor said.

"You don't have to worry about Molly," the fat girl said. "She's only going to be here until—" She shut up.

Eleanor and I looked around the room again, but we knew it was over. They hadn't frozen up, the way they had the night before, but they had definitely stopped talking. The looks they gave us were almost pitying, as if they not only knew something we didn't, but something we should. That made me very, very nervous. The most worldly-wise of these girls was still very young, and very naive. The toughness was a facade I had once put on myself. I knew how deep it didn't go.

I looked at Eleanor, thinking she was still close enough to what they were to have some idea of what to do. She was shaking her head in resignation.

"You're all daft," she said. "You went to all that trouble to get away and now you're just asking to be sent back."

"We won't be sent back," Molly Larkin said gently. "Everybody who comes here gets away."

It wasn't the most comforting statement I'd ever heard.

Apparently, it wasn't the most comforting statement Eleanor had ever heard, either. She stayed on after I walked out, long enough so that I almost went back in and got her, and when she finally emerged she looked agitated and a little depressed. I led her down the hall to the stairs again, moving more quickly than I usually did. I had things to do and I wanted to get them done.

"Are you all right?" I asked her. "Did you try to give them another pep talk and fail?"

"No. There was a girl at the back—I didn't see her till the end—who'd been with me at St. Thomas's."

That was interesting. "Did you try to pump her? What did—"

Eleanor shook her head. "It wasn't anything. She didn't say anything, I mean. She just—" Eleanor turned away. "Whatever. She ran away a couple of weeks before I did. She seems to be fine."

Any other time, I would have pursued the subject. Eleanor was obviously uncomfortable, and all those broken sentences weren't like her. I was in a hurry and had my mind on other things. If I could get the murder business straightened out, the business with the girls would be straightened out, too. Solving one would solve the other.

We reached the foyer. It was deserted, and I was glad to find it that way. The last thing I needed at that moment was a visit from Mrs. Henry Copplewhite. I let us into the back hall and then into the telephone room. We were still alone. The telephone room was pitch dark. Mrs. Copplewhite was saving electricity by keeping the overhead lights turned off in the daylight, even though there weren't any windows to give light.

I found the switch and gave us what faint illumination we could expect. Then I dragged Eleanor over to the wall of photographs and pointed at them.

"You said he reminded you of someone," I said. "Think. *Who?*"

Eleanor blinked. "I told you," she said. "I don't know. I never knew any little boys, really. St. Thomas's was a girls' school."

"I'll tell you who he reminds me of," I said, "and it's not a little boy. It's a man who followed us home from Foyle's the night we went to buy the godmothers' books. He stayed outside our gate the entire rest of the night. Just stood there."

"You're not joking? You didn't tell me anything about that."

"You were spooked enough already," I said. "And I didn't know what to say. But I'm going to make a guess. Who he reminds *you* of is the woman who followed you to the Connaught."

221

Eleanor started. "Oh, God," she said. "But it isn't possible. This is a little boy—"

"This was a little boy," I said. "These pictures were taken at least thirty years ago. They don't do prints like this, anymore. And I'll tell you where the resemblance is, too. It's been driving me crazy since I called you last night and first got a look at these pictures, but now I know. It's in the eyes."

Eleanor looked again. "He does have her eyes," she said finally. "Do you mean this is her son? Or her brother—"

"No, you fool. I mean this is her."

Eleanor blinked. "You mean, she *was* in drag."

"Yes, when you saw her—I mean, him. When *I* saw *him*, he was just being himself: Mrs. Copplewhite's son Charlie."

"Oh, dear Jesus."

"I think I have it worked out," I said. "Mrs. Copplewhite's been running a scam for some time, selling the girls for something. I don't know what yet. Whatever it is, she feeds them a good cover. They'll stay with her no matter what. She probably feeds them good backup, too. Letters from the girls she ships out. Things like that. In the meantime, her son grows up, and he gets adolescent urges. Not normal ones. He does something to one of the girls. Rapes her, certainly. He may have killed her, but I doubt it. If he had, the police would be looking for him instead of bothering Ben. Whatever it is, it's bad enough to get him sent away to Dartmoor. That sends him right over the edge, making him crazy enough to kill. So he does his three years in Dartmoor and he comes out, and when he does he's got a problem.

"He's got a reputation by now, you see. The people in the village probably don't want to have anything to do with him. Unemployment's high up here anyway. With this thing hanging over him, he couldn't get a job if he paid himself. And he *is* over the edge. He *does* want to kill them. In the beginning, I think he just did it. Dragged them out back or something and then buried them in the weeds. Mrs. Copplewhite would have told the other girls that the one who'd gone had gone on to whatever they'd been promised, and they wouldn't think anything of it. The people in town wouldn't think anything of it, either. The girls at Mrs. Copplewhite's come and go. They aren't seen much in the village. Mrs. Copplewhite makes sure they don't go there. When one of them disappears, there's nobody to know it's happened. At least, not anybody who could do anything about it.

"I think he probably got nervous about killing them so close to home. It's remote out here, but it's not the Sahara. He probably thought if he kept digging graves in the weeds, he was going to end up caught. Then he had problems with the town. Emigrating felt like a good idea, going someplace entirely new."

"But they didn't emigrate," Eleanor said. "Mrs. Copplewhite's still here."

"Yes, she is," I agreed. "But I give you a bet half the town thinks Charlie is in New York. Or Sidney. Or Liverpool. Probably nobody's seen him around for months. When he shows up here, he shows up as Mrs. Ewern. An ugly, unpleasant old woman nobody wants to get any closer to than they have to. And he has taken a few trips. He took one to Boston, where he picked up Julie Matthews and murdered her and didn't work too hard at concealing it, probably because he thought nobody would get on to him. But Ben did."

"And he found out Ben did," Eleanor said.

"Exactly. Because Ben wasn't being too subtle about it. He was bashing around asking questions of everyone he could find. Ben's a writer, not a private detective. So then, when he found out Ben was coming to England—"

"How?" Eleanor demanded.

"Easiest thing in the world. His mother told him. He made a reservation to stay here. She got in touch with Charlie—"

"But that would mean she was in on it," Eleanor said. "It would have to be the two of them together."

"Why not? One of the godmothers told me in one of those interminable discussions we were always having about crime that most forms of schizophrenia are hereditary biochemical conditions. Especially the violent kinds."

"She's crazy and she gave it to him," Eleanor said. "At birth. And he's not just crazy. He's some kind of genius."

"He's not a genius," I said impatiently. "He's an ass. Look at all the things he's pulled. Julie was a bad choice. If what Ben says is accurate, Charlie knew her two months before he killed her. He must have known she had family, a fiancé, all those things. He left her where she was sure to be found and then he pinned that rose on her, like some street jerk spray-painting on a subway wall. That must be some kind of compulsion he can't control, his signature. That's stupid. And then all the things he's done with us: sending me all those roses, following you, following me. Making himself as obvious as possible. He's got delusions of invincibility. He's manipulating us, but he's leading us to him, too."

"And she's feeding them to him?" Eleanor said. "She's sending them off so he can kill them?"

"Deliberately," I said. "They've probably been doing it for years."

"All the publicity," Eleanor said doubtfully. "If those girls—Sheila Ann Holme and them—the girls upstairs would have known them—"

"The girls upstairs probably don't even know there's a Ripper in London. Mrs. Copplewhite won't have a telly. The pub won't let them watch there. The nearest neighbor is a mile-and-a-half trek into the village. As far as I can tell, Mrs. Copplewhite doesn't take any newspapers, either. The girls wouldn't read them if she did. And look around you. She does everything possible to discourage guests. She's on every tour guide's blacklist from here to Hong Kong."

"And she took us because she thought it would have looked suspicious not to," Eleanor said.

"Exactly."

"I want to get out of here," Eleanor said. "If that was this Charlie, I can go back to the Connaught. You can come with me. We'll be safe there—"

"Eleanor, if they end up convicting Ben of all this nonsense, none of us will be safe anywhere. Charlie's just going to go on doing what he's doing. He'll go back to hiding the bodies where they won't be found for a couple of years. He won't stop killing. I don't think he can stop killing, and I don't think he wants to. And he knows where we live."

"What are you going to do?"

I had sat down, without realizing it, on the bench next to the phone. I stood up and stretched.

"The first thing I'm going to do is go talk to Ben," I said. "That is, if I can get in to talk to him. I need to know what made him know where to look for those bodies. I hope to God he didn't just see them out his bedroom window. We need something solid to take to the police. After that, it depends."

Eleanor looked down at her hands. "I'm going to be sixteen in not too long. It won't matter after then. I want you to be alive then."

"I want to be alive a lot longer than that," I said.

"I guess you do." She straightened up. "I know something you ought to know. Something Lisa told me upstairs. That girl I was with at St. Thomas's. It wasn't much. She just came up to me and whispered in my ear, *'it's all true.'* And I know what it means."

"What does it mean?"

"There used to be rumors at St. Thomas's," Eleanor said. "Rumors about people who could put you in touch with your parents. The idea was sort of that the welfare system took you away for reasons—well, crazy reasons. Like fairy-tale-witch reasons. Because they liked to hurt people and because they were evil. And there were these other people who were like an underground who helped you escape and helped your parents find you. Because your parents weren't dead even if they told you they were. I mean, I know it sounds stupid—" She gave me a desperate look. "Nobody with half a brain would believe it and I never did, but you know what those places are like. You know what we're like. And a lot of the girls did believe it and Lisa was saying it was here."

"Oh, dear God," I said.

Eleanor had started to sniffle. "You're just so small and you're just so scared and you just don't *know* anything."

─── TWENTY-ONE ───

By the time I got outside, the day was clouding over. Another storm was moving in. There was too much electricity in the atmosphere. I set out on the road to the village in a state of half-collapse. My conversation with Eleanor had been nerve-wracking even when I was in control of it. Once Eleanor took over, with all that business about secret undergrounds that reunited children and parents, I'd been devastated. Some things, like suspiciousness and defensiveness and anger, you eventually lose. Some things, like the desperate hunger for the love of the one person you will always remember perfectly, you never do. I couldn't decide what I thought was worse: that the Copplewhites were killing them, or that they were filling them with this cruel and impossible hope.

When I got to the edge of the village, I asked directions at a sweet shop, a cramped, musty place that looked like it hadn't seen a customer in half a century. The woman behind the counter gave me a searching look—there had been a murder in St. Edmund Cavateur, after all—but she also gave me directions. Before I knew it, I was walking down a side street crowded with trees and white rose bushes. The road, like the roads in the rest of the town, was only intermittently paved. The bald patches between the cobblestones seemed to sum up everything that had gone wrong in St. Edmund Cavateur. Things were not done thoroughly here, by Public Works or the police.

The police station turned out to be a small brick building set back in a modest courtyard, the one courtyard on the block without a single white rose in it. The building was less elaborately Victorian than most of its neighbors. It had a spire here and a curlicue there, but the effort seemed half-hearted. The tiny parking lot at the side held three bright new shiny Austins with CID plates and one broken-down mini, going to rust. The mini belonged to our local constable. It looked as dilapidated and ineffectual as he was.

I walked through the front door and found myself in a small square room with a desk in the middle of it. The desk was sitting on a platform three inches higher than the floor, the way teachers' desks used to in the thirties. I looked around for someone to talk to and found myself alone. There was a metal bellhop bell on the desk, though, so I stood on tiptoe and pounded that.

A few minutes later, a door at the far end of the room opened and a man stuck his head out. He looked like London, all well-tailored suit and city air. He didn't look happy to see me.

"Constable's away for the moment," he said. "You'll have to wait."

"I came to see Benjamin Grade," I said. "I'm not sure the constable's the person I need to talk to."

He stared at me for a moment, curious, and then came all the way into the room. He was a tall man with thinning hair and a ruddiness of face that suggested too much fondness for real ale, but he had all the authority of a serious police officer. He stopped in front of me and held out his hand. The gesture was polite but pointed. He knew as well as I did that I was the one who was supposed to offer a hand, but we were going to do it his way, no matter what.

"Detective Inspector Jamison," he said. "You are—"

"Avra Mahon," I said.

"Miss Mahon. Are you a friend of Mr. Grade's?"

I didn't know how to answer that. "I know him," I said. "I'm playing tour guide for some women who are friends of his and are staying at Mrs. Henry Copplewhite's." I stressed the "Mrs. Henry Copplewhite's" slightly. "They're interested in knowing how he's doing."

227

This time, Detective Inspector Jamison's inspection was long. "Are you talking about Miss Caroline Matthews?"

"And Miss Belle March and Miss Mariliee Bonnard," I said. "Except I think they all call themselves 'Ms.'"

"I don't doubt they do. I will say, however, that I don't think they're very good friends of Mr. Grade's. They're the ones who called us."

"I know."

"Would Mr. Grade know your name if I gave it to him?"

"Oh, yes."

Detective Inspector Jamison lapsed into thought. After a while he said, "I thought you might be from the consulate, although it's early for that. Mr. Grade did put a call into them, however. It would be against the law, of course, for us to listen in to a conversation between Mr. Grade and his consul. Or his solicitor. Would you like to tell me what you'd want to speak to Mr. Grade about?"

"I should think that was obvious," I said. "I want to talk to him about his finding the bodies."

"His finding the bodies in particular," Jamison said. "Not the murders in general."

"Not the murders in general," I agreed. "I don't have to talk to him about the murders in general."

"You don't think he committed them." It was not a question.

I said "no" anyway.

Detective Inspector Jamison went back to staring at me. It was not a hostile stare. He might have been working out a logic problem in *Games* magazine.

After a while he stepped back and said, "Please wait. I'll return in a moment." He turned around and disappeared through the door he'd come in by.

I walked around the room, too restless to sit down. It wasn't the reception I'd expected, but I could read it well enough. It *would* be perfectly legal for the Detective Inspector to listen in on any conversation Benjamin Grade might have with me. Letting me see him, therefore, might prove useful. He had probably gone back to talk it over with the other drivers of shiny Austins with CID plates.

I stopped at the windows and looked out at the street. I

didn't mind the idea of Detective Inspector Jamison listening in on what I had to say to Benjamin. For one thing, I intended to give my theory another full airing. Without proof, that wouldn't get Benjamin off the hook, but it might at least plant an idea. An idea well planted could make a great deal of difference when the press showed up.

Which reminded me—where *were* the press? I scanned the street carefully. The only cars on it were in the police parking lot, and the houses that took up the rest of the space looked as blank and uninhabited as the houses had on Roskell Road the night I'd come home to find the cat. The police had to be keeping this under wraps with a vengeance. I'd always thought the *Sun* had a mole at Scotland Yard. The crime had received so much publicity, even the suggestion of a suggestion that the police might be close to solving it was going to generate a media circus.

I caught movement to my left and turned slightly in that direction, still thinking about newspaper reporters and front-page headlines. There was a hedge between the station and the house on that side, a huge mass of evergreen that looked oddly lively among all the dying bushes. I stared in its general direction, noting absently that there must be a wind coming up. The evergreen branches were shuddering and swaying in a fitful breeze.

I caught on only seconds before he decided to show himself. I pressed my face flat against the window and concentrated—and then, all of a sudden, there he was. Or she was. He was dressed in sprigged print cotton and a powdered wig, but I would have known him anywhere. The man who had followed me from Foyle's.

He'd followed me here. Of course he had. If everything I'd theorized about him was true, he would have had to.

I stepped away from the window, wondering what I was supposed to do. As long as I was in the police station, I was safe. After that, I was going to be on my own. I didn't have a hope in hell of convincing them with nothing but theories.

Behind me, Detective Inspector Jamison coughed and said, "If you'll come this way, please, Miss Mahon."

He took me to what looked like the conference room for a failing corporation. There was an oversize table and a set of matching chairs, but the table was peeling and the chair seats had been padded with green plastic. I sat down on one of the chairs and waited. There was an ashtray in the middle of the table. I drew it toward me but didn't do anything about lighting up. The longer I stayed in the room the less I liked it. It was cold and curiously snide, as if it had heard too many false protestations of innocence.

The English are a very civilized people, newspapers notwithstanding. When they brought Benjamin in to me, he was without handcuffs or leg braces or restraining paraphernalia. His guard—or maybe it was his escort—was without a gun. He showed Benjamin into the room, looked me over once, and then disappeared.

Benjamin said, "You ought to be my lawyer. I wanted you to be my lawyer. I was *hoping* you'd be my lawyer."

"They didn't tell you who was here?"

"Of course they told me," he sighed. "I even believed them. Avra, what do you think you're doing?"

"I'll get to that in a minute. And if it makes any difference, they're probably monitoring this conversation. That man, Detective Inspector Jamison, said something outside—"

"I'm sure they're monitoring the conversation," Benjamin said. "This isn't New York. They can monitor practically anything they want to. They're monitoring my nature calls. You still haven't told me what you *want*."

"Do you mind if I ask how you are first?"

"I'm about the way you'd expect me to be. They've got a beautiful theory. You want to hear it?"

"I can guess," I said. "They think you killed Julie Matthews, but they think that's probably an anomaly. They think you've been running over here every year and killing girls. A few this time, not so many the times before. You come to England once a year. They can prove that. Your London hotels have your files, but all that those say is that you paid for a room for a couple of weeks every year. They don't testify that you were actually in it. Then Mrs. Copplewhite comes along and says you've been coming up to stay with *her* every year—"

"How the hell did you know that?"

"Let's just say it logically follows," I said. "I even know how she's going to get away with it, or thinks she is. She's out of the village. All she has to say is that you drove up instead of taking a train. I bet you've rented a car every time you've been in England. You could have come up the west side and never been seen in St. Edmund Cavateur at all."

"Do you work for the CID, or have you just decided to trade touring in for mystery writing?"

"Believe it or not, I came to help you out."

He subsided, looking defeated. It wasn't something that sat well on him. "You know," he said, "before I met Julie Matthews, I don't think I'd ever been in a situation where I'd really failed. I'd lost a few things, but nothing important. I came from a nice, normal middle-class family. I lived a nice, normal middle-class life. I was looking forward to the future. The books have been that successful. Then I fell in love with a girl, and asked her to marry me, and the next thing I knew, my life had gone to hell."

"No thanks to our fairy godmothers," I said.

"No thanks to myself," Benjamin said. "I'm the one who had to come chasing over here after that—that maniac. I'm the one who couldn't leave well enough alone. I'm the one who didn't have the brains to hire a professional—I could have gotten a private detective. I had to do it on my own. I think I was confusing myself with my hero. He's always doing things like this and winning big."

I looked at my hands and the empty ashtray in front of me. The problem with not smoking is that there's no way to create a diversion. I needed one. Benjamin's voice kept rocking back and forth between anger and despair. The anger wouldn't have been so bad if it had been directed against Mrs. Copplewhite, Charlie, or me, but it was directed against himself. I didn't like that at all. That was just one step away from giving up.

I had intended to pump him first about what had sent him searching in the back garden. That was the important thing, and I didn't know how long the police would let us have. Now I changed my mind. Benjamin needed some good news, and I had it. I at least had something that might get him thinking about other possibilities besides his own.

I leaned toward him, raising my voice a little. I wanted to get his attention, but I also wanted to get the attention of whoever was listening in on us.

"Let me tell you a story," I said. "It's the only story I know that takes *every little thing* into account."

When I'd finished telling the story, the world beyond the interrogation room's barbed-wired windows was dark. I wondered what time it was. Dark comes early in England in the late fall, but in October it usually holds off until after five o'clock. Either they were giving us forever to talk to each other, or the storm I'd noticed while walking over had moved in fast. On the other side of the table, Benjamin looked shell-shocked. It was a good kind of shell-shock. It was caused by the fact that he was furious with me.

"Did you tell *anybody any* of that stuff? The roses? The guy following you? Did you just mention it to one other person? Were you trying to get yourself killed?"

"Ahh," I said. "We've returned to normal here."

"Don't change the subject," he said. "You've got to be out of your mind. What are you doing up here?"

"He could have killed me just as easily in London as here," I pointed out, "and he probably would have if I hadn't come. Me or Eleanor. Or both. That's not the point. The point is—"

"The point is," he said, "that I may not be Derek Hayes, Boy Detective—my hero; he's thirty-seven—but I've got a better shot at it than you do. You're—"

"A woman?"

"Scrawny," he said. "Don't be trite."

"I won't be trite if you won't be unreasonable. We've got to get you out of here, at the least. At the best, we've got to get Charlie Copplewhite picked up. And his mother. What were you doing out in the garden? How did you know the graves were there?"

"I didn't," Benjamin said. "Oh, hell, Avra. I was counting windows."

"What?"

He put his hands in his hair. "The address in Julie's book wasn't just 'Mrs. Henry Copplewhite.' There was a room number: *236.* Last night, right before I found you downstairs, I went prowling all over the second floor, looking for the room. It wasn't there. Then when I took you up to your room, the corridor on three just seemed—longer, somehow. It wasn't that big a difference. Maybe there isn't a difference. It just seemed like there was. It was too dark to do anything about it then, so I waited until morning. I went into the village, while everybody else was having breakfast at Mrs. Copplewhite's, and ate at the pub. They have a restaurant section they open for morning coffee. I talked to some people and then I walked back. I knew how many doors there were on two. Every room has two windows facing the same direction. I went out to the garden to count windows. And I just—fell on them."

"So you decided to dig them up?" I said. "That's crazier than anything you've accused me of doing."

"Excuse me," Benjamin said. "I write action-adventure."

"Don't get sarcastic," I said. "You were right. There is another room on that floor. You can only reach it by the back stairs. I assumed it was Mrs. Copplewhite's bedroom."

"Mrs. Copplewhite's bedroom is on the ground floor, off the back near the kitchen. She invited me into it."

"Did she?" I said. "What was your answer?"

"Give me a break."

I gave him a rest, at any rate. I sat there, thinking. I finally decided to smoke, after all. I curled into my chair and got a cigarette going and put it down again. I was using the things for incense.

"If it's not Mrs. Copplewhite's bedroom," I said carefully, "it must be Charlie's. Wouldn't you think so? And if it's Charlie's, there might be something—"

"Avra," Benjamin said. The dangerous note was back in his voice, the one I'd noticed that first day in my office. "Don't do anything stupid. I'm serious. This is going to work out."

── TWENTY-TWO ──

Detective Inspector Jamison offered to drive me home. That was the only indication I had that he'd listened to my conversation with Benjamin. I'd heard no telltale beeping or whirring of machinery while I'd been in the conference room. I saw no extraneous people in the hall when I came out. The only thing that seemed to have changed, besides Benjamin's frame of mind, by the end of that conversation, was Detective Inspector Jamison's attitude. His icy, prying formality disappeared. If it hadn't seemed ludicrous in the extreme, I would have thought he was worried about me.

The clock in the front room said *5:23*, late enough for full dark, but the dark was being helped out by the weather. The rain was heavy. The whining gurgle of water sluicing down the roof gutters made it sound as if we were standing under a draining bathtub. The rolling thunder reminded me of the old legend about giants bowling in the sky. There was no lightning that I could see. The streetlamps here, with the exception of the one directly over the police station gate, were as inadequate as the ones at Mrs. Copplewhite's. If Charlie Copplewhite was still out there waiting for me, I wasn't going to be able to see him. Of course, if he was still out there waiting for me, he was going to drown.

I took Detective Inspector Jamison up on his offer anyway. I didn't want to get soaked, and I didn't think it was beyond possibility that Charlie might still be out there. My theory was a beautiful thing, but as far as Charlie's personal-

234

ity was concerned, it was *just* theory. I knew how Charlie should behave, given everything I'd been told and everything I'd read in the past few weeks about psychopaths, but I didn't know how he *would*. If science knew everything there was to know about these people, there wouldn't be any serial murders. The nuts would be caught long before they had the chance to cause that much havoc.

I let Detective Inspector Jamison drive me right up to Mrs. Copplewhite's gate and then come around to my side of the car to let me out. He had a big black umbrella to shield me from the rain and an expression on his face that reminded me of MacGruff, the cartoon hound-dog from the "Take a Bite out of Crime" campaign back in the States. He got my door open and I jumped out of the car, trying to get as far under his umbrella as possible. I landed in a puddle in the process. Filthy water sprayed up over my slacks and his trousers. We both smiled.

"Looks like nobody's home," he said, wafting a hand toward the house.

He was right. There wasn't a light on anywhere, not even over the front step, and bed-and-breakfasts *always* have a light on over the front step. They need it for late-arriving guests. Mrs. Copplewhite's looked shut up and abandoned. It was that dilapidated. Somehow, its rotting condition was more evident in total darkness than in partial light.

"They must all be in the back," I said.

"Maybe they've all left," Detective Inspector Jamison said. "Maybe you should leave, too."

"I brought a tour group of people up here," I said, making the godmothers sound like the hordes of Attila. "I can't abandon them without knowing where they are."

Detective Inspector Jamison shrugged and leaned past me to open the door. The knob turned easily in his hands. "Maybe you're right. Maybe they are in the back. Wouldn't leave the door wide open with a murderer in the neighborhood, would they?"

"Why wouldn't they?" I said. "When the murderer's already been caught?"

He leaned past me, felt around on the inside wall, and got the foyer light on. "It's a funny thing about people," he said.

"Some man shoots his wife at noon on the high street in full view of twenty people, we run him right in, and the whole village *still* lives behind closed doors for a month."

"Do they really?"

"It's the fear," Detective Inspector Jamison said. "The only people who leave their doors open after things like this are the ones with nothing to fear."

"Which is supposed to mean what?"

He backed away, taking his umbrella with him. Then he bowed slightly from the waist. "Good evening, Miss Mahon."

His car was the red Austin. In the light from Mrs. Copplewhite's foyer, it looked like a vibrating drop of blood as it drove away.

By the time I closed the door, I knew there was no one in the house. It had that odd feeling houses get when they're empty, a kind of super-silence. Everything echoed: the rain on the roof, my footsteps in the foyer, that rustly flapping noise of curtains near an open window. I opened the double doors to the living room and looked inside. It was dark and uninhabited. The night before, it had radiated the presence of someone I couldn't see—Ben, probably—and I'd been frightened. Now I just felt flat. It was a dirty, shabby, empty room with nothing in it to interest me.

I closed the doors and turned away and headed toward the stairs. The light switch was at the bottom near one of the elongated windows beside the door, and I flipped it to *on* without much thought. I wondered where they had all gone. I couldn't believe they'd gone out together, but they'd almost have had to to leave the house empty. I wanted to believe the girls had finally seen reason and bolted, but I didn't believe that, either. The way they'd been that afternoon, nothing would have budged them but a full-scale war.

I stopped on the second-floor landing and looked at the police barrier. It was a piece of string stretched across the hall, anchored to two portable aluminum posts. I could have walked right past it. The sergeant who had been there when I left for the police station this afternoon was gone. Apparently, the police no longer thought they were going to find anything important in Benjamin's room. I thought that meant they were convinced of Benjamin's guilt. If they had had doubts, they'd have kept something posted just to insure nothing was *planted* there.

I went up to three, knocked on the godmothers' door just for form, and then went down to my own. I went into my bedroom and sat on the bed and got a cigarette lit. I pulled my feet up under me and got the books I'd brought from London off the night table shelf. Barbara Cartland, Jude Deveraux, Jackie Collins: My taste runs to romance and glitz-and-glitter, love and sex and sin.

I took out the Deveraux—*The Maiden,* just out in the States and just shipped to me by a woman I knew in New York—because I liked her best and usually had no trouble getting lost in her plots. I settled back against the pillows and read the first line. I thought about the fact that I hadn't eaten all day. I was starving. I thought about the fact that love seemed to be something I wasn't very good at: What was it, exactly, that I felt for Benjamin? I closed the book and put it down beside me and swung my feet off the bed.

Somewhere at the core of me there was a little pulse. It was saying: hurry, hurry, hurry.

Hurry and do *what?*

I felt useless and ineffectual and stupid. I felt I ought to be doing something when I couldn't think of anything to do. I felt directionless and impotent. Benjamin's mood when I first saw him that afternoon now made perfect sense to me. I was in the same mood myself, and I didn't have all the social pressure men did to be competent and aggressive and on top of things. Ben must have felt like hell.

I looked down at my hands and saw I was holding my pack of cigarettes, shredded. I didn't even remember picking it up.

The fact was I could think of something to do, I just wasn't sure how to go about doing it.

There was that, and there was the simple fact that the whole idea scared me to death.

I was already in the back hall when it first occurred to me the house might not be empty after all. The room I had found on the second-floor landing was closed off to every other part of the house. There was a thick wall between it

237

and the corridor Benjamin's room opened onto. Somebody could be locked away in there without making any sound I could hear.

I had stopped in the living room on my way through to get a poker from the cast-iron stand beside the fireplace. I had some vague idea of battering the door down with it. I stopped again in the telephone room to listen. There was nothing to hear. The telephone room and the hall beyond it were dead dark. I went to turn on a light and stopped myself. If there was somebody up in that room, I didn't want to alert him—or her—to my being in the hall.

I went to the bottom of the stairs and stood still, listening again. Nothing, nothing, nothing. The house just felt empty. I don't put much credence in that kind of thing. The universe I believe in is rational, straightforward, without stray psychic quirks, and devoid of miracles. Logically, there was no reason why that room should not be occupied. But the house *did* feel empty, and that counted. It counted enough to relax me a little. Relaxing made it easier for me to think.

I held the poker in the air so it wouldn't knock against the floor or walls or banister and climbed to the landing. There was a little light coming from somewhere, I didn't know where, and it hit on the brass knob and key plate, making them gleam. Singled out like that, they reminded me of the grinning doorknobs in Disney's *Alice in Wonderland*. I had to stifle a nervous giggle. *Alice in Wonderland, Sleeping Beauty:* When I was twenty and waiting to leave New York for London to work for Amelia Mortimer-Jones, I spent an entire week going to all the Walt Disney movies I'd missed as a child.

I looked at the door and then at the poker and then at the door again. That was stupid. I was never going to get through that door with a poker. I'd have had better luck with hairpins, even though I didn't know how to use them. If I wanted to break the door down, I'd do better with a chair.

I put the poker on the floor, leaning against the wall beside the door. Then I tried the knob, just in case.

I don't know what surprised me more: that the door didn't creak when it moved, or that it opened at all.

Rain and thunder, wind and the sigh of moving fabric, the

smell of roses; *especially* the smell of roses. When the door opened, the scent washed over me like an angry surf. It was warm and thick and cloying. I felt the bile rise in my throat and pushed it down, down, into that well of denial that is supposed to be the unconscious. I couldn't afford to throw up on the floor.

I was standing in the hall with the door wide open, right there for anyone to see. I stepped into the room and closed the door behind me. The roses had put me off balance. My heart was thumping wildly and all the blood seemed to have deserted my head for my feet. My breathing was labored, hitching and painful, as if I'd chain-smoked two packs of cigarettes and then gone for a two-mile run. I closed my eyes and counted, slowly, doing my best to get myself under control. My best wasn't good enough. When I opened my eyes again, I was shaking.

Evidence, I told myself. *You have to find evidence. Evidence will solve everything.*

I closed my eyes again. I didn't know anything about evidence. I always stopped reading long before I got to that part of the godmothers' books, although Eleanor had told me that was the *best* part. I hadn't the faintest idea how to search a room or what to look for while I did it.

I did know I wasn't going to be able to search it in the dark.

I got my eyes open again and felt around for the wall switch. My hands brushed against petals and thorns, slime and edge, and I shivered again. I had no control over my body. My mind had departed for the land of panic minutes ago.

The wall switch was directly behind a vase of roses that had been pushed up against the wall. There had to be another light, the one Charlie or Mrs. Copplewhite or whoever habitually used, but I didn't have the patience or the self-possession to search for it. I didn't have the time, either. I shoved the vase out of the way and went for the overhead light switch.

The light took so long to go on, I thought the bulb might be out. Then there was a flickering and a sputtering and a little spark—if I'd known anything about electricity, I would have realized there was something wrong with the fixture—and a glare started up in the middle of the room that was as blinding and merciless as an arc lamp in a morgue.

It took me a while to adjust to the light. When I did, I realized why the smell of roses had been so overpowering.

There were hundreds of them. Literally hundreds of them. The room was broad and deep and high, and the roses covered every available surface except the top of the bed. They spilled out of vases and wilted against the hat stand and climbed the walls on wire hangers. They were old and getting older, going to rot. The rot had a smell of its own that underlay the rose smell like foul breath.

I ran to the window closest to me, threw it open, and took a great gulp of air.

Once I got used to it, I could make out furniture under the flowers. There were a bureau and a dressing table and a chair, as well as the bed. Everything had been dusted and cleaned and polished. Even the wastebasket had been recently emptied. The only litter in the room was rose petals.

I went back to my counting act. I thought of it as an exercise in futility, but it was the only thing I knew to do. Maybe because I'd had more shocks than I could handle, the exercise finally worked. I felt my heart slowing down and my breath coming more easily. The girdle of steel wires my rib cage had turned into began to soften and melt. I turned my head back and forth, casing all that buried furniture. I could just make out the shape of a jewelry case on the dressing table's glass cover.

Evidence, I told myself firmly. I walked over to the dressing table and pushed the roses out of the way. The vase at the end edged over the side and fell, clattering to the floor. I winced at the sound, but I didn't stop. Obviously, this wasn't going to be one of those expert searches where the person searched never knows his room has been invaded. I'd moved two things I knew about and probably a dozen I didn't. I took a pot of roses off the dressing table's chair and sat down.

The jewelry case was nothing special. It was one of those leatherette-covered, paper-padded ones you can buy in any Marks and Sparks for five pounds fifty, and its design was unimpressive, gold tracing on black. I fumbled around for the catch and sprung the lid. I looked down at a collection of trivialities: plastic costume pins, plastic costume brooches, plastic costume bangles. I stared at all the garish primary colors and bright fake-looking beads. I couldn't imagine what anyone would have wanted with any of it.

Something at the back of my mind said: *It's wrong. There's something wrong with it.*

I looked into the box again. Bangles, brooches, necklaces, rings, earrings for pierced ears—what?

Something clicked into place. It was a *mess,* that was what. Everything else in that room was as orderly as the shelves of the Library of Congress, but the things in that box were jumbled.

I put my hand inside and started to take things out. I dumped feathered earrings and Mickey Mouse pins in a heap. I pulled out plastic-piece-after-plastic-piece-after-plastic-piece. I was almost to the bottom when I found it. Sister Tom had to be right. There had to be a God. I should have missed it. I'd been pulling things out of that box on the assumption that the things themselves didn't matter. I thought they were camouflage. I was going to find something hidden under the lining, at the bottom.

But there it was, small and delicate, looking like a virgin in a whorehouse. A tiny gold locket on a thin gold chain, with a great curling *W* engraved on the front of it and two smaller initials engraved on either side. MJW. Margaret Jane Willeford. Margaret Jane Willeford had had a locket she'd worn everywhere, with a picture of her mother in it. It hadn't been found with the body.

It was here.

Evidence.

I turned toward the sound behind me with no feeling of apprehension. I saw Charlie Copplewhite standing in the doorway, all dressed up in his Mrs. Ewern clothes and grinning like a rabid dog.

Charlie was holding something I didn't recognize in front of his chest, a slim cylinder he had grasped in both his hands. He moved his hand against the edge of it and there was a sharp *ping.*

What he'd been holding was the haft of a flic knife.

What had just come up was the blade.

——— TWENTY-THREE ———

There are a hundred ways to handle things like this. You can read about them in any murder mystery not written by a little old Englishwoman. I didn't know about any of them. All I could think about was the fact that the light in the room was so damn bright. There were no more than the customary four corners, only the door Charlie was standing in, and a twenty-five-foot drop to the ground. I couldn't climb out the window I'd opened and jump to the ground.

Charlie was doing odd things to himself. He had taken off his white wig. Without it, but with all his heavy makeup still in place, he looked bizarre, alien, almost like a mime. His real hair was sparse, stiff brown, cut short. Under it, his eyes had changed color. They had gone from slate gray to silvery, like the kind that glow in the dark.

My original impression of him, garnered on the bus to Putney, did not hold. He looked nothing at all like a downtrodden bureaucrat. I couldn't imagine how I'd ever thought he did. He wore his insanity like a Mardi Gras reveler's flamboyant costume. It shook and shivered and gleamed.

He took one more step toward me and pushed the door shut behind him, grinning.

"Party time!"

The words came out of him like the booming roar of a cannon. If it hadn't been for the thunder, they might have heard him on the high street. My eyes darted around the room in shock. What did he think he was doing? How out of control was he? The house had been empty when I'd come in. It might, except for us, be empty still. It wasn't likely to stay empty forever. People would be coming back eventually: the godmothers, the girls, Eleanor. For all he knew, they might be walking through the door right now. Didn't he care?

I got off the chair and started moving backward, although what I was going to do for myself on that end of the room, I didn't know. The idea that Charlie Copplewhite had finally come completely unhinged nearly unhinged me. It was my very worst terror: something coming at me to hurt me that couldn't be reasoned with, couldn't be talked to, couldn't even be made to hear. I backed up all the way to the open window and then stopped, holding on to the sill. I could feel rain on my shoulders and fingers and cold on my spine. I never took my eyes off Charlie. I didn't dare.

I'd expected him to lunge for me. He didn't. He walked to the chair I'd abandoned and sat down in it.

"I've been watching you for weeks," he said pleasantly. "I've been watching you forever."

Conversation, I thought. Fine. Wonderful. That had to be a good sign. I pushed myself back a little farther, until I was sitting on the sill. It made me feel better to know that, if I had to die, I had a choice. I could go out the window and break my neck before Charlie could get at me with the knife.

"Why?" I asked him. "Why have you been following me?"

He looked surprised. "Because I love you," he said. "I told you that before. I love you."

"You love me," I said.

"I sent you flowers." His voice had gone petulant. It was coming at me in a low-pitched whine. "I sent you dozens and dozens of roses. White roses, just like you like. I put them up in your room. I put them everywhere. I even put them in your underwear. You were supposed to like them."

"I do," I said automatically. "I do like them." Obviously, he was mistaking me for someone else. That first girl, the one he was supposed to have raped? I supposed so. He was no longer in this time and place. I didn't know where he was and I didn't know if I had time to find out.

His nervousness was segueing into other things: agitation, nervousness, reproach. He'd started jumping and twitching in the chair, moving in arhythmic little tics like someone with a nerve disease. His face was as emotionally open as an infant's. The smallest shred of feeling contorted it.

"You were supposed to like them but you didn't," he said. "It was all your fault. We were supposed to run away together and you wouldn't come. You were supposed to meet me, but you didn't."

"But I did," I said desperately. "I'm here."

He faltered. "You're here," he repeated, doubtfully. His face brightened. "You're *here*," he shouted. "You're *HERE.*"

"Exactly," I said. There was too much eagerness in my voice, but I was beyond caring. I couldn't control it anyway. I just hoped Charlie was beyond caring, too. He looked it. His eyes were shining sightlessly. He looked so happy he almost seemed angelic.

"Charlie," I said, "if we're going to run away, we ought to do it. We ought to go right now. If we wait too long, she might catch us."

The "she" was an inspiration. I didn't know what Charlie's relationship with Mrs. Copplewhite was, exactly, but I couldn't think of any reason for him to run away if he wasn't running away from her. Apparently, for once I'd been right on the mark. He got very businesslike.

"It will be all right when it's done," he assured me. "She won't say anything then. She doesn't want to lose me, you see. I'm very important to the business."

"I know," I said.

"I'm the one makes the contacts," he said. "It's all Arabs now, you know. A woman can't do business with Arabs. They don't like it. I'm the one has to do the work there. They all know me now. I'm very important."

"It's one of the things I love about you," I said. "How important you are."

"You'd be wasted on the Arabs," he said. "They wouldn't know how to value you. They don't think about anything but the dirty part. They just put the girls in rooms and sell them to whoever comes in. You'd be wasted on that."

"I know," I said. "I know, I know, but Charlie—"

He turned suspicious. It happened fast, and it was total. *"How* do you know?" He was shouting again. *"How* do you know? You're not supposed to know anything. You're supposed to think you're going to see your mother. HOW DO YOU—"

"Charlie," I said.

"Avra?"

Charlie and I both jerked around and stared at the door. That was Mariliee Bonnard's voice we'd heard, floating up the back staircase. Once we started listening, we could hear other things, too: the clatter of footsteps, the muffled curses of someone bumping into the walls. We jerked our heads back simultaneously, like a pair of marionettes tethered together.

Charlie flipped into a white rage. I'd heard of people's eyes bugging out of their heads, but I'd never seen it before. Charlie's face had gone red and was on its way to purple. His muscles had locked down hard and tight, like stone.

"You," he screamed at me. "You were supposed to be here and you weren't. You didn't come. YOU DIDN'T COME."

I snatched up one of the vases on the floor under the window and threw it at the overhead light. It connected with a pop, sending up a shower of sizzles and sparks, like fire coming out of the sky.

"Mariliee," I yelled. "Mariliee, I'm on the *second floor.*"

The door wasn't locked. I held that to me like a security blanket. Charlie had pushed the door shut as he was coming into the room, and he hadn't done any fiddling that might lock it. That was another old-fashioned skeleton-key lock. It needed a key to work.

God bless Benjamin Grade for giving me *that* piece of information.

Charlie had started moving, fumbling against the furniture and the roses. I got down on my hands and knees just as he tripped over a vase. The vase crashed against the floor and sent out glass slivers that reached me all the way at the window. I inched sideways, keeping my hands stretched out in front of me to detect planters and roses and stray snags. Charlie could afford to break a vase, but I could not. I couldn't do anything that would let him know where I was.

"Crap," I heard somebody say. "He's flipped. We can't *wait* for Jamison."

Benjamin Grade.

Charlie had stopped moving. I could still feel him in the room, but he was a still presence. He must have thought Benjamin was safely out of the way, tightly locked up.

I got down flat on my stomach and started to crawl. Time, that was what I needed. They were right below me and they knew what was happening. All I had to do was stay away from the knife long enough for them to get to me.

I put my palms on the floor and started to pull myself forward. I was headed for the bed. It was a good high bed, an old-fashioned four-poster. There would be plenty of room under it. It would be difficult to get at me there.

"You didn't come," Charlie whispered in the dark. "You really hated me."

There were rose petals all over the floor, a thick carpet of them. They were working their way under my clothes and up my nose. Every once in a while I got one in my mouth. They tasted like sour mayonnaise.

I was going to sneeze.

Outside the door, Benjamin said, "What use would Jamison be, anyway? The police in this country don't even carry *guns.*"

Then a lot of things happened at once: Charlie reached the lamp on the other side of the bed and turned it on, Ben walked through the door, and I sneezed.

A second later, Charlie came hurtling over the bed, knife out.

A sane man would have run, or stopped, or something, but Charlie wasn't a sane man. Whatever remnants of sanity he'd managed to hold onto through his years of killing were gone. He didn't give a damn about Benjamin. He didn't give a damn about the police. He didn't give a damn about anything but getting to me. He came leaping over the bedspread like a polevaulter, manic and wild but deadly accurate. I tried to twist away. I didn't make it. The knife hit the floor half a second before his body and cut into my hand. Then he just fell on top of me, knocking the wind out of me.

He was a middle-aged man, not constitutionally strong. Another time, I might have been able to fight him off. This time, my hand was pinned to the floor by the knife and I couldn't breathe.

He pulled the knife out, ripping my skin and muscles. He rose above me like a phantom and came down again, slashing. I moved just in time. He cut a slash in my cheek but didn't get any deeper. He was panting and furious, savage. I was scared out of my mind. He raised his arm again, and I moved again, drawing my knees up to my chest, fighting against the pain. I wanted to pass out. Any break in my will and I would have. He came at me again a moment too soon. I hadn't managed to get my feet in position, so that he'd fall with the soles of them against his chest. I pushed with my knees anyway. It jogged him but didn't stop him. The knife came down against my shoulder and tore into the soft flesh of my upper arm.

The air in front of my eyes rippled, looking suddenly like liquid. The pain was red and hot and sharp and washing over me in waves. I jerked my legs up one more time and got my feet where I wanted them. Then I kicked out toward his chest.

If I'd waited, I'd have got him. Instead, I kicked up while he was still rising, and my legs had too far to go. They caught him at the hip and staggered him, but they turned the stagger into a gymnast's whirl. The whirl became an arching dive. He was going to crack his skull when he landed, and he just didn't care.

He was also going to get me right in the center of the chest. I could see it coming. It seemed to go on coming, for hours. Blade, body, light, roses: Everything was hanging above me, as if suspended in jelly, taking forever to move.

The first thing I'd expected to feel was something sharp cutting through the bone over my heart. What I felt instead was a sharp flat pain in my side and a push. The next thing I knew, I was rolling, over and over and over, bumping along the floor of that room like a ball pushed downstairs. The pain was terrific, running through my shoulder and my cheek and my hand like fire. I blacked out twice and came to twice, thrown in and out of consciousness by shock. I came to a halt lying on my back, staring up at the bare springs under Charlie Copplewhite's bed.

It was hard to move, but I did it anyway. I kept thinking I had to know how it all turned out, even if it didn't seem to have anything to do with me. Besides the pain in my shoulder and hand and cheek, I had one in my ribs. It felt scratchy and poking, as if something were broken there.

I got my head turned around until my cheek, the injured side, was lying on the floor. It hurt, but I didn't want to move it. I could see a pair of heavy work boots I recognized as Benjamin's, and that made me feel better.

What didn't make me feel better was what I could see of Charlie, which was nearly all of him. He was lying on the floor, one arm flung away from him with the hand on the end of it bent at an unnatural angle. He had broken his wrist.

His other arm was still moving, arching up, slamming down, using that knife to turn the floor underneath him to splinters.

Then I closed my eyes and let myself faint.

—— EPILOGUE ——

We celebrated Eleanor's birthday on the first warm day of spring, one of those days when you can forget that London ever has a winter. It was only April, but there were flowers in all the parks and new green leaves on all the trees. Coming over Putney Bridge toward the tube stop, we could see, spreading out on the grounds of the little church nestled on the other side of the Thames, a bright yellow riot of flowers that reminded me of children. It was a good omen. The police inquiries were over, my bandages were gone, and my money problems were being solved by the newly inaugurated tourist season. Jasmyn Cole had finally walked out on Amelia Mortimer-Jones, come to work for me, and brought a dozen clients with her. Eleanor, having turned sixteen, was now officially beyond the clutches of England's Department of Health and Social Security. The only problem I had was figuring out what to do with Molly Larkin and Delia Torr, her round little friend from Mrs. Copplewhite's. At the moment, I was stashing them in much the same way I'd once stashed Eleanor, and I knew that couldn't go on forever. Oh, well. I'd told Benjamin Grade once that I wanted to go into politics, to form an advocacy group for foster children and ex-foster children. Maybe this was the beginning of it.

We were headed over Putney Bridge toward the tube station, but we weren't going *to* it. We were riding in Caroline Matthews' brand new Rolls-Royce Corniche, being shepherded from the dowdy middle-class confines of the Roskell Road to the party Caroline was having catered for

Eleanor at Claridge's. The Copplewhites had done some good for somebody, after all. All three of the godmothers had had books come out in the past few months, and the books were selling briskly. Mariliee not only had a new coat, she was making noises about buying a ninety-nine-year lease, which is the British version of a condominium. Belle had spent an entire day in Harrod's, buying shawls. Caroline, whose book was not only selling briskly but holding steady at number two on *The New York Times* bestseller list, was spending money like water. Rolls-Royce Corniches. A driver who looked like he could have played Bunter in a stage production of a Dorothy L. Sayers mystery. A twenty-four-piece antique Georgian tea service bought at auction at Christie's for ten thousand pounds. It was mind boggling, especially since I'd picked up enough about publishing in the last few months to realize none of them had seen any money yet.

I got out my cigarettes, ignored Eleanor's hostile stare—I was supposed to be quitting—and said, "I still think it was unkind of Jamison to say I was an ass to think he was really going to hold Ben. It looked like he was going to hold Ben."

"Don't talk to me about it," Eleanor said. "It looked like that to me, too."

"So tell me what else I was supposed to do," I said. "If you'd thought what I'd thought, wouldn't you have searched that room?"

"I'd have been on the first plane to Hong Kong," Eleanor said. "I told you that."

"I know you told me that. But you wouldn't have really."

She gave it up. I shrugged and said, "Well, it's just a good thing you went and got him when you did. And it all turned out all right, anyway."

Eleanor made a face. "You," she said, "have the memory of someone with severe brain damage."

I let that one go, too. We were swinging through Knightsbridge, and the streets were full of tourists in overbright clothes. Usually that made me cringe, but today it made me as happy as the Rolls-Royce Corniche. Europeans, even the English, think Americans are terribly unsophisticated to wear all those reds and blues and greens. I'd got into the habit myself during my years in England, but now I changed my mind. I loved reds and blues and greens. They looked happy and healthy and innocent and fun.

We shot through Cadogan Square, down a side street, past a park, and came to a stop at the edge of the curb about half a block from the hotel. Between us and the canopy were a lot of other cars, mammoth expensive fuel hogs that probably belonged to famous people. But not people who were too intrusively famous—Claridge's is very particular. I let the driver get out and help me to the street, and then I waited on the curb while he hauled Eleanor out after me.

Eleanor was in the middle of thanking him when the expression on her face changed and her eyes fixed upon something, and I looked curiously in the direction she was staring in to find we'd been joined by a stout middle-aged woman. As I've said, with things like this, I've got radar. I could have spotted the type from four blocks away. I didn't need to be standing right next to her.

The middle-aged woman had a face the color of stale raw meat and a shabby set of tweeds that needed mending. Her shoes needed mending, too. They were getting run-down at the heel.

Eleanor said, in a strangled little voice, "Miss Denbar."

Miss Denbar said, "Nell? Nell *Pratt?*"

It was the "Nell" that gave it to me. I knew who Miss Denbar was. She was Eleanor's headmistress from the home in York. The one who'd told Eleanor all sorts of things about her mother.

Since Eleanor was in no shape to handle this, I put my hand out to Miss Denbar and gave her a great big smile. "How do you do," I said. "I'm Avra Mahon. You were Eleanor's headmistress at St. Thomas's, weren't you? We've all heard a great deal about you."

Miss Denbar started to give me a suspicious look, but it soon melted into uneasiness. I was dressed too well, and I was being too damned aggressive. She checked over each article of my clothing in turn, and then turned on Eleanor. She was beginning to look frantic.

"Nell," she said.

"Is on her way to her birthday party," I interrupted. "Her *sixteenth* birthday party. Don't you think sweet-sixteen parties are fun?"

"What?" Miss Denbar said.

"Eleanor's Aunt Caroline thought she really couldn't do less than Claridge's," I said. "You're only sixteen once, aren't you? But I'm being rude. You really will have to come along. It's the least we could do after all the help you've given Eleanor."

Eleanor was on the verge of exploding. I nudged her, silently urging her to watch. She did. It was quite a sight.

Miss Denbar turned red and purple and then green. She checked our clothes again. She checked her own. She looked at Caroline's driver still waiting beside the Corniche at the curb and coughed.

"Claridge's," she said. She choked on it. "A sweet-sixteen party in Claridge's."

"Won't you come along?" I asked again.

She didn't even bother to swear at me. She just turned on her heel and stalked away, pushing people out of her path with the flat of her hand. I started to laugh. Once I started, I just couldn't stop.

"Oh, dear," I said. "I've always wanted to do that. I've never had so much fun in my life."

"That was *wonderful*," Eleanor said. "You've got to teach me how to do that. It'd come in handy."

"What would come in handy?" Benjamin said. We turned to find him standing behind us, loaded down under a great square box wrapped in silver paper. "Birthday present," he said. "Who was that?"

"Nobody important," I said. "Just somebody Eleanor knew once. What's in that thing?"

"It's a surprise," he said. "You see the papers this morning?"

"No."

"The high court just passed on Mrs. Copplewhite's contention that she's mentally ill. Turned it down flat."

"Well, that's good to hear." I started moving us toward the hotel canopy. "If you wouldn't mind, though, I'd really rather not think about any of that. It gets me aggravated. Where are the godmothers?"

"Right up ahead," Benjamin said.

They *were* right up ahead, waiting for us on the hotel's steps, completely oblivious to the pedestrian traffic swirling around them. They looked small and happy and bright and cheerful and altogether fairy-godmotherish, which was just the way I liked them. When they saw us, they started waving excitedly. They even waved at Benjamin.

"Listen," Benjamin said, "we've got to talk about this. I can spend the year in London, but I can't afford to spend two years. You've got to come to some decision, Avra."

"About what?"

"Don't do this to me."

Eleanor had stopped and turned back toward the way we had come. She was looking up the street in the direction Miss Denbar had disappeared.

"Come on," I told her. "Forget about it."

"I don't want to forget about it. I want a videotape of it."

I linked one of my arms through Benjamin's and used the other to drag Eleanor up the hotel steps to where the godmothers were waiting for us. Godmothers.

The dreams of abandoned children sometimes come true. There really is magic out there waiting, if only they can find it.

253